"I WON'T SELL THIS FARM," BRITT SAID.

"Mrs. Hansen, you're in considerable debt already, with little chance of fighting your way out. If you sell, you can pay all your debts and still have enough left over to start four college funds."

She did not appear appeased. "You even know how many children I have."

"Details are an important part of my job," he said without apology. "You owe us a lot of money, Mrs. Hansen. One of us better do his research."

She marched across the kitchen, yanked the door open and fixed him with a lethal stare. "I'm a 34B, I love silk underthings, mocha fudge ice cream, and I root for the Milwaukee Brewers. Anything else you'd like to know?"

Temporarily defeated, Jake smiled politely and went to the door. "We'll deliver your supplies," he said as he stepped out, "as soon as your bill is paid."

To Joe and Sally Rohne,
who have a beautiful farm, and a beautiful romance

Special thanks and acknowledgment to Muriel Jensen
for her contribution to the Tyler series.

Special thanks and acknowledgment to Joanna Kosloff
for her contribution to the concept for the Tyler series.

Published November 1992

ISBN 0-373-82509-9

MILKY WAY

MILKY WAY

Muriel Jensen

Harlequin Books

TORONTO • NEW YORK • LONDON
AMSTERDAM • PARIS • SYDNEY • HAMBURG
STOCKHOLM • ATHENS • TOKYO • MILAN
MADRID • WARSAW • BUDAPEST • AUCKLAND

WHIRLWIND
Nancy Martin

BRIGHT HOPES
Pat Warren

WISCONSIN WEDDING
Carla Neggers

MONKEY WRENCH
Nancy Martin

BLAZING STAR
Suzanne Ellison

SUNSHINE
Pat Warren

ARROWPOINT
Suzanne Ellison

BACHELOR'S PUZZLE
Ginger Chambers

MILKY WAY
Muriel Jensen

CROSSROADS
Marisa Carroll

COURTHOUSE STEPS
Ginger Chambers

LOVEKNOT
Marisa Carroll

TYLER

American women have always used the art quilt as a means of expressing their views on life and as a commentary on events in the world around them. And in Tyler, quilting has always been a popular communal activity. So what could be a more appropriate theme for our book covers and titles?

MILKY WAY

This charming collection of tiny squares and twinkling triangles that form stylized stars captures the frontier quilter's vision of the galaxy. A long-ago seamstress, perhaps in a lonely Wisconsin farmhouse, could have been inspired by the golds and blues of a night sky to name her creation after our own small corner of the universe.

Dear Reader,

Welcome to Harlequin's Tyler, a small Wisconsin town whose citizens we hope you'll soon come to know and love. Like many of the innovative publishing concepts Harlequin has launched over the years, the idea for the Tyler series originated in response to our readers' preferences. Your enthusiasm for sequels and continuing characters within many of the Harlequin lines has prompted us to create a twelve-book series of individual romances whose characters' lives inevitably intertwine.

Tyler faces many challenges typical of small towns, but the fabric of this fictional community created by Harlequin will be torn by the revelation of a long-ago murder, the details of which will evolve right through the series. This intriguing crime will culminate in an emotional trial that profoundly affects the lives of the Ingallses, the Barons, the Forresters and the Wochecks.

A hot baseball game is going on across the park, and, as usual, the whole town is turning out for the Fourth of July picnic. No doubt they'll be sampling Britt Hansen's delicious new yogurt products.

And there's startling scuttlebutt as well. The investigation of Margaret Ingalls's death takes a dramatic turn. In fact, it seems Alyssa Baron is preparing to take over the family business. Judson just hasn't been the same since the news....

So join us in Tyler, once a month, for the next four months, for a slice of small-town life that's not as innocent or as quiet as you might expect, and for a sense of community that will capture your mind and your heart.

Marsha Zinberg
Editorial Coordinator, Tyler

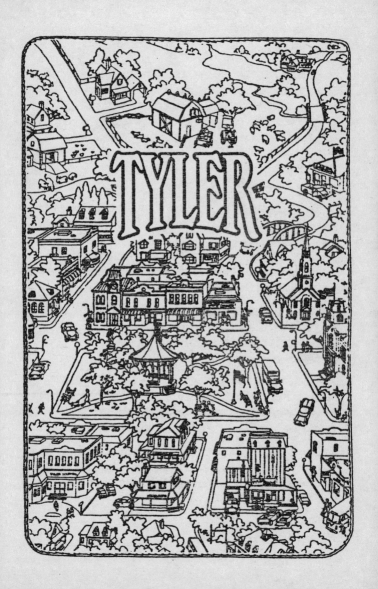

CHAPTER ONE

JAKE MARSHACK TURNED his red Ford Explorer off the highway onto the gravel side road marked with the Wisconsin Department of Transportation's official brown-and-yellow Rustic Road designation. The signs identified stretches of thoroughfare that retained the charm of days gone by, when life and travel were slower, when there'd been time to smell the wildflowers and listen to the birds. But the rich, verdant pasture spreading out to his left, dotted with grazing Holsteins, and the tall, lush green crowding in on his right went unnoticed. He didn't see the gray clouds against the stormy spring sky, heralding rain, or the fat black-and-white Canada geese flying toward Timber Lake, a quarter of a mile away. His mind was ticking over figures.

As Winnebago Dairy's sales manager in southeastern Wisconsin, Jake spent most of his time in a Chicago office. But several times a year he went on the road to collect outstanding receivables. He could be charming and firm, understanding but unshakable in his resolve to have the district with the best numbers. Still, the percentage of uncollectible debt was growing among the smaller farms in his district, and the struggles of their owners to hold on to what little they had left touched him as few things in life did.

But business was business. However much he hated this part of his job, he had to do it. When the big red barn and the white Victorian farmhouse beyond it came into view, he pulled over to review his notes.

"Hansen widow trying hard, but still unable to pay," Buckley, the sales rep, had reported after his last call at Lakeside Farm. "Renting out large parcels of pasture in March and promises to pay outstanding balance at that time."

Jake checked his printout. March had come and gone and there'd been no payment. In fact, there'd been no payment since the previous September. Policy was clear. The widow Hansen was cut off pending payment in full.

Jake closed his folder with a groan. Great. A widow. He had to stop feed delivery to some little old arthritic thing who'd probably lose the farm before the year was out and be forced to move in with one of her kids.

He shook his head as he pulled back onto the road and headed for the lane to the house. He'd never understand why generation after generation of farmers broke their backs and very often their hearts over a piece of land that was subject to every joke God, nature and the government could play. It was masochistic and senseless. He couldn't imagine dedicating one's life to something as completely unpredictable as a harvest.

Now, numbers made sense. Columns that balanced were easy to understand. A future that depended solely on what an individual could do was the only course worth plotting, as far as he was concerned. Needing and depending on others or on the beneficence of nature always led to a predictable end—disappointment.

Jake didn't believe in disappointment. He believed in success.

He pulled to a stop behind a muddy blue GMC truck at the side of the house. A yellow Lab lying at the top of the porch steps raised an intelligent face to watch him. Jake leaped out of the vehicle, careful to miss a puddle, and took a moment to look around.

The house had a peaked roof with gingerbread finials and a wraparound porch. It was tidy but in need of a fresh coat of paint. A heart-shaped wreath of dried flowers hung on the front door, and scarlet May-blooming tulips and bright forget-me-nots trimmed the foundation and the porch steps. He imagined the little widow kneeling on a rug and pampering her flowers.

Maybe he'd get lucky, he thought, and she wouldn't be home. He could send her a registered letter telling her she was customer non grata. No. He had the best numbers in the company because he dealt with people face-to-face. He made things turn out his way, but he did it openly.

He took two steps up toward the porch and was greeted by a hair-raising growl from deep in the Lab's throat and a clear view of impressive canine incisors. The dog hadn't moved, and Jake got the distinct impression it was because she didn't feel she had to.

Accustomed to a fair amount of hostility, Jake had perfected an understanding manner and a conciliatory tone of voice that usually worked on dogs as well as people. He extended a cautious hand and asked, "Good dog?"

The Lab changed demeanor instantly. Rolling onto her back, she tucked her feet in in eager surrender, her strong tail wagging madly. She whined in helpless adoration as Jake reached up to scratch her sturdy mound of a chest. An upside-down tongue flicked at the sleeve of Jake's suit jacket.

Jake laughed. "You are a good dog," he praised. "You're not much of a security system, but I'll bet you're a great friend."

The dog rolled onto four big feet and followed him as he went to the front door and knocked. She sat on his right foot as he waited . . . and waited.

BRITTANY HANSEN STOOD on tiptoe on top of an eight-foot wooden ladder and groped for the shingle that was just beyond her reach. She growled impatiently when the tip of her longest finger refused to close the gap.

"Come on!" she said aloud. "One more shingle! I am not going to climb down and move the ladder again for one more shingle!"

She withdrew her aching arm and studied the shingle with hostility. Rubbing her aching biceps, she tried to remember why repairing the hole in the porch roof had seemed so important this afternoon. Because she wanted to put the porch swing out, she reminded herself, and a large drip had developed where she usually placed it near the kitchen window.

And because Jimmy had always brought the old swing out for her at the first sign of spring, and she wanted to prove to herself that although he wasn't here to do it, it would still get done.

Sneaky, strong emotion rose up to sting her eyes and clog her throat. Having it out would be no fun, and she'd probably choke up every time she looked at it, but it would be in its place because *she* had put it there. It would be one small victory after a long dark winter of silent, corrosive grief.

Britt drew a deep breath, leaned her weight against the roof and stretched her right hand out as far as she could reach—and felt the toe of her right foot push the ladder out from under her.

She screamed, the palms of her hands scraping over the rough tiles as she slid down, then caught the rain gutter with her fingers.

Great, she thought with a gallows humor she was surprised to find had survived the winter. *Hanging by my fingernails. Literally. The bank should see this.*

She groped with her feet for the porch railing, but the extended roof had her too far out to reach.

She considered letting go, but the drop to the ground was considerable. She could not afford a broken limb at this point in time, and the way her luck had been running, a multiple fracture was bound to result.

"Dammit, Jimmy!" she shouted at the air. "Do something!"

JAKE AND THE LAB, still waiting at the front door were galvanized into action by a crash followed immediately by a piercing screech. With one loud *Woof!* the dog ran around the porch to the back of the house. Jake followed, his mind already in sympathy with the poor little arthritic old lady.

He jerked to a halt at the sight of a pair of long legs dangling at eye level. They were not arthritic legs. They were slender, shapely legs in snug denim. His brain took a moment to swap mental images and assimilate what was happening.

His eyes lifted to a baggy gray sweater and arms holding rigidly, desperately to the gutter. Pale blue eyes in a white face were wide with alarm and a curious resignation.

Jake wrapped an arm around a pillar to steady himself and reached out over the railing.

BRITT STARED at the man in the three-piece gray suit and wondered if her desperation had conjured him up. Before she could decide, he had a fistful of the front of her sweater.

"Kick a leg out toward me," he ordered.

She blinked. He didn't disappear. "Who are you?" she asked.

She heard his gasp of exasperation. "Does that matter at the moment? Kick a leg out."

Reflexively, she complied, and felt a muscular arm wrap itself around it.

"Now drop a hand to my shoulder."

She wanted to, but even the threat of falling couldn't blunt the effect of a large male hand wrapped high around her inner thigh.

"I haven't got a good grip on you," he said when she hesitated. "If you fall now, we're both going over. I don't know about you, but weeks of traction wouldn't fit into my schedule."

"I . . . can't hold on with one hand."

"When you let that hand go, I'll have you."

"You're sure?"

"Absolutely."

She believed him. She wasn't sure why. Possibly because she wasn't in a position not to. Closing her eyes, she dropped a hand and reached out blindly. She uttered a little scream as her other hand lost purchase and she fell, landing solidly against hard muscle. Sitting on his arm, she was swung sideways over the railing, then deposited on her feet.

For an instant she couldn't breathe or speak. All she could do was stare.

Her Good Samaritan was long-legged and lean, with just enough thickness in the shoulder to make her grateful he'd been the one to come along and not spindly Chuck Stuart, who rented part of her pasture.

With eyes the color of maple wood and dark blond hair side-parted and perfectly groomed, he bore a startling resemblance to Kevin Costner. His recent exertion hadn't disturbed his good looks at all. There was a confident, capable air about him that was comforting and alarming.

She watched him shrug his coat back into place and straighten his tie.

She began to emerge from her trance when she noticed the subtle elegance of everything about him. His finely tailored suit probably cost more than her monthly food budget. And he wore cuff links—gold and jade, if she wasn't mistaken. Antiques, probably. His shoes were shined to perfection.

She pulled herself together and folded her arms. "You're from the bank," she accused.

"No," he said.

"An attorney, then."

"No."

She frowned, her shoulders relaxing. "Then who are you?"

Jake had never seen hair that color. It rioted around her face in soft curls and ended in a fat braid that rested on her shoulder. It was the shade of a ripe peach, a sort of pink-orange with gold highlights. He judged by the generous spattering of freckles on her face that the color was natural.

Aware that he hadn't answered her question, he offered his hand and a smile he was sure had to be at least a little vague. "Jake Marshack," he said. "And you are...?"

She studied him uncertainly for a moment, then shook his hand. Her fingers were long and slender, but her grip was firm. "Britt Hansen. Thank you for rescuing me."

He indulged in a poignant memory of an armful of soft, round hip, then immediately dismissed it. "The...widow Hansen?" he asked.

She laughed lightly at the title. "One and the same. For a minute I thought you were the villain come to tie me to the railroad tracks. Instead you turn out to be a genuine Dudley Doright. Come on inside. A gallant rescue deserves at least a cup of coffee."

She beckoned the dog with a slap to her thigh. "Come on, Daffy."

Jake hesitated on the threshold as she opened the back door. Dudley Doright he was not. "Mrs. Hansen..."

But the ring of a telephone at the far end of the kitchen made her hurry inside. She gestured for him to follow and pointed to a chair at a large round table. The dog settled under it.

Feeling an annoying little niggle of guilt, he sat. He'd left his notebook in the car because he'd found that official papers and copies of bills always made people defensive, and he wanted them willing to work with him. Of course, in her case, he doubted she had anything to work with.

Chatting happily to someone he judged by the conversation to be a neighbor, she washed her hands, poured coffee into two mugs, then walked the full extension of the phone cord to hand one to him. He stood and reached across the table for it.

"No, I was happy to lend it to you, Judy," she was saying, "but if you're finished with it, I'll come pick it up. I was trying to repair the porch roof with my short ladder and almost broke my neck!"

She grinned at him, and he heard a loud expression of dismay from the other end of the connection.

"No, no, I'm fine. Dudley Doright rescued me."

"Who?" came across the line loud and clear.

"It's a long story. I'll tell you about it when I pick up the ladder. I'm going to town tomorrow—want me to bring you anything?"

While she made notes on a pad stuck to the refrigerator, Jake sipped his coffee and studied the enormous kitchen. It was a large square room papered in a soft blue-and-cream pattern. The woodwork was Williamsburg blue and the high cupboards were oak. Children's artwork and schedules covered the beige refrigerator, and something with a rich, beefy fragrance simmered in a deep pot on the stove.

The table at which he sat was bordered on two sides by sparkling countertops. The third wall was painted creamy white and covered with what appeared to be antique kitchen implements and an ancient pitchfork that must have been hand-carved all of a piece. He was wondering who had used it how long ago when three kittens, one white and two spotted black-and-white, suddenly ran across the kitchen from the room beyond. They tumbled over one another in a rolling heap, then raced back the way they'd come.

He had turned his attention to the pitchfork again when the widow Hansen joined him at the table.

Pale blue eyes smiled at him over the rim of her cup. "My great-grandmother pitched hay with that," she said, "and once held an amorous neighbor at bay while my great-grandfather was off hunting. I believe her father carved it. Would you like something to go with your coffee?"

"Ah...no, thank you." He straightened in his chair. It was time to state his business. "Actually, I'm from Winnebago Dairy. I'm here to talk to you about..." He looked into her eyes and experienced a glitch in his thought processes. His brain disengaged and he couldn't remember simple words. All that seemed to work were his eyes, which couldn't stop looking into hers.

They were like Lake Geneva under a cloudy sky, softly gray-blue and suggesting unimagined depths. He felt pulled in, like a diver who'd forgotten to draw a breath before jumping.

"About?" she prompted. She lowered her cup and a subtle change took place in her cheerful, friendly expression. That helped him pull himself together.

"About your bill." He forced out the words and groped for his professional persona. "You're eight months overdue, Mrs. Hansen."

She looked at him levelly across the table, her eyes now like the lake in February—with a six-foot, impenetrable ice crust. "So you're not Dudley Doright, after all," she said, pushing away from the table.

Jake half expected her to order him to leave. Instead, she went to the sink, a deep old porcelain one with ancient faucets, around which a more modern counter and cupboards had been built. She looked out the window, and he supposed she could see the cows grazing.

"You're here to cut me off," she guessed.

He mentally went through all his options. It didn't take long. There weren't any. "I'm afraid so," he said finally. He added, "The moment you pay the outstanding balance, I'll send a truck out with the order you put in two days ago."

She turned and leaned against the edge of the sink, both hands behind her, gripping it. "I can't pay right now, but I've been to the bank about a loan. I should have an answer in a few days. And I'm getting a desserts business going on the side for extra money. I—"

"Our rep," he interrupted quietly, "said you thought you'd be able to pay when you rented out pasture."

She nodded. "It went to the mortgage. I thought having my payments almost current would give me a better shot at getting a loan."

Robbing Peter to pay Paul was a sign of real trouble. But Jake knew that was how half his customers made it from year to year.

He shook his head regretfully. "I'm sorry. We'll ship to you the moment—"

"But I could have the money for you in a week," she said, trying desperately to keep the plea out of her voice. She wanted to convey competence, reasonableness.

"Or the bank could turn you down," he said gently.

She tilted her chin. "I believe they'll approve me."

Jake stood. If he had to hurt her feelings, he felt he had to do it on his feet. "I've seen your credit file, Mrs. Hansen. I think you're deluding yourself."

Anger sparked in her eyes, which were suddenly like the lake in an electrical storm. "At the moment, hope is all I have, Mr...." She hesitated over his name.

"Marshack," he provided.

"Marshack," she repeated. "If you're going to tie me to the train track, let me at least hold on to the hope that the *real* Dudley will come along."

Jake wanted out of the warm, cozy kitchen and out from under her judgmental glare more than he wanted anything else at that moment. Yet something rooted him in place. He guessed the reason was that she looked so touchingly brave that he couldn't do anything cowardly.

So he decided to tell her what he thought. "Mrs. Hansen, small farms run by strong men are going under left and right. Why continue to fight the inevitable? We've offered to buy you out twice. Maybe it's time you considered it."

She was now rigid with anger, but he gave her credit for controlling it very well. Had their roles been reversed, he'd have had her on the porch by now, on the business end of the pitchfork.

"This is a heritage farm," she said, her voice very quiet. "It's been in my family for four generations— five, counting my children. I'm not interested in turning it over to a dairy that now owns more of Wisconsin and Illinois than the state park systems."

He nodded. "I've been empowered to raise the offer." He named the sum Stan Foreman, vice president of sales, had brought to his office that morning with the subtle reminder that acquiring her property for the company would speed Jake's rise up the corporate ladder. The offer was generous and was intended to knock her off her feet and out of her stubbornly negative stance. It didn't.

For an instant the blue eyes widened and he saw a flash of longing, then it was gone and he was treated once again to the February lake. "You don't understand," she said, her patience obviously strained. "Four generations of Bauers were born here. It's been like a gift passed from hand to hand. I couldn't sell this farm any more than I could sell one of my children."

"How are you going to provide for those children's education, Mrs. Hansen?" he asked. "You're in considerable debt already, with little chance of fighting your way out without selling—or marrying a wealthy man. Would you rather the bank got your memories?"

She paled, holding both arms rigidly to her sides. "How dare you worm your way into my kitchen—"

"You invited me in," he reminded her quietly, "after I prevented you from breaking your neck."

"—drink my coffee," she shouted over him, "then proceed to call me a deadbeat?"

This wasn't going at all the way he'd hoped. "I said no such thing," he denied, pushing the chair he'd occupied back to the table. "I mentioned only what is public record. If you sell, you can pay all your debts, buy a nice little place somewhere and still have enough left over to start four college funds."

She did not appear appeased. "You even know how many children I have."

"Details are an important part of my job," he said without apology. "You owe us a lot of money, Mrs. Hansen. One of us better do his research."

She marched across the kitchen, her braid flapping against her upper back. She yanked the door open and fixed him with a lethal stare, her cheeks pink, her voice wavering a bit as she said darkly, "I'm a 34B, I love silk underthings and mocha fudge-nut ice cream, and I root for the Milwaukee Brewers. Anything else you'd like to know?"

Jake tried to accept defeat gracefully. But his life and career were on a timetable, and her inability to pay her debts, plus her refusal to sell, were holding things up. The Winnebago Dairy board would be making the vice-presidency decision at the end of summer. He'd hoped to be district quota buster by then, or to have reeled in her property for the company so that he'd be the only possible choice.

On such short acquaintance he'd decided he liked her, even though she was making his life difficult. He'd try again. There had to be a way to reach her. But he had to regroup first.

He smiled politely and went to the door, resolutely keeping his eyes from the charming dimension she'd announced. "We'll deliver," he said, "as soon as your bill is paid."

He stepped out onto the porch, but was swept back into the kitchen when a wave of children collided with him, then carried him along as they burst into the house. He heard the four of them yell, "Hi, Mom." Four lunch boxes clattered onto the table, then the wave dispersed in four directions—the refrigerator, the cookie jar, under the table where the dog lay and to the small television in the opposite corner. A bouncy cartoon ditty filled the room. The kittens raced back in, seeking attention.

A slender boy about twelve or thirteen polished an apple and studied Jake from a careful distance. He wore jeans and a plaid flannel shirt open over a T-shirt. "Your wheels in the driveway?" he asked.

"Yes," Jake replied.

The boy nodded. "Cool." Then he looked from his mother's frowning face to Jake's unfarmlike attire and asked with an edge of hostility in his voice, "You from the bank?"

Britt put her arm around her older son's shoulders and forced herself to smile. She tried so hard not to let her financial woes affect her children, but money, or the lack of it, had become so large a part of her life lately that the subject intruded everywhere. Determined to keep it from gaining more ground as long as she could, she said cheerfully, "Matt, this is Mr. Marshack. We were just talking about...about Great-Grandma Bauer."

Jake saw the transformation take place on the widow Hansen's face as, snacks secured and the dog and kittens petted, the children gathered around her. He guessed it was maternal reflex at first; she didn't want them to know she was upset. Then the youngest boy and girl flanked her, each leaning in to her, and she seemed to visibly relax.

"This is Christy," she said, putting a gentle hand atop a pre-adolescent with hair the same shade as hers. The child wore glasses with red frames and had eyes that studied him with the same suspicion her mother's showed.

"David," she went on, moving her hand to a boy about eight. He was the only one in the group with dark hair, and his blue eyes verged on green.

"And Renee."

"I'm six," the plump little girl reported. She was the spitting image of her mother and sister, but with the rounder features of early childhood. She smiled up at him. "You look like Robin Hood," she said.

Britt's eyes met his and said without words, *But you're more like the Sheriff of Nottingham.* Aloud, she said, "Mr. Marshack was just leaving."

"Stay cool," Matt advised.

"Nice to meet you," Christy said.

David waved at him from his mother's side, and Renee followed him out to his truck.

"I'm in first grade," she said, hopping on one foot beside him, then racing to catch up as he got ahead of her. "My birthday is in October. You know, January, February, March, April..."

She went all the way through to October while following him around the truck and watching him open the door and climb in.

He let her go on without comment because he never knew what to say to children. He always got the impression that, despite the less-sophisticated vocabulary and the smaller stature, they were smarter than adults. And this one fairly glowed with curiosity and intelligence.

As he consulted his calendar to check his next call, she pointed to the portable office that sat on the passenger seat. "What's that?" she asked.

"Files," he replied.

"What's that?"

"Papers and stuff."

"Oh." Satisfied, she stood on tiptoe to study the dash.

"Renee, honey," the widow said, appearing from around the hood and taking the child by the hand, "Mr. Marshack has to leave."

She stepped away from the truck, pulling the little girl with her. "Goodbye, Mr. Marshack," she said, her eyes hostile again. "Next time you wish to speak to me, please write or phone."

Jake put the truck in reverse, checked that his rearview mirror was clear, then stepped on the gas, determined that the widow Hansen hadn't seen the last of him.

The sound of metal crunching and glass popping under his rear tires made him slam on the brake.

CHAPTER TWO

"MY BIKE!" Matt stared down at the pile of contorted metal that had been his beloved twelve-speed, his dark blue eyes reflecting his horror. The other three children also stared, openmouthed.

"Maybe Mom can fix it," Renee suggested.

"I think it's dead," David said.

"You were supposed to put it on the porch," Christy pointed out. "Mom told you—"

Matt rounded on her. "You shut up!" he ordered, then turned back to the "body" with a gasp of distress.

Jake, riddled with guilt, put an arm around his shoulders. "I'm sorry," he said. "I'll buy you another one."

"No." Britt's voice was firm, though her expression was sympathetic. "He always leans it up against the most convenient prop, then forgets it. I've barely missed running over it countless times. He's supposed to lock it up on the porch. He knows that. It wasn't your fault."

Jake had expected her to be grateful to have something to blame on him. He was surprised into feeling responsible.

"Look," he began, "I'll be happy to—"

"No," she insisted, pulling Matt out from under Jake's arm and putting her own around the boy. "We all have to pay the consequences of our actions. That's one of life's primary rules."

"What about my paper route?" Matt asked plaintively.

"You'll have to use my bike," Britt replied.

He rolled his eyes in distress. "Mom, come on. Your bike is dorky! I can't—"

"What are your alternatives?" she asked.

Jake could see the boy struggling manfully not to cry as he continued to stare at the twisted tubing. "I could ask Howie to take over my route."

"Then he'll get the money and not you. How are you going to pay your way on the Scouting trip?"

Jake bit his tongue. He'd never been a parent, but he considered her unreasonably stern. It didn't seem fair to remind the boy of other things he couldn't have while he was standing over the corpse of his bike.

"Could I speak to you for a moment?" he asked the widow.

She gave him a cool, reluctant glance, then shooed the children toward the house. "Matt, put the bike in the back of the station wagon," she said. "I'll see if Brick can do anything with it."

As the children moved away, Jake took her elbow and pulled her down the drive, out of earshot of Matt, who was bending over the bike.

"No," she said quietly before Jake could say anything.

"Look," he countered reasonably, "I backed over the bike because I didn't see it. I feel—"

"You didn't see it because he parked it in the wrong place after repeated warnings."

He folded his arms and frowned down at her. "You chew nails, too?" he asked.

She glowered at him for one long moment, then sighed and squared her shoulders. "Do you have children?" she asked.

"No, I don't," he admitted, "but if I did, I wouldn't rub their noses in their mistakes."

She shook her head at his naïveté. "How do you suppose they learn not to make them?"

He opened his mouth to answer, but she cut him off. "By having to live with the results. Perhaps you can afford to be more understanding because if your child made such a mistake, you could simply buy him another bike. Matt's reality is that I can't afford to do that, so he has to take special care of the one he has."

"I feel partly responsible." Jake thrust a thumb at his chest. "And I can afford to buy him another one. Doesn't that change the equation just a little?"

"No," she said, "because you won't be around to buy him yet another one when he forgets and leaves the new one in the wrong place because the message never really got through."

Jake turned his head to watch the boy heave the wreck into the back of the car. "Do you really think he'd let that happen again?"

"Twice or three times more," she said without hesitation. "Kids are thick, Mr. Marshack. Now, if you'll excuse me." She glanced at her watch. "Christy has a piano lesson, David has a t'ai chi class, Renee has ballet and Matt has to deliver his route." She started to walk up the drive but he caught her arm.

He was surprised by how small it felt in his grip. Her bicep was muscled and firm, but he could easily close his hand around it. She looked up into his eyes and he felt that shock again, as though water had closed over his head.

Then, unexpectedly, her eyes gentled and she gave him a half smile. "I know you mean well," she said, "and I appreciate the generosity of your offer when you know it really wasn't your fault. But it's important that Matt live with this for a little while." Then her smile took on a slightly wry twist. "Just as I have to live with the results of my inability to pay my bills. Life is hard, and that's a truth no one escapes. Goodbye, Mr. Marshack."

She caught up with Matt and put an arm around his shoulders.

Jake saw the boy stiffen stubbornly, refusing to respond to some teasing remark. Now he felt sorry for both of them.

She certainly had a lot to contend with—the fairly recent loss of her husband, the brink of financial ruin and four children, one of whom was on the threshold of puberty with all its attendant confusion and volatility. Not to mention a porch roof that leaked.

Jake got into his vehicle again and backed down the drive. There was nothing else he could do here. He'd delivered the company's offer, then its ultimatum. He'd upset the widow Hansen and made her older son a pedestrian. That was quite enough for one day.

WITH CHRISTY, David and Renee piled into the station wagon, Britt drove the three miles into Tyler. While the children teased and argued in the middle seat, she pushed in a Clint Black tape about "living and learning" and turned up the volume. The music didn't deter the children one bit but it helped her ease the knot of worry that had begun to grow in her stomach a year ago when Jimmy died, and that now threatened to cut off her breath and smother her heartbeat.

Not that she and Jimmy hadn't struggled before. Life for the small farmers all across the country had come down to a basic truth: success was being able to break even; profit was an impossibility. And for her and Jimmy, debt had been a fact of life since she inherited not only the farm when her father died, but the high cost of new milking equipment. The four days Jimmy had spent in intensive care after the accident had almost bankrupted her.

When he'd been there by her side, dark-haired and lanky and determined to look on the bright side, she'd felt as though she could handle anything. But since he was killed, she'd lost sight of the bright side. Lakeside Farm's cash flow was down to a trickle, and it was impossible to hire someone to do all that Jimmy had done. Already putting in a full day herself, she tried to take over as many of Jimmy's chores as she could manage and still be there for her children. But she felt like something from one of the taffy pulls described in Great-Grandma Bauer's diary—as though she'd been stretched so far she was now stringy and limp.

"Mom!" Christy shouted. "You passed Miss Gates's house!"

Britt broke out of her thoughts, quickly checking her rearview mirror before braking to a halt.

"She's not Miss Gates anymore," Renee corrected importantly. "She's Mrs. . . . ?"

"Mrs. Forrester," Britt supplied, backing up to a curb canopied by tall old maple trees just acquiring green buds. "No, Chris!" she cautioned as her daughter would have opened the street-side door. "Get out on the curb side."

"David's in the way."

"David, honey, tuck your feet in."

"If she wasn't so fat—"

Whap! Sheet music to "Dance of the Butterflies" connected with David's cheek as Christy stepped over him and past Renee, who had raised both feet onto the seat and covered her head.

"Christy," Britt began to scold, but the child was already running up the walk to her piano teacher's charming cream-colored house. She knew she should correct David for insulting his sister, but lately it'd become such a major event when he said anything that she hated to discourage him, even for saying something negative. She decided to conserve her energy on all counts. She was bound to find something that would require it later.

"I'd like to live here," Renee said as they proceeded along the street. Britt glanced out at the fussily trimmed and gabled Victorian houses, some with orderly picket fences and others with gardens that would soon be ablaze in a riot of colors. Already daffodils and tulips were blooming everywhere.

"You couldn't play with the calves if we lived in town," Britt pointed out, fighting the concern she felt when any of her children expressed a desire to live anywhere but on the farm. "And you couldn't walk down to the lake."

"Yeah," Renee agreed vaguely, gawking out the window, "but I could walk home from school for lunch. And I could go to the drugstore and buy candy bars after school like Jenny Linder does. Can I buy one today after ballet?"

Pleased to be able to grant a modestly priced request, Britt turned toward the commercial district, then pulled up in front of the newly built concrete-block building that housed the Y.

David leaned over the seat to kiss her on the cheek, then climbed past Renee and pushed the door open.

"I'll pick you up in an hour," Britt reminded him. "Wait right inside for me."

David waved assent, then ran into the building.

A block farther Britt stopped again, this time in front of a pink Victorian trimmed in purple with a wooden sign marked Teddy Bear Tap and Ballet.

Renee leaned over to peck her mother's cheek and said, when Britt opened her mouth, "You'll pick me up in an hour and wait right inside the door." She smiled impishly. "Right?"

Britt patted her curls and held her face against her own for an extra moment. The most cheerful of her children, Renee had unknowingly saved her sanity more than once during the past year. "Right, baby. Have fun."

Britt wondered how many errands she could fit into the quiet hour afforded her. She had to stop by Brick's to see if he could do anything with Matt's bike, but that would still leave her time to check at the bank about her loan application. She decided against that instantly. She didn't have the heart to face more rejection this afternoon.

She would visit Judson Ingalls and see if he'd completed the nutritional evaluation of her cheesecake sample.

A little stir of excitement distracted Britt momentarily from her worries. Her cheesecake was wonderful; everyone said so. It sold out regularly at the lodge, and Marge Peterson claimed that customers arrived early or else had to fight for the dozen cheesecake Danishes sold every morning at the diner.

As Britt drove to Ingalls Farm and Machinery at the edge of town, she frowned at the road, thinking that there had to be something *big* she could do with it. At the moment she was simply toying with the idea of wider distribution. But that meant more time baking and less time running the farm. She simply couldn't spare the hours.

Unless the nutritional breakdown was so outstandingly low fat, low calorie and superbly nourishing that she had no choice but to market aggressively. Britt laughed as she pulled into the F and M parking lot. At least her sense of humor was still alive.

SHE FOUND JUDSON in his office in a rear corner of the building. He was in shirtsleeves, his tie pulled away from the open collar of his shirt, glasses far down on his nose as he studied a piece of correspondence. He looked up at Britt over the glasses as she peered around the door.

"Britt! Come in," he said, standing and coming around the desk to draw her into the office. "I was going to call you in the morning. I put a report together for you today."

"Wonderful." She smiled, touched by his gallantry as he retained her hand until she was settled in one of the two chairs that faced his desk. She could haul fence posts by herself and he knew it, but he considered it important to see her properly seated.

Descended from one of the Tyler founding fathers, Judson was a generous, well-respected citizen who worked hard for his community, but whose favorite place was the laboratory off his office where he'd tinkered and dreamed most of his life.

Tall, gray-haired and gravelly voiced, he was possessed of a touching kindness and caring that reminded Britt sharply of her father. Judson had worked with her dad on several service projects. Despite the differences in their social standing, they'd become friends. When her parents were killed in an auto accident right after Matt was born, Judson had taken care of all the expenses the insurance hadn't covered. When Jimmy died, he'd paid for the funeral. Those were kindnesses she would never forget.

"How are you, first of all?" she asked, sincerely interested. There was always a hint of tragedy and sadness behind the kindness in his eyes. Now, since the traumatic discovery of his ex-wife's body during the renovation of Timberlake Lodge, once Judson's home, he'd seemed to retreat even more deeply within himself.

Tyler was abuzz with speculation. Britt ignored it, figuring the truth would come out one day, and that it probably wouldn't be the lurid tale gossip had embroidered.

Though she didn't believe for a minute Judson had been in any way involved with his wife's death, recent developments in the case were bizarre and inexplicable. She just wished the whole mess would go away. She wanted to see that haunted look gone from Judson's eyes, wanted to know he was happy.

"Not bad, not bad," he said in answer to her question, his smile broadening quickly, "for a man my age." Just as suddenly he sobered and studied her closely.

"You're looking a little peaked," he said. "I saw Brick at the lodge." A cloud passed quickly over his features, then was gone. "He says you're working much too hard."

She shrugged a shoulder. "It's that or lose the farm. I just can't do that to all the Bauers who worked so hard to pass it on to *me*." She smiled at Judson. "You know how that is."

He nodded, fixing her with an expression of paternal affection. "The past keeps its hold on us, all right. I just hate to see you work yourself sick against impossible odds. The world's different now, Britt. Your ancestors fought Indians and the elements and the market, but they never had to deal with monster dairy conglomerates who could outproduce and undercut you a hundred times over."

She leaned forward in her chair. "So, is my cheesecake recipe going to make me a contemporary food industry marvel and help me save the farm?"

He pulled a thin folder out of a lineup of books and cleared a place for it, opening it on the desktop. "I've got good news and bad news," he said.

She leaned an elbow on the armrest and grinned. "Just tell me the good news. Bad news always finds me anyway."

He folded his arms on the report. "First, I think you do have something with potential here. It's delicious. We're all agreed on that." He consulted the report, running his index finger down a line of figures. "Using low-fat milk and cheese brings it in at a caloric and nutritional level that should thrill the gourmet dieter.''

Britt felt her adrenaline begin to flow. She knew it! She resisted the impulse to leap across the desk and hug Judson, and instead asked with what she hoped was professional cool, "Then you don't think I'd be crazy to develop more yogurt products and widen my market base?"

He considered a moment, removed his glasses and nodded with obvious reluctance. "Yes, I think it would be crazy."

Britt's adrenaline flow reversed, blocking a gasp in her throat. "I . . . don't understand."

Judson leaned back in his chair. "Britt, the market's already clogged with low-calorie, high-nutrition products. All the big dairies are jumping on the bandwagon. You might do all right, but not well enough to outsell, say, Land o' Honey Foods. And there's the extra time and effort this will cost you just to put yourself in a position to try to compete."

"Those products aren't really all that healthy," she argued. "The producers play games with numbers and trick the consumer with labeling. They call a product 95% fat free, but when you check the breakdown, with 150 calories the product has 9 grams of fat. At 9 calories a gram, that's 81 calories of fat—more than half the 150. How can that be called 95% fat free?"

He smiled at her vehemence. "You can make numbers mean anything you want. They're talking about a percentage of the product's weight, not of its calories. A product like milk, for instance, has a large amount of water and minerals that add to its weight, but not its calorie count."

"My product really is better for people. I've used low-fat everything and a sugar replacement."

Judson sighed. "You know how much it'd cost you in advertising to let the consumer know that?"

Britt got to her feet and paced the office, trying to organize her thoughts. "Judson, I've researched the market. *Fortune* magazine says the consumer's self-indulgent phase is winding down. The new shopper is eating his cancer-fighting cruciferous vegetables, having his cholesterol tested and striving to prolong his life. He isn't buying gourmet ice cream anymore."

Judson shifted in his chair and consulted the report again. "I'm not denying there's a market for it. I'm just trying to tell you that scores of food manufacturers have gotten there before you."

She folded her arms. "Is their cheesecake as good as mine?"

He chuckled. "I seriously doubt it, but I can't say with any authority. Shall I send someone to the grocery store so we can conduct a taste test?"

She frowned good-naturedly. "Don't laugh at me. I've had a rough day and I've got to do *something* to get out of this chasm of debt."

"Britt, you have an excellent product here," he said. "But that freezer aisle in the store represents a cutthroat market. Your cheesecake is scrumptious, but I don't think you have the capital or the . . . the distinction to be noticed."

She continued to pace. "Distinction?"

"You know, something that makes you unique, that screams out at the buyer. A gimmick."

"Gimmick," she repeated thoughtfully, falling back into her chair. "Why should something delicious have to have a gimmick?"

He smiled sympathetically. "The world turns on gimmicks. For a little guy like yourself, the gimmick would have to be big to get you noticed. But I think if you could find it, you'd be successful, because your product is superior."

She looked at him suspiciously. "In your personal or professional opinion?"

"Both. Because I don't have to conduct a lab analysis to know what *you're* made of, Britt. If anyone can do the impossible, it's you."

Britt couldn't help herself. She was encouraged. And it was so long since she'd felt a spark of enthusiasm for anything but her children that she let herself enjoy the sensation. She would remember all the negative aspects Judson had pointed out later. Right now she'd just hold on to the fact that he thought her cheesecake was delicious, and that he had faith in her.

This time she didn't stop herself from hugging him. "Thanks, Judson. That means a lot to me." She stepped back to dig into her purse. "What do I owe you for the lab work?"

"A dozen cheesecake Danishes," he said, closing her purse and walking her to the door. "By the time I get to Marge's they're always gone."

She hugged him again. "I'll bring them by tomorrow. Thanks again for your help and your honesty."

"Any time. Good luck, Britt."

BRICK BAUER LOOKED into the back of the station wagon at the crumpled bike and halted Britt's efforts to pull it out. "Don't bother," he said, shaking his head. "I'm afraid it's DOA."

She hated to believe that, but Brick never lied to her. He'd been looking out for her since they were children, and Jimmy's death had made him even more caring and protective.

"You're sure?"

"Trust me. Someone did a very thorough job. Matt park it behind the truck again?"

Britt smiled at her cousin. "You have a detective's instinct. Insightful and cleverly deductive."

He grinned. "Of course. It's the Bauer way."

"Are you just coming home, or leaving for work?"

"I'm just off duty." He glanced at his watch. "Karen should be home in half an hour or so. I can't believe our shifts coincide for once."

Britt squashed the surge of jealousy she felt that his marriage was fresh and new and hers was so prematurely over. "Who starts dinner in a two-cop family when the wife's a captain, and the husband . . . isn't?"

He made a pretense of polishing his badge. "Why, the better cook, of course. Sauerbraten. Want to stay?"

"Thanks. I've got to pick up the kids."

Brick frowned. "Is Matt walking his route?"

"He's using my bike," Britt said, her expression wry. "A 'nerdy' comedown for him, I'm afraid. Marshack wanted to buy him a new one, but I wouldn't let him. Matt's got to take responsibility—"

"Marshack?" Brick asked.

"Winnebago Dairy's district sales manager." Her forced smile slipped a little. "He came to try to collect. When he left, Matt had propped his bike up against his Explorer and he backed right over it."

"Matt needs the route if he's going to go to that Boy Scout thing." He grinned apologetically. "And your bike *is* nerdy. Want to borrow my credit card?"

She frowned her disapproval. "It's the principle of the thing."

"I know." He put an arm around her and held her close for a sober moment. "How're you doing with him? Is he still moody and remote?"

She nodded, happy to lean against her cousin's strong shoulder. "Yeah. But then, so am I. He's fairly cooperative. No worse than any other prepubescent boy dealing with the loss of his father." She sighed, then pushed away, afraid of becoming too comfortable with Brick's support. "I appreciate your interest, but you've got your own household to worry about now."

"Karen has a meeting Friday morning and I'm off," he said, opening her door for her. "I'll come by and fix the porch roof for you."

She smiled sheepishly. "I already did. Sort of."

"Sort of?"

"Well, I was using the short ladder because I'd lent the twelve-footer to Judy Lowery, and I over-reached."

He frowned in alarm. "You fell?"

"No. Marshack caught me." She had a sudden, vivid memory of his hand wrapped around her inner thigh. A deep blush caught her completely unaware.

Brick noted it and raised an eyebrow. "Do tell, Brittany."

She got into the car, pulled her door closed briskly and lowered the window. "Nothing to tell. He just happened to arrive at a very timely moment. Cut off my supplies, but saved me from breaking my neck." She smiled and turned the key in the ignition. "That's life. You have to take the bad with the good." She blew him a kiss. "Love to Karen. See ya."

As Britt drove back through town, she cranked up her Clint Black tape to put thoughts of Jake Marshack out of her head. She couldn't imagine why images of him lingered there anyway. He was just another big-dairy bully making her life more difficult than it already was.

So he was nice looking. Actually, he was a lot more than nice looking. Since she was having to deal with serious realities lately, she could admit to herself that he was gorgeous.

Guilt and confusion filled her simultaneously. Why did that matter, anyway? And how did thoughts of him form when her entire man-woman awareness was always focused on Jimmy—or, rather, his absence?

"You're losing your grip," she warned herself. "Work with me here, Britt. Get your brain going on things that are going to mean money, not trouble."

"All right," she told herself. "Today was just fated to be a disaster. You can't fight that. But tomorrow things are going to be different. Tomorrow you are not going to try to fix the roof, you will not have to deal with Jake Marshack, there will be no more bicycles to be run over. Tomorrow you will deliver Danishes to the diner and to Judson, you will take cheesecakes to the lodge, you will visit Grandma Martha. And you will come up with a gimmick."

There. She felt herself relax. It always helped to hear her problems or her plans spoken aloud. It gave them substance, somehow, and made her better able to deal with them.

Jimmy had always laughed at her when he came upon her talking herself through a dilemma. "You should have gone into politics," he told her more than once, "then you could have gotten paid for filibustering."

She enjoyed the memory for a moment, smiling absently at the road, feeling warm and happy. Then the truth crashed in on her, as it always did. It was just a memory. It would always be just a memory. And she and Jimmy would never ever make another one.

Darkness threatened to suck her in like the core of a tornado. But she pulled to a stop at the side of Main Street, grinding her foot into the brake, holding her ground.

She drew one even breath, then another one. "You can do this," she told herself bracingly. "Four kids are counting on you to get yourself together. A hundred acres that have belonged to a Bauer since the middle of the last century are waiting for you to come up with a gimmick so they don't become part of some hybrid, megamonster farm."

Feeling the return of control, she drew another deeper breath and let the car roll forward. She was smiling when she pulled up in front of the ballet school to pick up Renee. "And the food industry is just *waiting* for your gimmick."

CHAPTER THREE

JAKE FELT the resentment the moment he walked into the diner. The place had been abuzz with conversation when he opened the door, but it fell silent in the few seconds it took him to walk to the counter. Men in coveralls and baseball caps, men in suits and women dressed for work in town watched him every step of the way. As he settled on a stool at the L-shaped bar, talk started up again, but he got the distinct impression he was the subject of it.

He tried to take it in stride. News got around fast in small towns, and he'd paid four calls yesterday, trying to collect. He was the good guy when he could provide products needed, but the bad guy when he had to collect for them in hard times. He was getting used to being treated like the biblical tax collector or the contemporary IRS auditor.

He indicated the pile of newspapers on the counter between himself and the police officer seated beside him. "Finished with this?" he asked with a courteous smile.

The officer gave him a long, measuring look, then nodded. "Help yourself."

"Thank you." Jake found the sports page and decided to lose himself in the Cubs' spring-training stats.

The woman behind the counter ignored him, while second-guessing the needs of everyone else. A second waitress raced from the kitchen to the banks of booths against the wall. He gathered from the teasing going on back and forth that the woman ignoring him was named Marge and that she owned the diner.

He finally commanded her attention with a loud but courteous "Ham-and-cheese omelet, please. Hash browns. Sourdough toast. And coffee with cream."

She glared at him and he added with a pointed look, "When you get around to it. Thank you."

She came to stand in front of him, the coffeepot held aloft. He got the distinct impression she intended to pour its contents on him if he made one wrong move.

"Fresh out of ham and cheese," she said aggressively.

He put down the paper. He pointed to the officer's plate, where half of a ham-and-cheese omelet lay fluffy and plump beside a wedge of wheat toast.

"What's that?" he asked.

Brown eyes looked back at him evenly. "That's *his* ham-and-cheese omelet. He protects the people around here. He doesn't take food out of children's mouths and make life miserable for young widows who are barely—"

"Marge," the officer said quietly, his expression mildly amused. "That's harassment. Get him his omelet or I'll have to take you in."

Marge put down the pot and offered both wrists across the counter. "Here. Do it now. Put me in solitary, but don't expect me to do anything for this monster who—"

"What is going on?" a familiar voice demanded near Jake's shoulder.

He turned to find the widow Hansen standing in the small space between his shoulder and the police officer's. She wore jeans and another baggy sweater, this one a soft blue that was the color of her eyes. She had a wide, flat plastic container balanced on one hand and a big purse hung over her shoulder.

"Hey, babe." The officer snaked an arm around her and pulled her to him, kissing her temple. He rubbed her shoulder. "Buy you breakfast?"

She smiled at him affectionately, and Jake felt the irritation that had been building in him since he walked into the place develop into anger. "Thanks, Brick. Had it two hours ago." She placed the container on the counter, then frowned from him to Jake to Marge, whose hands were still held out sacrificially. "You're arresting Marge?"

Brick grinned. "She refused to serve this gentleman his ham-and-cheese omelet. That's unconstitutional."

Britt blinked at Marge. "Why?"

"Because he—"

Jake folded his paper and put it aside. "Forget the omelet. I was just leaving." He tried to stand, but a soft but surprisingly firm hand on his shoulder held him in place.

Britt's blue, blue eyes flashed at him. "You stay right there." She turned to Marge. "Why won't you order his omelet?"

Everyone in the restaurant was absolutely still, waiting for her answer.

"Because I know he's from Winnebago Dairy, and that he cut you off yesterday because you couldn't pay. Nobody does that to *my* friends and gets away with it." Marge's eyes filled briefly, then she sniffed and swiped at something on the counter that wasn't there. "Not after what you've been through. So Officer Bauer here—" she glanced in his direction "—threatened to take me in."

Britt drew a breath and sat Jake down a second time when he tried again to get up. "Margie, he was just doing his job," she said reasonably, almost surprised to hear the words come out of her own mouth. It was one thing to feel personal resentment at the bind his actions had left her in. But to see him unfairly treated by her friends in a public place for having done nothing more than what was required of him made her furious.

"I ordered the stuff," she said, "and I couldn't pay. His company has waited eight months already, while still supplying me. Do you think I'd keep making Danishes for you," she asked, tapping the plastic container, "if you didn't pay me?"

Marge folded her arms and raised an eyebrow. "Yes."

Britt wedged herself in between Jake and Brick so that she could lean over the counter toward Marge and give her the full effect of her stare. Brick grinned at Jake behind her back.

"You get this man his ham-and-cheese omelet," she said firmly, placing a hand on top of the container, "or I won't give you these extra Danishes you ordered for the Kiwanis breakfast. Whoever told you I'd been cut off apparently neglected to mention that when Mr. Marshack arrived at my place I was hanging by my fingernails from the roof. He saved me from falling, at considerable risk to himself."

That was somewhat overstated, Jake thought, but Marge's spine seemed to relax a fraction. She looked suspiciously from him to Britt.

"That's true," Brick confirmed, taking a bite of toast. "She told me yesterday afternoon. Even blushed when she said it. I don't think she's half as mad at him as you are."

Britt turned on Brick and whomped him in the stomach with the back of her hand. He choked on the toast and had to reach for his coffee.

She turned back to Marge. "Get the omelet now."

With one last, distrustful look at Jake, Marge made notes on her order pad, tore off the check and, scooping up the plastic container, went toward the kitchen.

"Spoilsport," Brick said, finally recovered. "That would've been my first collar in a the week."

Britt rolled her eyes at him. "You're a nut, Bauer."

"Runs in the family," he returned. "Faulty chromosomes or something."

Britt gave Jake an uncertain smile. "You okay?"

He was having palpitations over the nearness of her eyes, but he suspected she wouldn't want to know that. "Fine," he said. "Thank you."

"Jake Marshack—" she swept a hand toward the officer "—my cousin, Donald Bauer, known among family and friends as Brick because his head bears a remarkable resem—" Her fingers traced a square in the air as Brick reached around with one hand to cover her mouth. He thrust the other toward Jake.

"Actually, it's a name from my football days. Pleased to meet you. And thanks for saving her neck. I offered to do that roofing job for her, but she finds it impossible to wait for anything."

Britt pulled Brick's hand from her mouth. "He's been promising for weeks. I'd hoped to enjoy the porch before snow sets in again."

Listening to their affectionate banter, Jake felt a wave of loneliness he usually kept at bay with long hours in the office and at his desk at home. But here in Tyler the pace was slower, and after calling on her yesterday, he hadn't been able to turn off his mind.

He wasn't even sure why he was still here. Though he'd made another call after visiting her yesterday, he'd easily have gotten back to Chicago in time for a late dinner. But it had started raining, and he'd told himself rush hour would be slick and ugly and he might as well stay the night.

He'd watched cable television in the small motel room he'd found on the outskirts of town and had wondered how in hell the widow Hansen could be expected to make it with no feed, four kids, and everybody from bank to grocer breathing down her neck.

Then he remembered Brick saying a moment ago that Britt had told him about being saved from the roof, and that she'd blushed while telling him. Every time he thought about grabbing her thigh in his hand and scooping her bottom toward him as she'd dangled there, he felt a catch in his chest, a hitch in his pulse. Something subtle had happened to him yesterday. And it was possible something had happened to her.

"I've got to go," Britt announced, her purse bumping him as she slipped out from between them. She turned to give him a quick smile, one that on the surface held only courtesy. But her eyes were so close to his that he saw deep inside a vague little longing that flashed when their eyes met, then was gone. "Safe trip home," she said. Then she leaned over to kiss Brick on the cheek. "Have a good day, cuz."

"Where you off to?" he asked.

"Worthington House to see Grandma and Inger."

When she was out the door, Jake couldn't resist asking Brick, "What happened to her husband?"

"He was plowing near a ditch," Brick said grimly. "Got too close. Tractor turned over on him."

Jake closed his eyes. That ugly accident happened all too often in farm country, but it was hard for him to think it had happened to someone Britt had loved.

"She'd gone to Milwaukee with a friend for a weekend of shopping," Brick went on. "The first time she'd ever left Jimmy and the kids alone. She carries a lot of guilt over it."

"God," Jake said quietly, feelingly.

"Yeah. You can see why Marge got testy. Britt's fighting an uphill battle, and we're all pushing and pulling for her."

As though on cue, Marge appeared with a steaming plate. The omelet was fat and beautiful, the hash browns golden and the toast buttered in every little corner. She poured coffee into a cup, put a pot of cream beside him and a jar of jam. "Anything else?" she asked, her tone a shade more congenial, but only just.

Jake looked down at his breakfast, then up at her again. "Something to eat it with," he said, "and I'll be a happy man."

"Oh." She looked surprised that she'd forgotten utensils. She retrieved knife, fork and spoon and a generous-size napkin, then leaned on her elbows across from him as he peppered the omelet.

"So you can't see your way clear to get her a month's extension?" she prodded. "She's got big plans, you know. She makes the best low-calorie cheesecake east of the Rockies, and she's going to pick up more clients and make more different products with her yogurt."

Jake frowned, knowing how overworked she had to be already. "By herself?"

Marge sighed. "That's how she does everything since Jimmy died."

Jake couldn't see how that was going to make any difference—provided she could even do it. Cheese-cake, however elegant, would have to be produced by the thousands to affect the kind of debt on her books....

Though she'd been gone ten minutes, he could still see deep into those blue eyes and that little flash of longing in them. Business was business, but it was hard to step on someone who was trying so hard.

Marge was still waiting for an answer.

"I'll try," he promised with a thin smile.

A cheer rose from Marge's Diner's clientele. Jake looked around from the counter to find himself being applauded.

Brick slapped him on the back. *"All right,"* he said.

Jake turned back to his breakfast, mystified. He'd visited Tyler a dozen times in the past few years, but he'd never stayed overnight, so he'd never stopped in for breakfast. He'd never spoken to anyone but the people from whom he'd been trying to collect, so he'd never gotten below the surface of the pretty little lake town.

Now that he had, it was a little scary. For a boy who'd lived with his mother in a tenement in Chicago, crowded in with an aunt who'd made it clear every day that they were there on the sufferance of charity, this warm caring of one person for another was something alien and new. As an adult, he'd certainly never seen it in the corporate world.

Marge topped up his coffee and gave him a brilliant smile. Brick picked up his tab. When Jake tried to protest, he offered his hand again, then was gone.

Jake dug into his succulent omelet, feeling as though his world had slipped a little out of orbit.

WALKING ACROSS the parking lot toward the rest home that sprawled on a corner of Elm Street, Britt tried to stop her mind's erratic jumping, from Jake Marshack to cheesecakes, to Jake Marshack to money, to Jake Marshack.

She'd seen a lonely man in the diner. Though she missed Jimmy abominably, she had friends and relatives who were always generous with emotional support or a more substantive helping hand. She hated to think of anyone trying to get through life without them.

Of course, why she was worried about a man with a secure, high-paying job when her personal economy was about to bottom out, she couldn't imagine. There was just something in his face that touched her.

Topping the stairs and blindly turning down the corridor, Britt collided with George Phelps, who was perusing a chart.

"I'm sorry, Dr. Phelps," she apologized breathlessly. "Did I hurt you?"

He grinned at the question. Tall and fit, with graying brown hair, he twirled the end of his elegant mustache in a parody of villainy. "Hardly. It was the nicest thing that's happened to me this morning. How are you, Britt?"

"Good. How are things with you?"

"I'm fine," he replied, his expression failing to match his words. He waved a typewritten sheet in the air. "Except for the resignation of Finklebaum, my nursing supervisor. She'll be missed around here. But how're the kids? I don't recall seeing any of your brood since back-to-school checkups."

Britt rapped on the paneled wall. "Knock on wood. I think they move too fast to catch anything." She began to back away. "I'm on my way to visit the ladies. Take care, Doctor."

Britt turned down the corridor toward Inger Hansen's room, bracing herself for the ordeal. She visited Jimmy's great-aunt before her grandmother because the woman's irascible personality made it more of a challenge than a pleasure. With that chore behind her, Britt could then relax and enjoy her Grandma Martha.

The theme music from "The Price is Right" blared from the television as Britt entered the room. The woman sharing the space with Inger, apparently cursed with good hearing, wore large orange ear protectors as she concentrated on her cross-stitching.

"Hi, Inger," Britt said, coming up beside her to put a bag of goodies on her bedside table.

"Shh!" Inger snapped, her sharp eyes focused on the television as she held Britt out of the way with one arm. "This guy's about to blow it. He is so stupid! You wonder how some people get by!"

The television audience cheered for a correct answer and Inger slapped her blanket in disgust. "One live brain cell. Big deal!" She turned to Britt and shouted over the loud television. "How are you? You look like a refugee. Don't you ever eat?"

Britt smiled and gave her a hug, tuning out her considerable annoyance quotient in deference to her age and her status as family.

"I'm fine, Aunt Inger. How are you?"

"Old. Arthritic. God knows what else. I hope that bag isn't filled with more cheesecake."

"No." Britt allowed herself a smile, grateful her small success didn't depend on Inger. It was interesting, she thought, how differently time and loss of loved ones aged individuals. Some, like her grandmother, drew others toward them. Inger pushed everyone away, as though telling the world that if she couldn't have the people she wanted, she didn't want anyone.

Britt delved into the bag and held out a Linder ball, a chocolate confection wrapped in colorful foil. They were Inger's weakness.

Inger's eyes softened for an instant, then she snatched the candy from Britt. "Thank you," she said, almost resentful at having a reason for gratitude. "How are your little monsters?"

Britt poured water into Inger's glass from the small carafe and tidied her tray. "Oh, you know. Monstrous. Anything I can get you?"

"No." Inger made a shooing motion toward the door. "Go on. Get back to your kids and your cows. And for God's sake, eat something before somebody puts old clothes on you and sticks you in a cornfield."

Britt leaned down to hug her again and felt the old woman's surprisingly strong response before she pushed her away and turned her concentration back to the television. When Britt paused at the door to wave, Inger had the bag of Linder balls in her lap.

She found an earnest game of gin rummy in progress in Martha Bauer's room. The tiny, fragile woman was propped up against her pillows, her white hair in a neat braid coronet atop her head, her bony shoulders adorned with a soft blue bed jacket.

"Brittany!" Martha's deep voice was slightly fractured with age. From the bank of pillows, her bright blue eyes smiled behind wire-rimmed bifocals. She patted the side of her bed for Britt to join her, then returned to the serious business of winning the hand. She tilted her head slightly backward to focus on the spread of cards she held. She considered for a moment, then placed everything in her hand in threes and fours on the swivel tray serving as a card table. "Gin!" she said with satisfaction.

Martha's round, gray-haired opponent occupied a room down the hall but visited Martha regularly to play cards and cadge treats. Britt knew her simply as Lavinia.

Lavinia looked at her full hand of cards, then down at the table in disgust. "I don't know why I drag my arthritic carcass all the way over here just to get beaten day after day. How much am I in your debt now?"

"Ah..." Martha consulted the score sheet. "Nine hundred and fifty-seven dollars."

"You cheat!" Lavinia accused with a smile. "If it wasn't for the food your granddaughter brings—" she winked at Britt "—I wouldn't come back."

She stood laboriously, and Britt went around the bed to help her untangle herself from the chair and position herself within the protective rails of her walker. Someone in Lavinia's family had made a colorful little calico pouch that snapped on the side of the walker, and Britt stuffed a bag full of soft cookies she and the children had made into it.

"Bless you," Lavinia said, leaning heavily on one hand to put the other arm around Britt in a hug. Then she started for the door, moving surely, but at a snail's pace. "Here I go," she said. "Like a turtle with her tail on fire. Out of my way. Watch my dust. That's not an explosion you hear, it's me, breaking the sound barrier. Hi, ho, Silver! Awayyyy..." Her voice trailed after her as she made her way down the hall.

Britt and Martha giggled.

"How are you today, Grandma?" Britt asked, settling herself on the edge of the bed again. "Do you really cheat?"

"Of course. She's a better player—it's the only way I can win." She looked more pleased with herself than apologetic. Then she tilted back her head to study Britt through the lower half of her bifocals. "How are you? You look more like your mother every day. Except for the circles under your eyes."

Britt delved into the bag she'd brought. "Well, I'm no spring chicken anymore, you know."

"Thirty-two. Still a baby."

"Thirty-three," Britt corrected, handing her the current supermarket tabloids. "Here's your *Globe, Inquirer, Star, Shalimar,* and a small piece of cheesecake."

Martha frowned at her playfully. "Small piece?"

"Got to watch that waistline." Britt put the cheesecake on her tray, pulled off the plastic wrap, then poured a cup of milky coffee from a thermos she'd brought.

Martha rolled a bite of cheesecake on her tongue and made an appreciative sound. Then she pointed at the cake with her fork. "You know, my mother used to love rich things. Torte with custard filling and meringue. And she made the most beautiful lattice crust you ever saw."

This was a story Martha loved to tell, so Britt smiled encouragingly and listened patiently as time rolled away and the old woman focused with misting blue eyes on her childhood. "'Course, she was only ten years old when her family came here from Germany, so she remembered life there very clearly. She was scandalized when stores started carrying cake mix in a box. She and our neighbor, Mrs. Olson, made a pact never to bake anything that was prepackaged."

"Hi, Martha!" An enthusiastic voice interrupted the old woman's reminiscences. "That's right, isn't it? I'm trying to learn names today."

Martha looked up with a bright smile, and Britt turned as a woman she guessed to be somewhere around her own age walked into the room. She was plump and red-haired, and was wearing the pale green uniform of the Worthington House staff. She spoke deliberately and with the childlike need to please of the developmentally disabled.

Martha beckoned her closer. "That's right, Freddie. You're doing very well. Come and meet my most favorite person in the whole world."

Britt stood and Freddie came forward shyly.

"Freddie, this is Britt Hansen, my granddaughter," she said, "Britt, this is Freddie Houser. Dr. Phelps just hired her a few days ago and she's fitting right in. She helps me with my bath."

Freddie beamed at the praise.

Britt offered her hand. "I'm happy to meet you, Freddie. I'm glad to know you're taking such good care of Grandma."

"I work very hard," Freddie assured her. "And I try to do everything just the way Mrs. Finklebaum showed me."

"Freddie?" One of the other aides appeared in the doorway. With a wave and a smile for Britt and Martha, she asked Freddie, "Can you come and help me with Mrs. Norgaard?"

"Okay." Before she left, Freddie whispered to Britt conspiratorially, "I'll take special care of Martha, don't you worry."

"Thank you, Freddie."

As the aides disappeared down the hall, Martha shook her head sadly, pulling Britt closer. "Poor Freddie," she said quietly. "She lived at home until her mother died. Lavinia told me Phyllis had been diagnosed as terminally ill, but lately had been in a kind of remission. Then, suddenly, she just died without warning. Now Freddie's all alone. Dr. Phelps hired her to help out around here and she's trying so hard." She sighed. "Imagine being not quite up to snuff and having nobody."

"That *would* be tough," Britt commiserated. "Well, she really seems to like you, so you keep encouraging her. Now finish that cheesecake so I can take the plate with me."

Martha tucked back into the treat with fervor. "My mother used to make something kind of like this. Though she never liked using cow's milk. She always wanted a goat, so that we could have goat's milk, but my father raised dairy cows and was horrified at the idea. She insisted goat's milk was healthier and tasted better. He said it tasted like—" She stopped abruptly and grinned. "I won't tell you what he said it tasted like. She tried to tell him goat's milk could be delicious if the goat ate the right things, and that it was easier to digest. Often, people who are allergic to dairy products can still drink goat's milk. But he wouldn't hear of it and she never did get a goat."

"I had goat's milk a couple of times in college," Britt said, trying to remember the circumstances. "We were on a health kick, I think, to get in bikini shape by the summer. We'd been impressed in class with how low in fat and..."

Something clanged in her brain.

Goat's milk. Lower in fat than cow's milk. Snob appeal. *Gimmick!*

Martha ate and chatted while Britt's heart began to pound and her brain ticked over with the idea. At the moment, yogurt was the ordinary consumer's fair-haired child. Goat's milk yogurt would probably bring them running. No. Would it? Would they go for it? Of course. All she had to do was think it through carefully and find the right approach.

She had to make some. Now. Today.

A BLOND EYEBROW went up disbelievingly. "You're going to make what?"

"Goat's milk yogurt," Britt repeated, taking her friend and neighbor, Judy Lowery, by the wrist and dragging her across the yard toward the pen where she kept three Alpine goats.

"You've got to be joking. You ever tasted the stuff?" Judy was a writer who kept the goats for company. She was a newcomer to the Tyler area and a cynic, but a wonderful friend.

"I'm going to scope it out in detail at the library, but my grandmother says goat's milk can be delicious if they're properly fed. Can I rent one of your goats for a couple of days? Long enough to get milk and make yogurt and try a few recipes?"

Judy, half a head taller than Britt, put her hands on her friend's shoulders and said gravely, "Why don't you come inside and lie down? I've seen this coming. You've blown a fuse. I knew this was—"

"Go ahead and scoff," Britt said, undaunted by her attitude, "but I'm going to produce a yogurt that's lower in fat and calories than anything currently on the market. And I'm going to make a bundle."

Judy folded her arms. "Why don't you just find a rich man and remarry? You've still got it, you know. Tight body, great hair, unconscious sex appeal. Why put yourself through this?"

This time Britt took Judy's arms and gave her a shake. She'd thought about her idea in the car all the way over here and it just felt right. "Judy, I've spent my life living everyone else's dream. I came home from college to take over the farm when my dad had a heart attack. I worked beside Jimmy toward *his* plan of what Lakeside Farm should be. This dream is mine. I'm going to save the farm with the hottest damned food product on the market."

Judy shifted her weight and cleared her throat. "Britt," she said, "as a dream, goat's milk yogurt kind of lacks the cosmic quality."

Britt swatted her arm. "This is going to work. Can I rent a goat or not?"

"No," Judy replied, "but you can borrow one. Take your pick."

"Which one's your best milker?"

"Mildred." Judy pointed to the doe in the middle, which was tan with white-and-black markings on her face and hindquarters. She was angular with prominent hipbones, thin thighs and a long, lean neck and body. Britt knew the uninitiated might consider her underfed, but a good dairy goat was neither fat nor meaty. Mildred looked like a good prospect.

Britt stretched a hand toward her and all three goats edged forward to nip at her fingers and sleeve. She patted Mildred between the stumps of her horns.

"Okay, Milly," she said. "You and I are going to take the world by storm."

Though Britt was pleased with Mildred, Mildred didn't appear to be thrilled with Britt. She complained loudly as the two women lifted her into the back of the truck. Britt raised the tailgate and locked it. Mildred looked at her with sad, accusing yellow eyes.

Britt patted her flank. "It's just for a couple of days, Milly. You'll have fun." Britt walked around the truck to the driver's side, then turned to hug Judy. "Wish me luck. If this works, it could be the end of my problems."

Judy smiled skeptically. "Don't be silly. This is life, Brittany. Problems never end, they just rest between eruptions."

"How's the book coming?"

"So-so. I think it needs more violence, but I'm not very good at that. I hate to hurt anyone I create."

"I'll lend you my *kids*," Britt said, grinning at her little play on words. "Fair exchange. They do violence to one another without a second thought or hint of remorse. Would that help?"

Judy smiled blandly. "Thanks awfully, but I'll pass. Let me know how it goes."

Britt waved out the window as she headed home.

Her mind glutted with ideas, she tried to make herself relax and take it one slow and careful step at a time. First, she'd make Mildred comfortable. Then she'd see that she had just the right things to eat to produce the perfect milk for her recipe. Then she would make the recipe work.

Everything would come together; she just felt it would.

Britt pulled into her drive, noticing the young spring green on the tips of everything, then turned into the yard.

She was just beginning to relax when she saw the red Explorer parked behind her station wagon. Her heart gave an involuntary and rather violent lurch. Jake Marshack was back.

CHAPTER FOUR

HE WAS SITTING on the top step of the porch, Daffodil beside him, licking his ear. The dog gave one loud bark and went running toward the truck. Jake got up more slowly and wandered down the steps while Britt came around the truck, eyeing him suspiciously.

She was as pretty as he remembered. After breakfast that morning, as he'd gone around on his self-appointed chores, he'd been plagued with a vivid memory of her, pink-cheeked and clear-eyed, insisting that Marge order his omelet. He'd finally concluded that she couldn't be as beautiful as he remembered. He was simply flattering himself because she'd come so wholeheartedly to his defense.

But he could see now that his memory had been sharp and true. She'd torn out the braid at some point since he'd seen her this morning, and her gold hair hung loose and a little wild in the early-afternoon wind. Her cheeks were flushed. Her eyes were bright, though he noticed a bluish bruised effect under them. That hurt him in a way he didn't entirely understand and couldn't have explained.

She stopped halfway across the yard as he came toward her. "Mr. Marshack," she said coolly. "What is it now?"

He fought an overwhelming urge to take her in his arms, carry her into the house and put her somewhere where she could rest undisturbed for a week. Instead, he moved past her to the truck and examined the goat, his hands in his suit pants pockets. "New transportation for Matt so he can keep his paper route?" he asked.

She fought a smile, then gave in. "No, he'll get by on my old bike. Actually, the goat's part of my plan to ruin *your* plan."

"My plan?"

"To make me sell."

It wasn't *his* plan, it was someone else's higher up the chain of command. But he didn't want to talk about that.

"That's not why I'm here," he said.

Her heart skipped a beat as she looked into his quiet brown eyes. She'd seen them over and over in her mind last night, then this morning after their meeting in the diner. There was a message in them she was afraid to read.

She dipped her head in mock apology. "My mistake. Why are you here?"

"Actually," he said, gently taking her arm and leading her toward the porch, "it's part of my plan to ruin your plan."

"I'm getting confused," she admitted. Then she noticed the bike leaning against the porch railing. It was a shiny new Huffy with a water bottle, a carry-bag attached to the frame and other options she couldn't even identify. She gasped at the beauty of it, smiled instinctively at the way she knew Matt would react to it. Then, when she'd had time to think, she frowned.

"I thought I explained—"

"You did," he said appeasingly, "and I understand and appreciate all your parental concerns. But the fact remains that your son wasn't completely at fault, and it bothered me all night. If you insist, he can pay me five dollars a month or something until it's paid off."

She looked at the spiffy top-of-the-line model with all the extras. "It would take him until he's twenty-one."

"Hardly."

"Mr. Marshack. I don't think..." she began half-heartedly, hating to deprive Matt of this beautiful bike, but knowing in her heart he'd be careless with it again and she'd never be able to come close to replacing it.

But the yellow school bus at the end of the lane expelled her children, and the dog ran to greet them. They were halfway to the house when their attention homed in on the bike. Matt shouted and started to run, the others following quickly behind, the dog weaving in and out of them in suicidal patterns. From the truck, Mildred complained loudly. Unnoticed by the other children, the goat brought Renee to a dead stop. At the sight of it she veered toward the truck.

Matt skidded to a halt at the porch steps, Christy and David flanking him breathlessly, all sets of eyes on the bike.

Britt watched Matt's face as his gaze caressed every shiny inch of it. He looked up at her, obviously afraid to draw any conclusions about what the bike's presence meant.

"Hi, Mom," he said. Then, apparently deciding his best behavior was called for in this uncertain situation, he extended his hand to their guest. "Mr. Marshack. Nice to see you again."

Britt melted as Jake shook hands with her son. Even knowing Matt had probably realized displaying good manners could only be to his benefit, it was such a deep-down, genuine pleasure to find that he'd absorbed something she'd taught him. She put an arm around him and squeezed.

"Mr. Marshack thinks the two of you should make a deal about the bike."

Joy flashed in Matt's eyes. He turned to Jake, and took the nobility just a little further. "It was all my fault," he said. "You'd never have seen my bike in your mirror. You aren't responsible." For good measure, he glanced at his mother. "Mom's got a thing about responsibility."

Jake nodded gravely, lifted the bike by the handlebars and seat from its leaning position against the steps and steadied it in front of Matt. "She's absolutely right. And most mistakes we have to pay for, but with some we deserve a break. I figure we can split the cost. You can pay me back for your half at five bucks a month. And you don't have to start until after the summer trip you're saving for."

Matt turned to his mother, his eyes wide with disbelief.

"Wow!" Christy breathed.

"Boy," David said, his voice filled with awe as he stared at the bike. "Are you lucky!"

"Hop on," Jake said. "Make sure everything works before I leave."

Matt watched Britt's eyes for the firm refusal he seemed to feel sure was coming.

She nodded. "You *are* lucky," she said, "to have had your bike run over by someone so understanding and so generous."

Matt smiled from ear to ear as he threw a leg over the bike. It was the first free, open smile she'd seen on his face in a year. He started to thank Jake and couldn't. He tried three different times, but the words refused to string together with any kind of coherence.

"Go," Jake said finally. "Be careful at first, though, just to make sure everything's all right."

They all watched as he did a careful circuit of the yard, then a faster, more complicated one. Then Matt shouted gleefully and headed down the drive to the road. "I'm gonna do the loop!" he called. "Be right back."

Christy and David ran to the fence to watch him.

"The loop?" Jake asked.

"A road around the woods that leads back here." She looked up into his brown eyes and saw satisfaction there. Making her son happy had made him happy. It was difficult to remain angry with him under those circumstances. "Thank you, Mr. Marshack. He hasn't been this thrilled about anything since . . . well, in a long time."

"It was my pleasure," he said. "And I have something else to tell you."

"What's that?"

Before he could reply, there was a squeal from Renee, who was hanging from the side of the pickup. Mildred had a mouthful of her hair.

With an exasperated groan, Britt ran to the truck. Renee dangled helplessly, giggling and shrieking. Jake supported her while Britt tried to ease her hair from Mildred's mouth. The goat nibbled at Britt's hand as she pulled gently.

Finally freed, Renee turned into Jake's arms, wrapping hers around his neck. "Hi," she said warmly, making no effort to get down. "You're back."

"Yes." She looked like her mother, he thought, with something in her smile that tugged at him the way Britt's did. There was openness in it, and a touching need.

"Did you bring the goat?"

"No, your mom did."

"How come?"

"Because we're going to make yogurt from Mildred's milk," Britt explained, stepping around a mud puddle. Taking Mildred's lead in one hand and opening the tailgate with the other, she added, "And use it in my cheesecake."

"Why?"

"Because it'll be lower in calories."

"Why?"

"Because there's less butterfat in goat's milk."

"Why?"

Jake admired Britt's patient answers to Renee's favorite question. But she was distracted now by Mildred's refusal to come to the back of the truck. Apparently deciding that the neglect of the past few moments didn't bode well for a stay of any duration in this place, Mildred refused to budge.

Britt climbed lightly into the truck and, putting a shoulder to Mildred's rear, pushed until she reached the rear edge. "Mr. Marshack," she said breathlessly, "would you grab her collar so she doesn't back away while I jump out?"

Jake put Renee down and complied. The goat looked at him with resentful amber eyes. Britt leaped down and wrapped her arms around Mildred's four legs. Mildred baaed unhappily.

Jake put a halting hand on Britt's shoulder. "What are you doing?" he demanded.

Surprised by his tone and a little annoyed with his interference, she replied over her shoulder, "Lifting her down. Get out of the way."

"You'll hurt yourself," he said, pulling off his suit coat.

Holding Mildred's collar, Britt straightened and looked at him with a raised eyebrow. "Mr. Marshack, I carry fifty-pound bags of grain, heavy bales of hay, even Renee...."

Ignoring her, Jake pushed her aside, wrapped his arms around the goat and lifted. Mildred stood quietly in his arms long enough to give him a false sense of security, then began to struggle wildly as he lowered her to the ground. He held fast, afraid a sudden drop might break a spindly leg.

Determined to break free, Mildred pitched forward. Jake overbalanced and they landed together in a shallow but messy mud puddle.

Britt caught Mildred's tether before she could prance away and handed it to Renee, who was giggling uproariously. Then she hunkered down beside Jake and considered him, elbows on her knees. Holding back the laughter was choking her.

"I could have done that," she said, "And without getting muddy."

The impulse to yank Britt down beside him was overwhelming. Had Renee not been standing there, he might have done it. Mud squished through his clothes and he felt splashes of it on his face.

"You're walking a fine line, Mrs. Hansen," he warned quietly, fighting his own urge to laugh. "A sympathetic hand up would be appreciated."

She straightened to her feet and offered her hand, still biting her bottom lip. "I told you I was perfectly capable of—"

"What can I say?" he groaned, taking her hand and using it only for balance as he pushed himself to his feet. "I was born and bred in Chicago—as a gentleman, I might add. I had this foolish, chivalrous notion that a woman shouldn't have to lift a goat."

"Farm women aren't like city women," she said, grimacing as she examined the mud covering most of the back of his elegant suit. "You're a mess, Mr. Marshack. You'd better come inside."

He stopped as she tried to lead him toward the house.

"Considering I've humiliated myself on your behalf," he said, "do you think you could call me Jake?"

She let her laughter loose then, looping her arm in his. He was forced to laugh with her and allowed himself to be guided up the drive to the porch steps and into the familiar kitchen.

"Keep Mildred company for a few minutes," Britt called to Renee. "I'll be right back."

The other three children piled into the house after them as Jake followed Britt through the kitchen to a dark hallway, then up the back stairs toward a long line of bedrooms.

"The bike's cool, Mr. Marshack!" Matt reported from the bottom of the stairs. "The thumb-shifters are radical, and the brakes *really* work." Then he seemed to notice the condition of Jake's clothes. "What happened?"

"I was trying to help your mother with the goat," Jake said. "I didn't do very well."

Matt frowned at Britt. "Yeah, I saw it. What's it for, anyway? Renee says you're gonna cook it."

"No," Britt called over her shoulder, stopping at the doorway to her bedroom. "I'm going to cook with the milk the goat gives us. I'm trying a new recipe for goat's milk yogurt."

"Oh." The word contained very little enthusiasm.

"Are you staying for dinner, Mr. Marshack?" Christy asked, eyes wide and interested behind her glasses. She and David had followed them up the stairs.

A dinner invitation hadn't been in Britt's plans, but she quickly decided that since his present predicament had been precipitated by a sincere desire to help her, it would be only hospitable to ask him.

But before she could, David said coaxingly, "We're having stew." David always checked the stove when he came home from school.

"Salad, corn bread," Britt added, "and cheesecake."

Jake got the impression the children really wanted him to stay. Britt was less easy to read, but he thought he'd be foolish to let that stop him.

"I'd love to stay."

The children cheered. Some strange emotion stabbed Jake in the chest.

Britt sent the children down to their after-school chores and led Jake into the bedroom. It was green and apricot, with a large window that looked out onto the pasture. Jake wondered if the furniture had come west on a covered wagon. The bed was a four-poster in a light wood with large cannonball-size finials. It had the patina that came from age and caring hands.

She pointed him to a bathroom at the far end of the room. "Shower's in there. I'll leave some of Jimmy's things for you on the bed." Her blue eyes did a quick, businesslike perusal of him from head to toe, one that made his pulse thrum. "They should fit . . . just fine."

She stammered as she looked into his eyes and saw something there she couldn't define but understood even so. It was related to the sudden acceleration of her heartbeat. The bedroom that had been practically like a convent for the past year, where she read and prayed and mulled over her problems, suddenly hummed with a curious power source. She wasn't sure where it had come from or why it had sprung to life so suddenly, but she suspected that if she were to touch Jake at that moment, electricity would arc between them.

She sidled past him, between his muddy body and her pristine bedspread, to the door. "I'll be in the kitchen when you've washed off the mud," she said, then ran from the room as though something had chased her.

JAKE FOUND showering in Britt's bathroom an unusual experience. The soap was scented, the shower curtain had green sea grass and pink seashells on it, and the bathroom counter held a modest lineup of cosmetics and colognes. It smelled like she did—vaguely floral and fresh.

On one level he felt uncomfortable because he didn't want to dirty anything, and he feared in his present condition that was going to be impossible. But on another level, the femininity was curiously comforting.

His condo was all brown and beige and leather. His cream-colored bathroom had a functional shower stall and brown towels. His counter was bare, thanks to a three-sectioned, mirrored cabinet.

He showered quickly, washed his hair and buffed himself dry with a fragrant pink towel. He found a pair of jeans, a chambray shirt and a set of underwear on the foot of the bed. The jeans were a tad short, but fit well. The shirt was perfect. Apparently Jimmy Hansen had been pretty much his size.

The thought had no sooner formed than he was confronted with its confirmation. Sitting down on the bed to put on the slippers Britt had left on the carpet, he found himself eye to eye with a photograph of the man himself in his wedding clothes.

He was surprised to find himself feeling suddenly aggressive. Jimmy Hansen had been nice looking in an unremarkable sort of way, tall and broad and smiling. What showed through and made Jake look twice was what must have been a basic kindness. It was in his eyes, in the way he held the laughing woman in the bridal gown, in the way Britt looked at him with complete trust and open-hearted love.

He felt their unity like a jolt. No wonder Britt could look so bright one moment and so fragile the next. A love like that would be a beacon, but without someone to direct it to, it would be a powerful force to deal with day after day.

He went downstairs feeling unsettled.

He heard the shouting before he reached the kitchen door.

"She is not!" a girl's voice said adamantly. He guessed it was Christy's.

"She is," a boy's voice said reasonably. David. "I heard her talking on the phone to Judy."

By the time Jake reached the doorway, Christy, wooden spoon in hand, was waving threateningly at her younger brother, who was placing silverware in orderly precision around the table. "Mom would never sell the farm. She couldn't. We'd have nowhere to live."

A quick glance around the room showed Jake that Britt and Matt were missing. Matt was delivering papers, Jake knew, but where was his hostess?

Renee followed David with plates and stopped to ask in horror, "You mean ... we're gonna go away?"

"Of course not!" Christy said with conviction, moving back to the pot of stew. "David's just being dumb."

"Then how come Mom was crying?" David demanded.

"She wasn't."

"She was."

As though in sympathy, even though the issue wasn't clear, Renee began to cry. "I don't want to go away," she wept, confounding Jake by turning to him, arms raised, as he walked into the room.

Panic seized him. He was alone with three children, two of them fighting and one of them crying. He didn't know what to do. He tried to tell himself this was no different from a sales meeting, and proceeded to take charge.

He picked up Renee and gently hushed her.

"I don't want to go away!" she complained, taking his neck in a stranglehold and weeping into it.

"I'm sure nobody's going away," he said, one-handedly finishing the placement of plates the child had started. "There. What else do we need to do?"

"Salt and pepper and napkins," Christy said, pointing to the caddy on the counter. Her own composure looked a little tenuous, Jake thought. "I'm sure Mom'll be right back."

The silverware placed, David followed Jake and Renee from the table to the counter, then back to the table. "She was crying," he told Jake, almost as though he wanted him to do something about it.

"Where'd she go?" Jake asked.

Christy turned away from the stove. "To the barn with the goat." Then she added in a very mature tone, "I think she just needed a minute to herself. The bank called."

David looked up at him with solemn dark blue eyes. "They're not gonna give us the money."

Jake felt a rush of unreasonable anger. He'd seen her credit profile. Loans-R-Us wouldn't lend her money. It was only good business. But she wasn't just a statistic in a ledger to him anymore. She was a brave and beautiful woman pitting herself against impossible odds to try to save her family's past for her children's future. Wasn't that what life was supposed to be about? Taking the love and knowledge of those who came before to make a better world for those who came after?

Jake was just about to put Renee down and check on Britt when the back door opened with a sudden crash. Matt strode into the kitchen, pulling off his delivery sack, its giant pockets emblazoned with the *Tyler Citizen* logo, and tossing it into a corner between the refrigerator and the wall.

"Mr. Marshack!" he said, his nose and cheeks bright red, a fresh out-of-doors smell clinging to his clothes. "The bike takes the hills like it's got a motor and I did the most radical wheelie you ever saw on the pad at the gas station."

Jake smiled at his ingenuous excitement. "Glad to hear it. Maybe we'd better get you a helmet."

"All *right!*" Matt agreed as he swept descriptive hands around his head. "One with an eagle with its wings swept back."

The back door opened and Jake looked up to see Britt walk into the kitchen. She'd apparently stayed in the barn long enough to make certain there would be no evidence of tears when she came back. But on just a little over twenty-four hours' acquaintance, he knew her well enough to know she felt lower than a hole.

Then she looked up, focused on him standing amid her children and stopped dead.

ALL THOUGHT CONCENTRATED on keeping tears and a crushing depression at bay, Britt walked into the kitchen with a phony smile on her face and all sensors turned off. Then she saw Jimmy standing in the middle of the kitchen with their children clustered around him, Renee in his arms.

She knew an instant's delirium. Of course! It had all been a mistake. He hadn't been meant to die. He'd been too young, too vital, too much in love with her and too proud of their children.

Then sanity returned and with it a chilling, paralyzing numbness. No. If she'd learned anything in the past year it was that death was permanent. It offered no glimpses of hope or possibilities of commutation. It was forever.

It took a moment for her brain to surface from shock, to remember who the man dressed in Jimmy's clothes and surrounded by Jimmy's children was. She watched him put Renee on her feet and disentangle himself from the little, uncertain crowd.

He came toward her, a hand extended. She took it because more than anything at the moment she needed a tie to reality, something to draw her out of that shocking little moment into the here and now. On top of the call from the bank, it was going to be more than she could handle.

Jake wanted to take her in his arms. He could see that she was hanging on by a thread, but he saw her eyes go past him to her children and knew she was calculating the emotional damage to them of seeing their mother fall apart in the middle of the kitchen.

He simply tightened his grip on her hand and pulled her into the room.

"What's wrong?" Matt asked with a frown.

Christy came to wrap her arms around her. "You okay, Mom?"

"The bank said no," David told Matt. "We're gonna have to go away."

"No!" Britt said sharply. When the boy's head snapped back at the tone of her voice, she put a hand to his dark hair and rubbed gently, pulling him to her side. "Who told you that?" she asked gently. "We're not going anywhere. We're going to stay right here. I just have to figure out how."

Christy made a face at David. "Told you."

Matt dug into the pocket of his jacket and extracted several crumpled bills and a handful of change. He held it out to Britt. "I did some collecting today. I got some tips."

Britt closed his fingers over the money and squeezed, feeling the backbone all mothers grow to keep their children whole and safe settle back into place. "Thanks, Matt, but you'll need that for your trip. This is just a temporary setback."

Matt's mouth took on a wry twist. "We've had a lot of those."

Inexplicably, absurdly, that made her laugh. "Yes, we have," she said. Suddenly realizing Jake still held her hand, she looked up into his eyes and saw genuine concern there.

She squeezed *his* fingers and dropped her hand. "How's the stew?" she asked Christy.

"Ready. But I haven't made the salad."

"Okay, I'll do that." Britt went to the sink and washed her hands, issuing orders all around. Jake found himself slicing tomatoes, while Renee, standing on a chair beside him at the counter, buttered bread. On his other side, David washed lettuce in the sink.

Christy wrapped the bread in foil and put it in the oven while Britt wielded a whisk in a small blue bowl. The spicy aroma of salad dressing rose to mingle with the rich beefiness of the stew.

Renee, now assigned to folding paper napkins in slightly lopsided triangles, leaned against Jake's shoulder as she told him about a calf named Spot she'd helped Britt bottle-feed.

At the crowded counter, Jake didn't have an inch to move in either direction. For a moment it reminded him sharply of his childhood and the claustrophobia he used to feel in his aunt's tenement.

But this was different. He wasn't made to feel out of place and unwelcome here.

Suddenly everything was on the table. Christy poured milk, Britt poured coffee and Matt prepared to offer grace. They joined hands around the table and silence fell.

The noise level never quite returned to the chaos of before supper. The children talked about school, Christy groaning over a farming notebook she had to have ready by the end of the school year. The kittens slept in a pile in a corner beside the dog.

David wanted to know more about the goat and what Britt planned to make with the milk. "I've never had yogurt from goat's milk," he said.

Britt smiled. "Neither have most people. My cheesecakes are doing pretty well, but we need something I can sell all over Wisconsin and maybe even in other parts of the country."

Renee frowned. "Kids don't like yogurt."

"Frozen yogurt's cool," Christy corrected.

"There's yogurt in the salad dressing," Britt said as Renee chewed a generous mouthful. Renee stopped chewing and looked worriedly around the table. Everyone laughed and she put both hands over her mouth as she joined in.

Britt rubbed her gently between the shoulder blades. "Careful you don't choke. Christy, will you get dessert?"

Jake had always considered himself a connoisseur of cheescake, but he'd never tasted anything like Britt's. It was tall and richly thick, with the subtle tartness of something citrus. The vanilla cookie crust was sinfully delicious.

"Why can't you just sell this stuff?" Matt asked.

"Because I was talking to Mr. Ingalls about it," Britt explained, "and he says the market is full of delicious, low-calorie products. I had to find something different and special. So I'm going to experiment with recipes using the goat's milk yogurt." She looked up at Jake with a cautioning smile. "Don't laugh, or I'll make you eat your words when I open a franchise in Moscow."

He picked up the crumbs with his fork. "I wouldn't laugh," he assured her. "If you realize there's a ripe market in Eastern Europe, you're doing your homework."

"Speaking of which..." Britt looked around the table at the children.

Groaning, they carried their plates to the counter, helped clear the table, then dispersed to their rooms. Renee resisted Britt's directives to take her bath.

"I want to stay and talk to Jake," she said, holding his hand, making his one-handed effort to wipe off the table difficult.

"You can come back down and say good-night."

Renee's eyes widened excitedly. "Is he staying?"

Jake looked up from his task, also interested in the answer.

Britt caught his eye, grinning as she replied, "Only for a little while. His shirt and socks are still in the dryer." She shook her head at him apologetically. "I put your suit in a plastic bag, but I don't know if the dry cleaner will be able to get all the mud out."

"It's all right," he said, crossing the room to drop the sponge in the sink. "It was worth it to have a home-cooked meal and the Tyler-renowned Britt Hansen cheesecake. What else can I do to help?"

She took down two fresh cups. "Pour coffee into these and take them into the living room. I'll get Renee going on her bath and be right down."

The living room extended across the front of the house and was rustic and warm. Here it was easy to tell that much of the furniture had probably arrived on a wagon. It was of good heavy German design and construction, and one cupboard had been painted with stylized tulips and decorative swirls. Though the cheerful colors were faded, they were reflected back in bright pillows on two full-size old brown sofas and in the dried flowers placed all around the room. In a corner near the window was a well-worn rocker with a new cushion in the blue, green and gold motif of the cupboard.

"You're welcome to sit in it," Britt said from behind him. He turned to find her moving around the sturdy coffee table on which he'd placed their cups. She sat in a corner of one sofa and reached for her coffee. Her shoulders had rounded a little, he noticed. He guessed it was because she was out of sight of her children. She didn't have to hold the world up for them at the moment.

Jake wandered toward her. "I was just wondering how many babies had been rocked in it."

"Many," she confirmed. "It's been in the family since Great-Grandma Bauer." She'd kicked off her boots and now stretched out her legs and crossed her feet on a corner of the table.

He sat beside her. "Your illustrious ancestor with the mean pitchfork."

Britt nodded and smiled. "My father remembered her and insisted she was quite a woman."

"Then she'd no doubt approve of your plan to take the food industry by storm."

She rolled her head toward him against the sofa back, her smile weary. "I think so." She added lazily, "You're welcome to put your feet up, too."

He kicked off the slippers and did. "You have the capital to launch this venture?" he asked.

She frowned into the cup now resting on her flat stomach. "If I can come up with a recipe that'll work, I'll need goats. I'll sell the Holsteins, and then I can rent out more pasture, because I can feed twice as many goats on half as much land." She gave him a grin that held no malice. "I can't feed the cows anyway."

He took a sip of coffee. "Do you remember before dinner, when we were standing outside, I told you I had something to tell you?"

"Oh, yeah."

"I got you a month's extension. Your feed delivery's coming in the morning."

"Jake!" She sat up, holding the coffee away from her to avoid spilling it. She put down the cup and turned to him, her eyes bright and pleased, but at the same time confused. "But why? Nothing's changed. In fact, it's gotten worse."

That was true. He hadn't known about the bank turning her down when he'd made the call to Chicago, but he doubted now that that would have changed his mind. There was something in her he simply couldn't squelch.

"You think the yogurt thing's a good idea?" she asked hopefully when he seemed unable to provide an answer.

He grinned skeptically. "I don't know. I've never been much for designer food. I don't think anything beats good old vanilla ice cream with chocolate syrup, but then, what do I know?"

"Then why'd you do it?"

Jake considered himself a good salesman, but he'd never sold anything he didn't believe in. He could promote like a carnival barker, but he couldn't lie.

"I'm not entirely sure," he said, looking into her eyes. "It wasn't a business decision, it was purely personal."

She stiffened just a little. "Pity?" she asked.

He couldn't help it; he laughed. "Hardly," he said finally. "You inspire a lot of feelings in me, but pity isn't one of them. Admiration, maybe. Belief, I guess, that if it can be done, you'll do it."

For a moment Britt was speechless. A month's grace might just buy her the time she needed. And he'd given it to her on the basis of a personal decision. After the kind of day it had been, the kind of *year* it had been, her throat closed and she couldn't find the words to thank him.

"You've got until mid-June," he said. "We'll just hope your instincts are trustworthy."

Britt studied him with new insight. He'd come out of the shower impeccably groomed, the ends of his dark blond hair curling slightly over his ears and at the back of his neck. But now she detected a trace of five o'clock shadow, and the casual clothes lent him an approachable air he didn't have in the suit. Or maybe that was her personal reaction, she thought. It seemed as though everyone who wanted money wore a suit.

She was one cushion closer to him now, and turned toward him. She leaned an elbow on the back of the sofa and rested her head against her hand.

"What is it you like about Chicago?" she asked curiously.

The question startled him. Or maybe the fact that he didn't have an answer startled him. He sat up, leaning forward to put his empty cup on the coffee table.

"I don't know. I'm not sure I do, I just live there. I was born there."

"But when you graduated from high school," she prompted, "didn't you want to do what all kids do? City kids move to small towns and country kids go to the big city, certain life is better there than what they've known."

He shook his head, smiling. "I guess I'm not that imaginative. I just wanted to learn enough to earn enough to get out of my aunt's place and never have to live on someone else's sufferance again."

She dropped her hand to the sofa and tucked her legs under her, feeling truly comfortable with him for the first time. "Were you raised by your aunt?"

"No. My father died in a construction accident when I was ten," he said. "He left no insurance and we had no savings, so my aunt invited my mother and me to come and live with her. Her husband had been killed in Vietnam, and it seemed like a good idea at the time that two women alone should pool their resources. My aunt worked, and my mother kept the apartment clean and cooked and watched my three cousins and me." He frowned, his eyes unfocused as he thought back. "It was crowded, and kids being kids, we fought. It wasn't long before my aunt considered my mother and me to be the root of all her problems. I wanted desperately to leave, but Mother had always been taken care of by someone, and she was terrified at the thought of having to make a living on her own. And though my aunt loved to complain, she really depended on Mom to keep the house going and watch us kids. We stayed until I graduated from high school and got a full-time job.''

"So you went to work right out of high school?"

"For a year, then I went to school for a year, worked another year, got some financial aid and went to school another year. It took me almost seven years to get my degree."

Britt stared at him, shaking her head. "And I was sure you'd been born with all the advantages."

He shrugged a shoulder. "The first ten years were pretty good. We weren't wealthy, but we ate well and my dad was a great guy. The years with my aunt made me swear to myself that I'd never sacrifice my independence or my privacy for anyone else."

She asked casually, "You never married?"

"No," he replied. "Then my life would be all entangled with someone else's, and I'd have to do whatever she wanted to with hers, because that's what marriage is." He turned to look at her. "Isn't it?"

She had to think about that. "Sort of," she said finally, "but in a loving marriage you're usually after the same thing. The details might be different, but the essence of what you want is the same. So you don't really surrender your needs to serve the other, you just sort of pull together."

He sighed. "Well, that doesn't sound like my style. I like my quiet condo and my unstructured life. I guess I'm just selfish enough to want things my way."

She laughed softly. "I'm sure you've got a lot of company there. Most of us simply know we can't have it and are forced to adjust."

"How do you cope," he asked seriously, "with four kids needing you to be a tower of strength, even when you need to scream and cry yourself?"

There was no answer to that. At least not one a nonparent would understand. "I can't tell you," she said with a self-deprecating shrug. "It's nothing for which I can take credit. It's instinct. From the moment you know life is growing in you, your focus changes...." She smiled quickly, a smile that would haunt him later and often. "It's like someone's given you a new pair of glasses. This child becomes the axis on which your world revolves. You hug and get hugged back, you hold and experience this being's utter dependence that makes you feel superhero powerful and completely humbled all at once. You laugh and they laugh. You cry and they cry—so you just keep laughing, whether you feel like it or not, because you know they're going to get to where you are soon enough and then you won't be able to protect them from the things that make them cry. So as long as you can . . . you do."

Guided by his instinct and a very personal, very overwhelming need, Jake reached out gently to cup her head in his hand and bring her to him. He saw surprise flash in her eyes but she didn't withdraw. He tilted his head to put his mouth on hers, feeling a curious, tender amazement that fate had crossed his path with hers. Nothing could come of it, but it was amazing all the same.

So he simply kissed her, gently but with all the warmth and surprise she inspired in him. He tried to lend her his strength, if only for the moment. When he drew away, he caught that look of longing deep in her eyes. But on the surface, reading like letters six inches high, was guilt.

"I—I—" she stammered.

Britt's brain refused to form a clear thought. It was busy registering the sensation on her lips, where his had touched, at the back of her head where his hand had held her, at her knee bumping against his. Everything tingled. And inside her was a gentle, expectant excitement.

She tried to shut down the sharp awareness. This wasn't Jimmy! This was another man in Jimmy's clothes. She couldn't enjoy his kisses; Jimmy still occupied every little corner of her heart. God! She was acting like some love-starved spinster!

She leaped to her feet, staring down at Jake in dismay, unable to explain herself. Then, like a diversion from heaven, the dryer buzzed.

"Your things are done," she said. "I'll get them for you. Would—" She had to clear her throat and start again, because her voice came out high and broken. "Would you like another cup of coffee?"

Jake looked up into her guilty, horrified eyes and made himself deal with the facts. She was a widow with four children in an impossible financial situation, and she was still in love with her dead husband. He was a loner who couldn't deal with the chaos of family life. The kiss had been nice, but the lady was trouble. And it was his policy to stay cool.

"No, thanks," he said, standing also. "I'd better be on my way."

He remained calm all the way across the kitchen, while she folded his shirt and socks and underwear into a brown paper sack and brought out his muddy suit wrapped in a plastic sleeve from the cleaners. She handed it all to him.

"Thanks for Matt's bike," she said, walking him to the door. She was edgy, anxious for him to leave. "I won't let him forget to pay you."

"Don't nag him," he said, reaching down to pat Daffy, who came to lean against him, tail wagging. "Just let him enjoy it. Well . . . good luck with the yogurt thing."

She folded her arms and smiled at him, then glanced away. "Have faith. I'll pay you just as quickly as I can."

"I know you will. Goodbye, Britt."

She followed him onto the porch, stopping at the edge of the top step. "Goodbye, Jake."

"Wait!" Renee suddenly appeared beside her mother, feet bare, small body draped in a flowered flannel nightgown. "You said I could say goodbye!" she complained.

Jake came back up the steps halfway and leaned down for her hug, holding the muddy suit out of the way. "Bye, Renee," he said as she planted a kiss on his cheek. "Take good care of your mom, okay?"

"Are you coming back tomorrow?" she asked.

"No," he said, ruffling her hair with his free hand. "I have to get back to Chicago. You be good."

Before she could form another question, he'd moved down the walk and was climbing into the truck. Britt waited until he had backed onto the road, waved once at the farewell tap of his horn, then drew a pouting Renee into the house.

Later that night Britt went to check on Mildred, who'd been baaing pathetically since dusk.

Mildred stopped the moment Britt appeared. Her head was high and alert, her ears pricked. Britt climbed into the stall and fluffed the bed of chopped oat straw. "What's the problem, Milly?" she asked, rubbing the nubby stumps of horn. "Judy said you're supposed to be very happy in this stall."

Mildred nibbled at her sleeve and nuzzled her arm. Her breath puffed hot against Britt's hand as she rubbed her nose.

"Mmm, nummy, nummy," Britt said, taking a handful of the alfalfa, hay and grass mixture Judy had promised Mildred would love, and offering it to her. Mildred ate happily, her fringy little tail wagging at top speed. "There, now. Why don't you just curl up like a good little goat and go to sleep, so you'll be all rested and able to give me buckets of wonderful milk in the morning? We're in this together, Mildred. I need you to be good at what you do."

The hay eaten, Mildred nuzzled her in what Britt was sure was agreement. She gave the goat another handful of feed, one final pat, and climbed out of the stall.

The baaing began again before she was halfway across the yard to the house. She stopped in the dark night to take a deep breath of fragrant spring air. Maybe goats were like children, she thought. If you ignored their whining, they stopped. Deciding to operate on that principle, Britt went into the house, took a bath, tidied up, checked on her sleeping children and went to bed.

CHAPTER FIVE

AT 2:00 A.M. Jake sat in a Danish-modern rocker in a pair of decrepit navy sweats. It was a new rocker. No baby had ever been sung to sleep in it. He shifted his weight and sipped at the brandy in the cut-crystal snifter.

Beyond his tenth-story window, downtown Chicago shone like a jeweled canyon. Maybe that was what he liked about it, he thought. It was beautiful at night.

His eyes burned with exhaustion, and he closed them. The moment he did, a clear image of the widow Hansen bloomed in his mind's eye. He'd known it would. It had happened every time he'd attempted to sleep since eleven-thirty.

He tried to focus on the guilty, how-dare-you-kiss-me look she'd worn when she'd leaped off the sofa. But the picture in his brain insisted on laughing at him as she'd done when she'd leaned over him as he'd lain supine in a mud puddle.

He downed more brandy. It wasn't like him to long for things he knew would be counterproductive to his life's plan. He usually concentrated on moves that would improve his work and push him up the corporate ladder. Not because he was greedy, but because he wanted to secure his position and do his best.

Britt Hansen was planning to commit commercial suicide. He hadn't wanted to tell her that, but he saw it coming. No matter how good her product or how hard she tried, she couldn't compete with the big guys.

They had more capital than the whole town of Tyler put together.

Still ... he could see her powder-blue eyes fill with plans and determination, and he began to doubt what he knew to be true. There had to be something he could do for her.

BRITT WAS NOT SURPRISED that her principle was faulty. Ignoring her children's complaints hadn't *always* worked. There was no reason she should have expected it to work with Mildred.

At 3:30 a.m. she checked the children again, then put on her jacket over her nightgown, grabbed a flashlight and stepped onto the porch. Mildred's baas were now hoarse but still continuous. Britt went across the yard to the barn.

Mildred stood against the slats of her pen, head and ears pushing through the space between the white one-by-fours as Britt approached. Her amber eyes told Britt, "I want out of here, and I want out now!"

Britt climbed into the pen and fell wearily into a sitting position in the corner. "I need you, Milly," she explained. "We're going to make food history together. Try to cooperate."

Mildred ambled across the pen, nibbled at Britt's hair, sank onto her spindly forelegs, then lowered her rump with a mild thud. "All right," the yellow eyes said. "If I can't have out, then I want company."

Mildred laid her head in Britt's lap, huffed a little sigh and closed her eyes.

"Right," Britt muttered. Exhausted, she eased her upper body back into the chopped oat hay and went immediately to sleep.

JAKE TURNED at the Rustic Road sign. He was in a strange mood. He didn't remember ever feeling quite

this way before—aggressive with an underlying un-
certainty as to why. And just why he'd left Chicago at
6:30 a.m. to drive back to Tyler, which he'd left at nine
o'clock the night before, he had no idea.

He frowned as he turned into the Lakeside Farm
drive. He wasn't the kind of man who acted without a
reason. And he wasn't one to take a day off from work
and ignore his responsibilities on a whim.

He pulled the Explorer to a stop behind Britt's truck
and glanced at the paper bag beside him. The clothes.
That was why he'd come back—to return Britt's husband's clothes. Flimsy excuse, he thought, climbing
out of the vehicle, but it was something.

He walked slowly up the drive, considering what he
would say, when the front door to the house flew open
and Christy and Renee burst out, running toward him.
Renee was crying and held her arms up.

He picked her up, his heart thudding uncomfortably. Even calm, logical Christy looked panicked.
"Mom's missing!" she said, her voice tight and
strained. "She always calls us to get up for school, but
I woke up by myself, and when I came down to the
kitchen, she wasn't there."

Renee sobbed, "Maybe she died, too."

"Oh, don't be stupid!" Christy shouted at her sister. "You don't disappear when you die."

"You looked all through the house?" Jake asked,
frantically searching his mind for a logical reason why
Britt would have broken routine and frightened her
children. "You checked the barn and the pasture?"

Christy nodded, pointing to Matt and David, who
came running from the direction of the pasture.

"Jake!" Matt said with obvious relief. "I don't
know what's going on. Mom's gone. She did the milking and she turned the cows out to pasture, but I can't
find her anywhere. She'd never leave without telling
us."

"Her coat's gone," Christy reported grimly. "I don't get it."

"What about that friend of hers where she got the goat?" Jake suggested. "Could she have gone there?"

Christy shook her head. "I called."

"And the truck and the wagon are both here," Matt pointed out.

Jake resisted an insistent clutch of fear. Britt would never just walk away—he was absolutely sure of that. And he knew she'd never frighten her children like this unless something beyond her control was keeping her away.

"Okay." He put Renee down and sent the girls toward the house. "Check everything. Closets, basement, attic."

"Okay." Christy took Renee's hand and ran for the house.

"Check every inch of the pasture," he told the boys. "I know you've done it once, but...check again in case she's fallen or something."

They ran off obediently and Jake headed for the barn. All the stalls were empty. He climbed into the hayloft and inspected every inch. He climbed down again and did one more slow circuit of the stalls.

That was when he noticed Mildred, who lay against a brown blanket, contentedly chewing hay. Then he saw a faint splash of pale, honeyed red. He looked closer and realized that what the goat leaned against was not a blanket. It was Britt.

She lay on her stomach in the hay, snuggled into it so that she was practically indistinguishable as human, much less female. She was very still.

The clutch of panic tightened in him as he climbed into the stall. Then she murmured, shifted slightly and drew a leg up. She was asleep.

Relief swept through him and he sank into the hay beside her. He felt his panic die, but something even more alarming was taking its place. Deep inside him he shuddered at the realization that she was just fine, that for some reason known only to her she'd simply fallen asleep in a goat pen. He saw himself as though from a distance—saw how profoundly important it was to him that she was safe. That had ramifications he'd have to consider sometime, but not now. Now he had to let the children know she was all right.

Feet scampered into the barn just as he prepared to stand.

"Jake, we've looked every..." Matt and David came to an abrupt halt at the goat pen, falling to silence when Jake raised a finger to his lips and pointed to Britt.

"She's asleep," he said quietly.

Matt relaxed visibly; David stood on the bottom slat to look over the top one. "What's she doing in there?" he whispered.

Jake shook his head. "We'll have to ask her when she wakes up."

Christy and Renee appeared, hand in hand, eyes huge. "We still can't fi—" Christy stopped abruptly as Matt pointed into the pen.

Before anyone could stop her, Renee pushed her way inside and fell on top of Britt. "Mommy!" she shouted, shaking her. "You were lost!"

Mildred escaped to the farthest corner of the pen.

Jake pulled Renee back. "I think your mom needs to sleep," he said quietly.

Britt stirred, then awoke with a start. She sat upright, straw in her hair and stuck to her coat, her eyes heavy and disoriented. They focused on Renee with a frown.

"Hi, baby," she said, her voice thick and raspy. She put a hand to her head. "What time is it?"

"Breakfast time," Renee said, an accusatory tone in her voice. "Time for school!"

Britt took a moment to assimilate that information, looked around in confusion and frowned, rubbing at her forehead.

"You okay, Mom?" Matt asked.

Britt looked up, apparently noticing her other children for the first time. Then her eyes fell on Jake, a few feet from her, Renee in his lap, and she finally came awake.

"What happened?" she demanded.

"We couldn't find you this morning," Christy explained. "We looked in here, but didn't see you. Jake found you."

Britt frowned at him. "What are you doing here?"

"I came by to return the clothes you lent me, and arrived just in time to join the manhunt." He raised a puzzled eyebrow. "What are *you* doing *here?*"

She leaned back on her hands. "Mildred cried most of the night," she recalled. "I got up around three to try to quiet her down and..." She frowned, trying to think. "I guess we fell asleep together. I got up earlier to do the milking, then I came back to milk Mildred." She yawned mightily. "I had a few more minutes before I had to start breakfast so I just settled down with Mildred again." She pushed her coat sleeve back to check her watch and encountered bare wrist. "What time is it?"

Jake consulted his. "Almost eight." He stood Renee up, got to his feet and pulled Britt to hers. "How about if I fix breakfast while you get everybody ready for school?"

Their world back in order, the children headed at a run for the house. Jake let Britt out of the pen before him and latched it. She took two steps and winced, feeling her left hip protest. She rubbed at it, sending Jake a grinning glance.

"Guess I'm getting too old to spend the night in the barn."

Without stopping to consider, Jake swept her up in his arms and carried her down the long concrete aisle to the barn door.

She wrapped both arms around his neck, her eyes still heavy. "I thought you'd left for Chicago."

"I had," he said. "I just came back to return the clothes."

"I told you not to worry about it."

"I know. But it's a good thing I did. There might be an APB out for you at this very moment if I hadn't come along."

Unable to help herself, Britt let her head sink onto his shoulder, her body lean into the cradle of his arms, and she closed her eyes, giving up control if only for as long as it took them to reach the house. For the space of however many seconds that required, she was in his care. It felt blissful.

As Jake walked out of the barn, two vehicles raced into the yard—an old black truck and a Fiat. Britt's cousin, the cop from the diner, jumped out of the truck, and a woman about Britt's age from the sports car. Both ran toward him and the limp burden in his arms.

"What happened?" Brick demanded. "Is she all right?"

"Just sleepy," Jake said. As Britt lifted her head drowsily to smile at Brick, he explained about the goat and the sleepless night.

"Day off, Brick?" Britt asked, leaning her head against Jake again as though holding it upright was just too much trouble. "Did you come for breakfast?"

"Judy called me." Frowning, Brick indicated his companion with a jerk of his thumb. "She said the kids called her in a panic. You're sure everything's okay?"

"Yes," Britt insisted. "Jake's fixing breakfast. Want some?"

Brick shifted his weight and folded his arms. "No, I don't want breakfast, I—"

"Well, I do," Judy said, studying the intimacy of Jake's hold on Britt with as much interest as concern. "This definitely looks like something I want to know more about."

"It isn't anything," Britt said with a drowsy laugh.

"It isn't?" Jake asked.

Britt raised her head and looked into his eyes. They were a mere inch from her own, deep and dark and potentially dangerous. She seemed to lose awareness of her surroundings, of the presence of her cousin and her friend. Even her children had moved to the fringes of her mind. Jake! her brain seemed to shout. Jake is here!

She went from sleepy euphoria to rude wakefulness with a start. No! she told herself. She'd decided yesterday this just couldn't be. She still loved Jimmy, her soul mate, the father of her children.

Jake saw the change take place in her eyes. He felt her stir against him, asking silently to be put down. But he held firm. If this was all he could have, the walk across the yard with her in his arms, then he was going to have it.

"I can walk," Britt said quietly, but with pointed firmness. She gave another little wriggle.

He tightened his grip and returned as firmly, "I'm taking you inside." He smiled at Brick and Judy. "Come on. I make a mean bowl of cereal."

Brick shook his head. "Thanks, but it *is* my day off and I've got a million errands to run. You're sure everything's okay, Britt?"

At the moment she wasn't. She wanted down desperately, but Jake didn't seem to get the message. Or he got it and was ignoring it. Either way, with his arms wrapped around her, she was feeling things she didn't want to feel. But there was nothing Brick could do about that.

She smiled at him. "Everything's fine. Tell Karen hi."

"Right." With one last look from Britt to Jake, Brick got into his truck, backed out of the drive and drove away.

Judy smiled at Britt. "You're not getting rid of me that easily." She glanced at her watch. "And if breakfast is up to snuff, I'll even drive the kids to school for you."

"IT WAS NOT an all-night tryst in the barn," Britt said, standing in a bra and jeans while she rubbed her wet hair dry. "I really went to quiet Mildred. I've gotten so little sleep lately that when I finally did conk out, my built-in alarm clock failed. The next thing I knew, Jake was sitting beside me in the pen."

Judy leaned forward, her eyes wide. "And?"

Britt rolled her eyes. "And, nothing. Renee was sitting in his lap. Apparently he'd come to return Jimmy's clothes and—"

"Jimmy's clothes?"

"He fell in a mud puddle yesterday afternoon trying to help me with Mildred, and I lent him a change of clothes."

"Hmm."

Britt flicked her with the towel before tossing it aside and pulling a University of Wisconsin sweatshirt over her head. "Will you stop? You'll have to get the romantic elements for your novel somewhere else. There's nothing here."

Judy sat on the rim of the tub while Britt brushed her damp hair. "Oh, yes, there is."

"Where?" Britt challenged.

"In your eyes," Judy replied. "Look at yourself."

Britt began to scoff, the ruffly band she intended to use to tie her hair back held suspended in her hand. There *was* something in her eyes, but it looked like simple perplexity.

"That's not romance," she said, affixing the band. "It's confusion."

"Is it so long since you've been in love that you've forgotten that's how it starts?" Judy stood, looking over Britt's shoulder into the mirror. "You feel suddenly off balance, curiously out of sorts, disoriented. All the things you knew to be unshakably true about yourself suddenly aren't. Things you thought you'd never be vulnerable enough to feel are suddenly racing through your system."

"No," Britt whispered to her reflection. "I ... don't feel that."

The lie was written on her face and flashing in her eyes. She was interested in Jake Marshack—very interested. More than interested.

A pleat formed between her eyebrows and Judy said gently, "It's all right, you know. You can love another man."

Britt turned away from the mirror, articulating sharply to herself as much as to Judy, "Don't say that. I don't want another man." She went into the bedroom to pull on her boots.

Intrepid, Judy followed.

"The last thing in the world I need at this moment is a man." Britt shoved her foot into a boot. "I've got four kids, a hundred acres literally running down the economic drain, and I'm about as solvent as the city of New York."

"Maybe the right man could fix all that."

"I'm going to fix it myself."

"It won't be half as much fun as finding solutions with the right man—that's guaranteed. So if you're not attracted, how come he carried you out of the barn?"

"Because I had a hitch in my hip from lying on the concrete floor with your neurotic goat."

Judy grinned at her. "Good old Mildred. Maybe she's going to be your salvation in ways you hadn't imagined."

Britt stood and pulled Judy with her, drawing her toward the bedroom door. "Come on. I'm putting hemlock in your orange juice."

HIS MISTAKE, Jake concluded, as he turned bacon in a frying pan while keeping his eye on a batch of French toast on a griddle, had been in giving the children a choice. He should have told them what he'd prepare for breakfast rather than asking them what they wanted. As a result of his inexperience, he had an omelet under way as well as bacon and eggs and French toast. Mercifully, Renee had opted for cereal.

The children were crowded around him at the stove, Renee holding a squirmy, spotted kitten, and he had to fight the claustrophobic feeling he'd had the night before. He marveled that Britt could live this way day after day.

"I think my French toast is done," David said, tugging at his sleeve.

Jake turned Christy's omelet, then reached across the stove to check the bottom of the French toast. David ducked under his elbow and held up a plate hopefully. Finding the French toast golden, Jake flipped it onto the plate.

"My eggs're getting over well," Matt warned worriedly. "I like 'em over easy."

"Right." Jake took Matt's plate and turned two perfect over-easy eggs onto it. He added three strips of bacon and passed the plate to Christy, who added toast.

Matt looked from his heaping plate to Jake with a grin. "Thanks. I'm gonna talk to Mom about hiring you."

Christy held up her plate with its perfect, diagonally cut toast already waiting. Jake placed the plump omelet right in the middle.

Behind her glasses, a little steamy from the stove, her eyes studied him with new interest. "My dad was a good cook, too," she said. "Sometimes he made pancakes after church on Sundays. Aren't you gonna have something?"

He poured himself a cup of coffee. "I'll wait for your mom and Judy."

The children ate like starved refugees, talking about Matt's bike, Christy's farming notebook, David's math homework. The noise level had diminished considerably, and Jake felt himself begin to relax. When Renee finished her cereal, she climbed into his lap.

"Are you going to be here for dinner?" she asked.

Jake shook his head. "No, I have to go back to Chicago."

Her brow wrinkled in puzzlement. "How come you keep going back there and coming back here? Why don't you just stay here?"

Good question. "Because I live there," he said.

"Do you have to?"

"My job is there."

"How come? Mommy said you came here on business."

He wondered if Britt would let him hire Renee for his sales staff. She had an answer for everything. Or another question. "Because part of my job," he explained, "is to visit the people who buy things from the company I work for."

She nodded knowledgeably. "The monster dairy." She leaned an elbow on his shoulder and looked into his eyes. "I thought only monsters worked there. You're not a monster. You're more like a prince."

"Dudley Doright," Britt said, appearing suddenly at his shoulder and lifting Renee into her arms. "And now Prince Charming?"

He looked up into her eyes and wasn't sure what he saw there. Amusement at her daughter's remark, and that familiar longing she probably didn't even know was there. And a little flare of fear.

He felt it, too. This could become something, but it would be just too much of a leap of faith for either of them.

She put Renee on her feet and shooed her toward the hallway. "Go brush your teeth and get dressed for school."

Renee stopped at the door to blow Jake a kiss, ponytail askew, smile wide. He waved back, his heart melting. The kitten chased her as she disappeared into the corridor.

As Judy poured two cups of coffee, Britt looked around the table at the children's plates. She frowned at Jake. "You fixed four different breakfasts?"

He nodded wryly over his coffee. "I asked them what they wanted. How was I to know they wouldn't want the same things?"

Matt carried his plate to the sink. "Great eggs, Jake. Thanks."

Christy forked the last bite of her omelet and held it up for Britt to sample. "Isn't that the best thing you ever tasted?" she demanded on her way to the sink.

Britt bit off the morsel and chewed. It was fluffy and delicious.

"I'd give you a bite of my French toast," David said as he passed her with his empty plate, "but I ate it all." He put his plate in the sink and patted Jake on the shoulder as he headed for the hallway. "Thanks. See ya."

Christy kissed Jake's cheek and disappeared after her brothers.

Britt put both hands on her hips in mock disapproval. "Thank you. Now they're going to expect that every morning."

He smiled ruefully. "They were very upset when they thought something had happened to you. I thought they needed something else to balance out the beginning of their day. Can I fix something for you?"

"Thanks, but I have to drive them—"

"I'll take them to school," Judy said, smiling speculatively from across the table.

"You're supposed to be writing," Britt reminded her.

"I'll get right back to it as soon as I get home. I think *you* should fix something for *Jake.*"

Britt's answering glare had no effect on her friend.

"Thanks, but I've got to go," Jake said, getting to his feet. "I just came to return the clothes. I left them in the car in all the commotion. Be right back."

The moment the door closed behind him, Judy glowered at Britt. "He carried you across the yard, made four different breakfasts for your children and you're going to let him leave without paying him back?"

He had wiped off the counter and stove as he worked, Britt noticed, and though she had three separate pans to clean, he'd tidied up everything else. Britt sighed, feeling strangely vacant. "Judy, I don't need this," she said, rinsing off dishes and putting them in the dishwasher.

"Didn't you see your kids react to him? Yes, you need this."

Britt ran hot water and squirted suds into the dishpan. "I've got to get this yogurt thing..."

"Yogurt, shmogurt," Judy said definitively. "I hope you develop a great recipe and it makes you a bundle, but that's not going to provide your kids with a father, or fill the other side of your bed."

Britt took the towel she'd dried her hands on, twisted it into a rope and leaned threateningly over Judy's chair with it. "Judy Lowery, if you don't—"

Jake cleared his throat noisily as he stepped back into the kitchen. Britt straightened with a guilty start, her cheeks reddening.

He moved slowly toward them, enjoying Britt's blush, then dropped the bag of clothes on the table. "You need a cop again, Judy?" he asked.

The kitchen suddenly exploded with sound as all four children erupted into the room again, jackets flying, arms filled with books.

"Oh, lunches!" Britt exclaimed, scrambling to the refrigerator.

"It's too late, Mom," Christy said. "Can't we just eat in the cafeteria?"

Matt elbowed her. "We don't have the money." He dropped his books onto the table. "I'll get my tips—"

"Don't do that," Jake said, reaching into his pocket.

"No!" Britt said, coming back toward him, her eyes both miserable and angry. "I'll get my purse."

He caught her arm as she would have raced to find it. "There isn't time. You can pay me back later." He handed a bill to Matt. "Can you change that and see that everybody gets lunch?"

"Sure." Matt pocketed the money importantly. "There'll be two dollars left. I'll give it to Mom."

Jake shook his head. "Get something you can share with whatever's left."

"Bye, Jake!"

"See ya, Jake!"

"Bye, Jake!"

"Bye!"

The chorus was monotonous as the children trooped after Judy and turned to wave. Britt blew kisses, then closed the door behind her, angry and tense.

"You didn't have to do that," she said, going to the sink, presenting him with her back.

He picked up a dish towel and waited near the drying rack. "If you insist, you can pay me back, but I'm sure I can deal with your slow-payment practices better than Matt's summer-trip fund can."

Britt turned to him, her color high with fulminating indignation, only to find his eyes filled with amusement and his lips determinedly steady. He was teasing her. She hadn't been teased in a long time. She felt one of her crusty edges crumble. All in all it had been a most confusing morning.

Jake saw her eyes soften and the line of her shoulders relax. It made him relax, too, and succumb to a temptation he'd resisted since finding her snuggled in oat hay in Mildred's pen.

He took her left hand from the basin of suds and dried it with the towel he held. "Or," he suggested softly, "you can find another way to repay me."

Britt was nervous, but not opposed to what she knew Jake had in mind. Still, she had to be honest.

"I'm a farmer, Jake," she said, her voice high and breathless as he reached for and dried her other hand. "It's woven into my chromosomes like the color of my hair. You live in Chicago."

He glanced up at her soft red hair, caught back in a ponytail, tendrils of it drying and curling around her face. Then he looked into her eyes, his own curiously resigned.

"I know," he said. "You've got four great kids, but I'm ..." He wasn't sure how to put it so that it didn't sound cruel or unkind. "I ..."

"Need your peace of mind," she said with a nod of understanding. "I know."

"I'm selfish," he admitted quietly.

It occurred to her that she'd probably never met anyone, except for family, who'd been so impulsively generous. "You're entitled to live in a way that makes you happy," she said. "Just as I am."

He tossed the towel aside and now simply held her hands. He sighed, frowning, as though subtly dissatisfied. "We have nothing to give each other, and I probably won't come back until it's time to collect the bill, and if you don't have it, I'll really have to cut you off."

She knew that and still laced her fingers with his.

"But I can't leave," he went on, "without kissing you."

She understood that with complete clarity. Everything they'd just admitted to each other stood in their way. And there was Jimmy—still very much alive in her heart, still very much a part of every waking thought and almost every dream. But Jimmy couldn't touch her, couldn't hold her, couldn't fill her kitchen with the comforting presence of his maleness.

Jake could. But that wasn't fair to him.

He lowered his head. Her heart beat fast. "I . . . love Jimmy, Jake. I'll always—"

"I know," he whispered, then closed his mouth over hers.

His lips were warm and undemanding. As he freed her fingers and took her lightly in his arms, she relaxed into his kiss, feeling comforted and protected.

She kissed him back gently, artlessly, as would a woman who'd been with only one man in her life. She meant to express her appreciation for his generosity and his concern.

Then some subtle, fine-spun change took place. Feeling the inclination of her body, the sweetly giving nature of her lips, the crush of her breasts against his ribs, Jake's intention to tell her simply that he cared became something else.

Heat rose in him, filling his chest and his lungs, tightening the muscles in his arms and everything else he possessed. Suddenly driven, he deepened the kiss, his tongue exploring inside her mouth, meeting hers with a thrill he hadn't known in a long, long time.

The part of his mind still thinking clearly realized how long it had been since he'd felt heat. Life, women, sex, had become lukewarm and unfulfilling. Nights were cold.

But here in his arms was a heat source unlike any he'd ever known. A widow still in love with her dead husband, with four lively, noisy children and a hundred acres destined to go the way of most small farms. This couldn't be. It was contrary to everything he wanted and needed. But he couldn't tear his mouth from hers, couldn't pull away.

Britt felt the change instantly. Her own reaction, as his tongue probed deeper and his arms tightened, was to hold him even harder and draw from his mouth like a woman at the end of a long fast.

She saw Jimmy's image and felt pointed and desperate guilt, but right beside it was relief from the physical and emotional loneliness of the past year. She remembered the long nights she'd stared at the ceiling, the times she'd finally fallen asleep, then awakened in cold misery when her body and her soul rolled to the other side of the bed and found no one there.

She clung to the back of Jake's shirt and put all that need into her response. For this moment at least, it would be satisfied.

Jake finally raised his head, afraid to indulge himself any further. His lungs gasped in air, and he felt her breathe deeply as she clung to his waist. He held her for a long moment, afraid to let go. Afraid he'd imagined the passion that had flared between them—afraid he hadn't.

CHAPTER SIX

THE LOUD SOUND of an engine in the driveway drew Jake and Britt apart. They stared into each other's eyes, startled, confused, resigned.

A loud rap sounded on the door. Britt forced herself to turn away to answer it. A tall, lanky young man doffed a baseball cap and put a clipboard in her hands. "Hi, Mrs. Hansen," he said. "Got your delivery." Glancing beyond her, he spotted Jake standing in the middle of the kitchen. "Mr. Marshack," he said in surprise. Then, glancing from his boss to his customer, and probably reaching conclusions Jake didn't even want to think about, he stammered nervously, "Hi. Didn't expect to run into you. Nice day, isn't it? Warm. Finally spring. Thank you, ma'am." He reclaimed the clipboard and, looking harassed, went back to his truck to stow his delivery in her feed bins.

Britt turned to Jake with a wry grin. "I have the feeling you're going to be the subject of office gossip."

He shrugged a shoulder, taking his jacket from the back of a kitchen chair. He hooked it over his shoulder on his index finger. "A little notoriety might be good for my image. You know where to reach me if you need anything."

She tilted her head in the direction of the barn. "Looks like everything I need's being delivered."

He crossed to where she stood and looked down at her, his glance mildly impatient. "I meant anything personal."

She nodded, sobering. "I know. Thank you. But don't worry about me. I have family and friends watching out for me and the children."

He had only to remember the incident in Marge's Diner for confirmation of that. But he still felt responsible. He didn't question why because he couldn't have explained it.

She stepped back from the door to let him through. "Take care," she said.

"Right." He went out onto the porch and was immediately bumped by Daffy, who wagged her tail and waited for his attention. He reached down to scratch her between the ears, then straightened and turned back to Britt. "I'll be watching the market for goat yogurt."

She smiled. "Do that. Bye."

"Bye, Britt."

She watched him walk away, a new emptiness making space for itself inside her. Watching the dust from his Explorer as he turned onto the road and picked up speed, she had the feeling that something precious had just been wasted.

"NOTHING IN HER FILE justifies giving her an extra month." Stan Foreman, vice president in charge of sales at Winnebago Dairy, looked grimly at Jake across his slate-topped desk, cleared of everything but a jet-and-silver pen set and Britt Hansen's folder.

Jake didn't react. His ability to remain calm had been his ace on the corporate ladder. In an opulent office on the tenth floor of the Carstairs Building, in the middle of downtown Chicago's cluster of high-rise canyons, he knew there'd been nothing to justify his action.

Eighty-five miles away in Tyler, Wisconsin, in the light from a pair of blue, blue eyes, he'd had a hundred reasons. Trouble was, all of them had been personal. Foreman would never understand that. He was a little hard put to understand it himself.

"I disagree," he said with creditable conviction. "Lakeside Farm has been a customer for sixty years. That should mean something when times are tight."

Gray eyebrows beetled over Foreman's eyes. "Times aren't tight, Jake. Times are inflexible. Lines are being drawn between survivor and victim. The little lady's going down and it can't matter to you or me how long her family's been trading with us." That soliloquy was delivered sharply, firmly—boss to underling.

Now Foreman leaned back in his chair and smiled. His tone became paternal. "You're the best damned sales manager I've ever had, with the best damned numbers in the best damned district Winnebago Dairy has ever seen. But you know and I know that the widow Hansen isn't going to be able to come through. If she declares bankruptcy on us tomorrow, your job is down the tubes, Jake, and I'm holding on to your shoes. Now's not the time to get cute on me. It's no secret that you're a front-runner for my job. You start looking like you're not watching the bottom line and Napier from central district'll walk away with it."

Jake wanted to gag. Napier was known among the sales staff as Napoleon because of his small stature, his cock-of-the-walk strut and his wild ambition. He made Jake's wish to find a secure place high in the business world and hold on to it look like a Monopoly move.

He made himself say reasonably, "The sum total of her bill won't be even a fraction of a percentage point of our total receivables. In the interest of goodwill and PR, I think we—"

"Goodwill and PR don't put peaks on our graphs, Jake. Cold hard cash does. Sales do. Collections do.

And you and I don't think—we do what we're told. We follow company policy." Foreman gave the file a cursory glance, then closed the folder with finality. "Don't do it again. That's all." He handed Jake the folder. "Ask Marlene to refile this."

The bosomy redhead in a sedate white silk blouse accepted the folder from Jake with a knowing smile. "Are you fired, or are you free to take me to lunch?"

The scope and accuracy of office gossip always amazed him. "Fired?" he asked innocently. "As though this place could hum without me."

Marlene put down the folder, leaned both elbows on it and regarded him, resting her chin coyly on her crossed hands. "Word has it you had one of our delinquent accounts humming."

Anger swept through him, hot and startlingly violent. The thought that a private moment with Britt was now hot office news enraged him. Marlene's smile died and she leaned back in her chair—away from him.

"You'll need another candidate for lunch," he said and walked away before he was tempted to do or say more.

It's your own fault, he told himself as he marched back to his office. *You knew the truck was coming with Britt's feed. You arranged for it. But you had to have that kiss. You had to hold her and pretend for just one moment that you could have her. That's what you get. Play games and you lose.*

"Is that more yogurt?" David, standing beside Britt at the kitchen counter, looked at the round device that had eight smaller lidded containers and was plugged in where the toaster usually stood. The large lid over the containers was beaded with moisture.

"I've got to keep working on recipes," Britt explained, consulting her handwritten notes and calculations taped to the cupboard door over her head as she stirred the contents of a china bowl.

"What's that going to be?" David pointed to the bowl.

"I'm trying a new cheesecake recipe."

"This is the stuff you made with Mildred's milk?"

"Right."

"It's the stuff that's going to make us rich." Books, paper, glue, pictures cut from magazines, stickers and a colorful assortment of pens and pencils were strewn around Christy on the dining-room table. She looked up to join the conversation, her farming notebook in full production. "Right, Mom?"

Britt smiled at her over her shoulder. "Right, Chris."

"You been doing that for two weeks. How long before you have the right recipe?"

"I've got the basic yogurt recipe down," she said, dipping a spoon into the cheese mixture and tasting. Delicious. It was coming together; it really was. "I'm just figuring out other things I can do with it so I can really wow them."

Renee, who'd cleared a small area across the table for herself and her coloring book and crayons, tried to sneak one of Christy's markers.

"Put that back!" Christy shouted vehemently.

"I just wanted to do the lips," Renee whined.

Christy pointed her index finger at her little sister as though it contained a laser. "Put it back."

Renee slapped the marker down in the middle of the table. "You're supposed to share!"

Wearying of the argument she'd arbitrated several times already that evening, Britt explained one more time. "Renee, Christy bought those with her own money to do her report. They're hers."

Renee closed her coloring book and sat back dejectedly, her jeans-clad legs swinging desultorily. "I wish

Jake would come back. I'll bet he'd buy me some markers."

"That's selfish," Christy said, expertly cutting the picture of a goat out of an old *National Geographic* magazine. "You just want to see him so he'll buy you something."

"No," Renee corrected, folding her arms. "I want to see him 'cause I like him. He reminds me of Daddy."

Christy looked up to catch Britt's eye. "He *is* nice. Is he ever coming back?"

"He makes great French toast," David said.

Britt smiled at her children, remembering Jake's remark about a childhood that had made him feel choked and confined. While a part of her understood his unwillingness to put himself in a similar position again, another part couldn't imagine life having significance without children to do and plan for.

Her own heritage gave life a kind of continuity that rolled on from generation to generation. The Bauers had never been wealthy or particularly influential, but they'd always been involved in an effort to make Tyler a fine place to live. They'd loved and laughed and suffered and endured, and that kind of involvement in life and living had to be passed on. She felt sorry for Jake that he'd never understand that.

And she felt a little sorry for herself that things couldn't be different. She thought about him so often. During the night, in the morning, in the barn, in the pasture, in the kitchen surrounded by her brood, her mind would suddenly block out everything else and she would remember his arms around her, his mouth on hers, his deep, dark eyes looking way down inside her, touching something she'd lived without for a year.

But now it was awake again—some little niggle of unease that longed for things a widow with four children shouldn't be thinking about. She shook her head and said calmly, "No, I don't think so. He was just here on business, remember. I think he'll be sticking pretty close to Chicago now."

"Maybe we could go see him," David suggested. "One more week and there'll be no more school for a whole summer."

A cheer rose from the table.

Britt laughed. "We're going to be too busy keeping goats and making yogurt to visit anybody."

David frowned. "I thought we were going to be rich."

Britt nodded and shared a grim truth. "We have to work very hard to make that happen. Then, when we're rich, we can go to Chicago if you want to, or maybe even Disneyland."

"Wow! Disneyland!"

Matt wandered into the kitchen, a baseball cap backward on his head. A tuft of dark blond hair protruded through the sizing hole. "I think we should go to New York to see the Yankees play. What do you say, Mom?"

She smiled at him over her shoulder. "I say we have a little time to make plans. It's going to be a while before the big money starts rolling in."

He frowned. "Then how are we gonna keep going in the meantime?"

"As soon as I get this perfected," she explained, "I'm going to take a load of this stuff on the road in a refrigerated truck, and hopefully, I'll make enough to convince the bank I deserve a loan after all."

"Cool," he said. "You're going to leave us alone?"

Britt gave him a grin. "Judy will be staying with you, so cancel all wild party plans."

He took a banana from the fruit bowl and, looking thwarted, headed back upstairs.

Britt poured the yogurt-and-cheese mixture into a waiting graham cracker crust, then carried the full pie plate to the refrigerator. She said a silent prayer over it as she slipped it onto the shelf. "Be delicious," she coaxed. "Come through for me. I need you to be wonderful."

She closed the door on it and said another silent prayer that in two more weeks she'd have enough money to pay Winnebago Dairy what she owed.

JAKE DROPPED his tux jacket on the chair and poured himself a Scotch and water. He walked to the floor-to-ceiling window that looked toward the Loop and the Chicago River several blocks away and yanked at his tie, then unfastened the top two buttons of his starched shirt.

His ears still rang with Pavarotti's powerful tenor. He'd thought the enforced civility of an off-season charity-sponsored night at the Civic Opera House with Bridget Chancellor would jog him back into line.

The marble columns and crystal chandeliers, he'd hoped, would surely remind him what he wanted out of life. And the Winnebago Dairy president's daughter would be very good for his career. Though she'd cultivated the relationship they'd enjoyed the past few months, he'd found her company painless, even stimulating.

But the evening hadn't worked. It had been elegantly refined and aesthetically chic. In a glimmering black dress that showed off her wonderful shoulders and her remarkable derriere, Bridget had been the perfect companion. She stayed close but she didn't cling. She conversed intelligently and she didn't chatter. She'd invited him for nightcaps at her place, telling him she'd missed him. He'd refused.

She'd blinked and begun to detail what she meant by nightcaps. He'd kissed her on the cheek to forestall an explanation and had gotten the hell out of there.

Looking down on the brightly lit city, he sipped the biting Scotch and rubbed the back of his neck. It wasn't like him to be tense. And it wasn't like him to be distracted. But all he'd thought about all evening in the heart of the sophisticated city was a little farm in Wisconsin and a woman with eyes so blue that looking into them was like drowning in the sky. He wondered if the notion of goat yogurt had worked. He even wondered about the children. Had Matt remembered to lock up the bike? Was Christy making progress on her notebook? Were the younger ones holding their own? He smiled out at the city, wondering if Mildred had settled down or if Britt might be curled up in the chopped oat hay right now to keep her company.

Something hurt in the pit of his stomach and it wasn't the Scotch.

BRITT STOOD on a vacant bench in the alley behind the bus depot, searching the disembarking passengers. Through the open doors of the small terminal a female voice announced arrival and departure schedules over the intercom.

Then Britt spotted the tall, shapely brunette who'd been her childhood cohort and her confidante through adolescence, and felt the warmth of friendship brighten her horizons. Cece was back.

"Cece!" she shouted, waving both arms. "Cece, over here!"

In jeans and a lavender quilted parka, Cecilia Hayes looked up and spotted Britt. Thickly lashed gray eyes brightened in recognition as she smiled and shifted her purse and tote bag into one hand so that she could wave back.

Britt wove her way through the little knots of people that separated them, then flung her arms around her taller friend.

Cece dropped her bags where she stood and returned Britt's hug with a fierceness that bridged the decade or so she'd been away.

They drew apart and Britt looked into her eyes, seeing the same warmth she felt. And something else, something new they had in common—the grief of widowhood.

Britt hugged her again, imagining what it must be like for Cece, who had no children to soften the loneliness and warm the memories. She pulled away and swatted her arm.

"How dare you come back here still slinky and pretty!"

Cece looked down at her jeans and bulky jacket. "Slinky?" she asked.

"Don't try to fool me. I know it's under there. You haven't gained a pound since senior year, right? You go off to a Third-World country and spend years working under God knows what kind of conditions in a refugee hospital and you have the nerve to come home with a peaches-and-cream complexion and perfect teeth." She turned Cece around and pretended to push her back toward the bus. "That's it. You're leaving. I'll be darned if I'm sharing Tyler's one eligible male with you."

Laughing, Cece turned and hugged her again. "God, it's good to see you. Will you please take me to my mother's if I promise to keep my coat on?"

"Well . . ." Britt appeared to consider.

"Besides," Cece said, picking up her bags and walking toward the side bay of the bus, from which passengers were retrieving their luggage, "Mom tells me you've got your own single male and he's not from Tyler. Jake somebody?"

Surprised, Britt allowed Cece to fill her arms with a large, string-tied box. "Marshack. And I don't *have* him. How does she know, anyway?"

Cece slipped a garment bag over her shoulder and picked up her purse and tote. She spared Britt a dry grin as she followed her to the station wagon. "Be serious. My mother knows everything. I think it has something to do with being postmistress."

Britt dropped the box and unlocked the wagon's tailgate. "But letters and packages are sealed. You think she steams everything open?"

Annabelle Scanlon, Cece's mother, did have a reputation for knowing the lowdown on even the vaguest gossip.

Cece shook her head as she helped Britt lift her things into the back of the wagon. "No, I think she has an uncanny kind of clairvoyance or something. All she has to do is run her fingertips over the registered stuff and she senses the contents." Cece lowered her voice dramatically. "And she passes on the news—foreclosure, unrequited love, orders for things that come in brown-paper wrappers."

Britt giggled, feeling seventeen again. She closed the tailgate, then opened the passenger side, leaning in to remove Renee's Barbie doll from the seat.

"There you go. Untidy but reliable. Just like my old Pinto, remember?"

Cece laughed as she slipped inside. "I remember that it wasn't all that reliable. Remember when it died on our way home from the Sadie Hawkins dance and we walked a mile and a half in our high heels?"

In the car, Britt buckled her seat belt and patted the dash. "That won't happen this time, I promise." She turned the key in the ignition and grinned at her friend as the motor purred healthily. "Brick keeps it running for me. Remember Brick?"

"Star of the Tyler/Belton game? Of course I do. He's in law enforcement, isn't he?"

"Yes. He just got married," Britt said, pulling out into the midafternoon traffic. "To Karen Keppler, his captain."

"That's great!"

"There've been a rash of romances around here," Britt said, glancing at the dash clock. "You won't believe it. Your mom won't be off work for an hour yet. Want to go to Marge's for a cup of coffee and my soon-to-be-world-famous cheesecake?"

"Is the diner still there?" Cece asked in surprise.

"Every booth and faulty fluorescent." Britt steered the car in that direction.

Cece turned toward Britt as far as her seat belt would allow. "So tell me," she said eagerly, "who's married to whom? Mom's caught me up on some of it, but mail delivery in Nicaragua's been a little sporadic lately."

"Okay, let me think." Britt split her attention between the traffic and Tyler's romantic news. "Marge and I are starting to think of this as Torrid Tyler. Liza Baron married this blueblood from New England who worked on the lodge."

"Somebody's fixing Timberlake Lodge?"

"Yep. It's wonderful. They're still working on it but I'll drive you by before I take you to your mom's if you want." Britt frowned. "There've been some strange things going on there."

Cece raised an eyebrow. "Between Liza and the blueblood?"

Britt gave her a scolding glance. "No. Just in general. A body was found by one of the workmen."

"Whose?"

"You won't believe this. Margaret Ingalls, Judson's wife."

Cece gasped. "I thought his wife left or something when Alyssa was little."

"That's what we all thought. Anyway, it's under investigation right now." Britt sent Cece a quick grin. "Hard to think of Tyler as a hotbed of passion and violence, isn't it?"

Cece shuddered. "Very. Let's get back to the romances."

"Okay. There's Pat Kelsey and Pam Casals, who came here to coach football."

"A woman?" Cece asked in surprise.

Britt frowned at her. "You went to the wilds of Nicaragua to stamp out disease and you're a woman."

"True," Cece allowed. "Go on."

"Nora Gates married Liza's husband's brother, Byron Forrester."

Cece squinted, trying to grasp the relationship, then nodded when she had it. "She didn't sell the store, did she? Gates has always been an institution around here."

"Still is," Britt said. "Nothing's changed there."

"Good. Who else?"

"Joe Santori—you know, the carpenter?" At Cece's nod, she want on, "He married Susannah Atkins, who has a television show in Milwaukee. And remember Renata Meyer?"

"Petite? Arty type?"

"Right. She married a Winnebago Indian, Michael Youngthunder, who came to Tyler looking for his grandfather."

Cece shook her head in amazement. "Is there something in the water? Are you next?"

"No."

"Why not?"

Britt shook her head and sighed, turning down the street that would lead to Marge's Diner. "Because Jake's gorgeous and very kind and there could be something to it if we were different people. But he feels stifled by children, and I don't think I'll ever get over Jimmy."

Cece's teasing smile dissolved and she turned back to stare out the windshield, her whole being seeming to settle just a little—as though her cheerful, enthusiastic demeanor had been a role she'd assumed for Britt's benefit.

"Does it ever get easier, Britt?" she asked heavily.

Watching the road, Britt reached out to touch her arm. "Not much," she replied. "I still head off to tell Jimmy something, forgetting that he won't be there. But my children have helped me a lot. They give me something else to think about."

Cece placed her hand over Britt's and held it a moment. "I feel as though I've had a limb severed or something—like I've lost something I don't think I can live without."

"I know," Britt said gently. She remembered that feeling. The absolute amazement that a new day could dawn and the world remain unchanged when your personal world had crumbled to dust around your feet. "But you have to go on. I'm sure Steve would want you to."

Cece nodded halfheartedly. "I know. If I could just get the picture of him lying in the rubble of our refugee hospital out of my mind, I might be able to go back to work."

Britt remembered watching film clips of the devastating earthquake on the evening news. Pictures of an enormous death toll and heroic rescues had touched her as distant tragedy touched everyone. Then she'd remembered Cece and Steve's hospital.

She'd called Annabelle that night and been told in a frantic voice that Annabelle knew nothing yet but would call her as soon as the Red Cross was able to come through with news.

It had taken three days, during which the town had gathered around Annabelle with food and expressions of concern and encouragement.

The news that Cece's husband had been killed had stunned everyone. They remembered the vibrant, impassioned young man they'd met only once, when he and Cece had visited Annabelle before flying to Nicaragua. He'd seemed a fine match for the idealist Cece had always been.

Britt, just learning to cope with her widowhood, had fallen apart all over again with grief for her friend.

Britt had to swallow to find her voice. "I know," she said once more. "I'm haunted by mental images of Jimmy in a ditch with the tractor on top of him. The doctor assured me Jimmy probably felt nothing, though he lived for four days in a coma, but I can't help feeling things would have been different if I'd been there when it happened." She sighed, her throat straining painfully with tears she refused to shed in front of Cece. "Anyway, I know in my heart that isn't true. I guess holding on to the pain is a way of holding on to them."

She pulled to a stop in front of Marge's Diner and drew in a deep breath. "Anyway," she said, turning to smile at Cece, "work helps a lot. Will you be around long enough to take on a job?"

Cece nodded. "I'm not sure how long I'll stay, but Steve didn't have insurance or anything. I thought I'd give myself a day or two, then look in at Tyler Memorial, see if they need help."

"You know," Britt said, snapping her fingers as she recalled her conversation with Dr. Phelps, "the nursing supervisor at Worthington House is about to retire. I'll bet Dr. Phelps would be thrilled to talk to you."

Cece considered, then nodded. "All right. Sounds worth a try."

"I've got big plans for great success in the food business," Britt said, sitting up to check her makeup in the rearview mirror.

Cece blinked. "You're going to compete with Marge?"

Britt pulled a lipstick out of her purse. "No, I'm going to become the star of the healthy treat—the

Häagen-Dazs of low fat." She hesitated a moment as she applied a mauvey-pink shade, rubbed her lips together, then dropped the tube back into her purse and grinned. "Hansen-Dazs. That has a cash-register ring to it, don't you think? I've borrowed a goat and I've developed the most delicious goat yogurt you've ever tasted."

Cece stared at her blandly, then put a diagnostic hand to Britt's forehead. "Britt," she said evenly, "I think you're in the throes of a fever."

Laughing, Britt swatted her hand away and opened the car door. "That's what everyone thinks and that's why I'm going to make a killing. It's going to surprise everyone—even the big dairies, who'll wish they'd thought of it."

Cece stepped out of the car and shouldered her purse, meeting Britt at the diner door. "You know, I hate to bring this up, but remember the time you were going to make your fortune by putting sesame seeds in pet food?"

Britt sent her a scolding lift of her eyebrow. "I was young and silly then. Life has aged me."

Cece pulled the door open. "But it hasn't made you any less silly."

CHAPTER SEVEN

"MOM, DO WE HAVE TO?" Matt asked, looking suspiciously at the gelatinous white stuff in the bowl Britt had set before him.

"Yes," Britt said firmly. She dispensed spoons around the table. Christy, David and Renee exchanged looks of dread, then once again studied their bowls with a lack of enthusiasm that equaled their older brother's.

"Can't we have some strawberry stuff on it?" David asked hopefully.

"After you try it plain," Britt said. "I know you don't believe me, but I'll bet you're going to like it. Come on now. Be brave. Dig in."

"What if I throw up?" Renee asked.

Britt sent her a threatening glance. "You're grounded for a month. Now just take half a spoonful and put it in your mouth."

Christy picked up her spoon, dipped it into the yogurt, regarded it doubtfully for a second, then did as she was directed.

"If she dies," Matt warned, "I'm not trying it."

Christy screwed her eyes shut, anticipating the worst. Then her mouth worked as her taste buds reacted, and her face relaxed. She opened her eyes and smiled almost reluctantly. "It's good, Mom," she said in surprise. Looking around the table at her siblings, she confirmed with a laugh, "It's really good. Try it."

Matt dipped his spoon in, glancing at her distrustfully. "You're lying, right? You're just trying to sucker us into—"

"Mmm!" David said, rolling a bite on his tongue. "It is good." He held his bowl toward Britt. "Can I try it with strawberry now?"

Matt put the spoonful of yogurt into his mouth as Britt put a dollop of strawberry sauce into each of their bowls. He eyed her noncommittally, mixed the strawberry into his remaining yogurt and tried it again. "It is good," he said finally, almost reluctantly. "But I don't understand why. It comes from a goat."

"It's 'cause Mom is smart," Renee said, eagerly spooning up the contents of her bowl.

Giddy with success, Britt went to the refrigerator for the cheesecake. "Now you all have to try this." She cut small pieces and served them onto plates. "First plain, then with sauce." The cheesecake met with equal success.

"Okay, one more thing." Britt ran to the freezer, excited by their approval. If she could get her children to admit liking something as exotic as goat yogurt, she was sure the yuppie, health-conscious market would lap up her product in large quantities.

She spooned a frozen pink concoction into small cones and passed them around the table.

"Strawberry frozen yogurt," Christy guessed.

"You got it." Britt took her chair and leaned across the table on her forearms, watching her children's expressions.

Matt took a lick, then a bite, stared at the ceiling, then looked at her gravely. "Mom, this is radical," he said. "I didn't believe it, but I think you will make a fortune after all."

Christy declared it excellent, David asked for another cone and Renee had it all over her face. Success!

After bowls and plates were cleared away, Britt sat across from her children again with a notepad and a pen.

"We need a name for our yogurt. Any ideas?"

David piped up instantly. "Teenage Mutant Ninja Turtle Yogurt!"

Everyone laughed, and Britt reached across to pat his hand. "Good idea, David, but the turtle name's already taken. The guys who thought it up own it."

"How about Hansen Yogurt?" Christy suggested.

Matt shook his head. "That doesn't sound very exciting. Doesn't it have to be something that will really make people want to buy it?"

Britt nodded. "We need something appealing and unique."

"What's unique?" Renee wanted to know.

"Something different," Britt explained. "Something that there's only one of, so people really notice it."

"What about Lakeside Farm Yogurt?" Christy asked.

Britt wrote it on the pad. "That's not bad and it identifies us. The only problem is there are so many products with the word *Farm* or *Farms* in the name."

The children frowned thoughtfully.

"It should be something with a *Y* in it," Matt said. "So that you get the same sound. What's that called?"

"Alliteration," Christy said.

Matt frowned at her. "Laser brain. I was talking to Mom."

"Amoeba brain," Christy returned.

"Matt has a good idea," Britt said, trying to forestall the argument before it developed. "That's a good advertising tool. Something that starts with a *Y.*"

The children began offering ideas.

"Yeowie Yogurt?"

"Yellow Yogurt." Everyone groaned.

"Yacht Club Yogurt."

Christy sat up as Matt offered that suggestion. "That would make people want to buy it, wouldn't it? They'd think it'd turn them into the rich people on the lake."

Britt marveled at their nimble little brains. They were on the wrong track, but they certainly had the right idea.

"It should be something that relates to us," she said, "or to goats, or something that expresses how important this is to all of us."

"Why is it important?" Renee asked. "I forget."

"Because if we make enough money," Christy explained, "we won't have to leave here and move to Chicago so Mom can get a job."

"We can swim in the lake in the summer," Matt said, "and skate on it in the winter, and keep the animals, and slide down Perry's Hill in the snow."

"Yes!" David shouted, punching a fist high into the air. "That's the best! We can—"

"That's it!" Britt shouted, looking from child to child. "'Yes! Yogurt.' It's short, it's alliterative, it has a positive feel, and *yes,* we can keep everything we have if it's successful!"

Christy beamed. "I like it, Mom."

Matt nodded. "Cool."

David grinned. "It was my idea."

Renee came to wrap an arm around Britt and lean against her. "I don't want to go away."

Britt hugged her tightly. "I know, sweetie. Neither do I. So we're all going to work hard together to make this work, okay?"

"Okay." The reply was slightly suspicious, but unanimous.

"Good. Now, what'll we have on our label?"

"Mildred!" Christy said.

"Goats are funny looking," Matt disputed.

"But everybody likes them. And Mildred gave us the milk that helped Mom develop the recipe."

Matt frowned thoughtfully. "Maybe a goat would be okay, but there should be something special about it."

Britt grinned. "What about if we put a flower in her teeth, just to be silly?"

Everyone considered that. David, intoxicated with success, stood and punched the air again. "Yes!" he said.

BRITT WAS STRADDLING the side of the goat pen, the heels of her boots propped on the bottom slat, when Jake walked up behind her. She tottered dangerously as she leaned forward slightly, a camera to her eye. Mildred, a fat red rose in her mouth, looked up at her with only a minimum of interest before snapping the stem in her capable teeth and proceeding to eat the flower.

The camera clicked repeatedly until the rose disappeared.

Jake let his eyes roam slowly up dusty, disreputable-looking boots, old jeans clinging lovingly to slim calves, tight thighs and hips tautened by her precarious position. His eyes found her as perfect as any model on a Paris runway.

"Have you changed her name from Mildred to Carmen?" he asked.

With an exclamation of surprise, Britt turned, apparently forgetting that her legs were wrapped around the slats of the pen. Jake caught a glimpse of blue eyes widened with delight before alarm took over and she overbalanced and began to flail at the air.

He caught her upper body against his shoulder, steadying her so that she could untangle her legs. An arm around his neck, her eyes pinned to his, she swung the leg that was inside the pen over the wall. He propped a foot on the bottom slat to make a rest for her hips.

It was so good to see her. Better than he'd thought it would be when he'd finally made the decision to come. Over the past two weeks he'd begun to think he'd imagined her fresh beauty and that indefinable something that wouldn't let him put her out of his mind. But as her color heightened, he saw that she was as real as his memories.

"You should consider a rocket pack," he said softly. "Or working with a net." And then, because he couldn't wait another moment, he kissed her gently, sweetly.

She kissed him back, then leaned against him with a little sigh of pleasure. "Hi, Jake." She smiled as her eyes moved over his face feature by feature. "What are you doing here? I've got another week before I pay you."

He leaned his cheek against hers. "I know. I'm off on weekends so I brought some brochures for Christy's report. And I thought I'd take you out to dinner at the lodge. Can somebody stay with the kids?"

"They're all invited to a neighbor boy's birthday party. They're going to have pizza and watch a Star Wars marathon. I'm supposed to deliver them at six and pick them up at eleven."

"Good." He raised his head and tilted hers up. "I'll pick you up at six-thirty."

He loved that her smile was openly delighted. She made no attempt to disguise the fact that she'd missed him as much as he'd missed her.

"I'll even wear my only dress."

"I can hardly wait." He held her against him to drop his knee and lower her to the floor. He realized instantly that the move had been a mistake. He felt the peaks of her breasts against his chest, the rub of her thigh against his as her feet groped for floor, saw the suddenly smokey, languid look in her eye.

She maintained her hold on his neck, and the longing deep down in her eyes seemed to surface without shame, telling him silently but precisely what he wanted to know.

Crushing her against him, he kissed her again, all the feelings he'd suppressed in the past two weeks igniting and threatening to consume him.

Britt lost herself in his arms, marveling that she could feel so safe and so vulnerable at the same time. He seemed to represent everything that was paradoxical—security and danger, excitement and a curiously soothing calm, a wariness of children, yet a capacity for great generosity with them.

Jake drew away, feeling devoid of bone and wit and anything else that gave him substance. He'd come to find out what this compulsion developing in him was all about, to analyze it and make sense of it so that he could fit it into his orderly life.

Instead, he was rapidly discovering that absence from Britt had strengthened rather than weakened it, and that any attempt to try to understand it seemed only to point out qualities that confused him further. But he'd never felt this alive or this . . . eager in his life.

That what he felt for her refused to be brought into line concerned him more than a little. But the way she made him feel overrode that, and for the first time since he'd left his aunt's home and made a logical, carefully plotted plan for his life and career, he ignored the warning signs and made an emotional rather than an intellectual choice—to let himself fall in love with the widow Hansen.

David and Renee squealed excitedly from somewhere outside. "Jake's here!"

David ran into the barn. Renee ran into his arms. Christy and Matt followed.

"Mom said she didn't think you were coming back," Christy said. "She's almost never wrong."

Shifting Renee onto his hip, Jake removed a long, narrow brown envelope from his jacket pocket. "I was looking through some new brochures in our office and found some things that might help you with your report."

"Wow!" Christy accepted the envelope, pulling out a dozen colorful folders about the state of Wisconsin and its industries, recreation facilities, government and agriculture.

"My bike's cool," Matt said. "And I'm remembering to put it on the porch."

"Great. How's the summer-trip fund doing?"

He shrugged a shoulder. "Not bad. I'm doing odd jobs besides my paper route—lawn mowing, stable mucking, fence painting, stuff like that."

Jake nodded approval. "Hard work always pays off."

"That's what Mom says. We've got this yogurt stuff all over the place."

"It's gonna be called Yes! Yogurt," David said, beaming, "and I thought of the name."

"All *right*. That's very clever."

"And Mom's taking pitchers of Mildred with a rose in her teeth for our leggo."

"Logo," Britt corrected, enunciating carefully.

"Mom knows a man who's going to draw the picture of Mildred for our label," David said. "When we get rich, will you still come and see us?"

"Of course," Jake assured him. "You'll be able to buy lots of Winnebago Dairy products then."

Britt glanced at her watch and began to shepherd the children toward the door. "Come on, guys. It's time to start getting ready for the party."

"It's Binky Howard's birthday," David explained. "He's going to be ten." He was obviously impressed.

Matt laughed. "He's going to turn stupid like Christy."

Britt waited for the inevitable retaliation, then looked over her shoulder when it didn't come. Christy, absorbed in her brochures, walked blindly beside Jake and Renee, oblivious to her brother's slurs.

"America's Dairyland..." she read aloud, looking up at Jake and saying knowledgeably, "that's Wisconsin." He nodded, appropriately enlightened. She continued to read. "...has 1.8 million dairy cows that produce a year's supply of milk for 42 million people, butter for 68 million and cheese for 86 million. Geez!"

Before anyone could comment, she went on, "Wisconsin's cranberry bogs produce forty percent of the nation's crop, and the state raises more green peas, beets, cabbage and sweet corn for processing than any other." She looked up at Jake. "I knew that."

"Of course," he said.

"Once-depleted..." She stopped walking to frown up at him. "That means used up?"

"Right," he replied. "Almost gone."

She continued walking. "Once-depleted timberlands have been replaced by Christmas tree plantations and private forests, which supply timber for Wisconsin's vast..."

Unable to stop himself, he put a hand on her head and gently ruffled her hair. The brochures that had been an excuse for him to see her mother obviously pleased Christy so much that, on a completely unselfish level, he was happy he'd brought them.

Unconsciously, Christy put an arm around his waist and walked with him, still reading. He caught Britt's eye and smiled indulgently.

Some little hope deep inside Britt's chest tried to unfurl, but she refused to let it. No. She couldn't be that lucky twice in her lifetime.

BRITT WORE A DRESS of powder-blue silk that made Jake feel as though her eyes were going to swallow him. Sitting across from her at a candlelit table in front of the lodge's fireplace, he felt as though he was lost in a dream.

Free of the responsibility of her children for a few hours, and enthused about her yogurt project, Britt was more relaxed than she'd ever been with him, more spontaneous and less suspicious.

"If this trip works," she was saying, calling him back from his lazy perusal of the play of candlelight and shadow on her face, "I'm going shopping for goats. They're more economical to feed than cows and produce proportionately more milk."

He was nodding his approval when it dawned on him. "Trip?" he asked.

"I'm going to hit the road myself for a couple of days," she explained, her face all peaches and porcelain as she leaned toward him in her enthusiasm. "To see what the reaction is. I've rented a refrigerated truck and I'm going to stop at sidewalk sales and flea markets and grocery stores."

He didn't like the sound of that. "What about the kids?"

"Judy's going to watch them."

"Can you afford motels and eating out?"

"It's a refrigerated truck," she repeated as though surprised by his questions. "I'll take my own food along, and I'll sleep in the truck."

He *really* didn't like the sound of that. "Britt, I'm not sure that's a good idea."

"It would be better if I could wait for summer and the dairy fairs, but I can't expect someone to watch my children when they'll have them *all* day." She grinned. "That would be cruel and inhuman."

"No," he said. She just wasn't getting the message. "I mean, I don't think it's a good idea for you to travel alone."

She raised an eyebrow and her expression took on a mildly defensive set. "I'm well prepared. I know what I'm doing."

He tried another tack. "I could put you in touch with a sales rep."

She shook her head adamantly. "I have to see and hear reactions for myself. No secondhand report from a rep will be able to convey an ugly face or a smile of enjoyment."

"Then why don't I go with you?" he suggested.

She grinned. "Because then I really would be in trouble."

Worried about her, he toyed with his spoon, resisting the urge to return her smile. "I'll bring my longies and sleep in the refrigerated part of the truck."

She giggled. It was a beautiful sound and forced his grin at last. "This is the only way I'm going to get the money to pay you back." She reached across the table and patted his hand. "Don't worry. Remember when you tried to help me pick up the goat?"

He scolded her with a glance.

"I only mention that," she said, obviously biting back another giggle at the thought of him in the mud puddle, "to remind you that I'm very capable and very strong—physically and any other way you want to consider. I come from crafty, stubborn German stock and was married to a hardheaded Scandinavian. I will come to no harm, I promise you."

If he wasn't going to be able to stop her, the best he could do was encourage her to take precautions.

"You should check in with someone every day."

"I intend to call Judy."

"And spend the night only in campgrounds or state parks. None of this just pulling off the road stuff."

"I do have a brain, Jake."

"It's not your brain I'm worried about. How far are you going?"

"All the way to Rhinelander," she said, then waited for further argument. That was almost to the Michigan border.

He studied her with resigned disapproval, but said nothing. He pulled a business card and a pen out of his breast pocket and wrote something on the back of the card. He handed it to her across the remnants of their trout meunière. "My home number's on the back," he said. "If you have a problem, call me."

She smiled and put the card in her purse. "I will. Now you have to try the cheesecake I've made with my new goat's milk yogurt. I think it'll reassure you that I do know what I'm doing, and that Yes! Yogurt will be in every refrigerated case before you know it."

Jake gestured for the waiter, then fixed a level look on Britt. "Just don't let it become more important than your common sense."

Her expression sobered. "It is *very* important to me. And if you're going to drop in on me unexpectedly and shoulder your way into my life, you have to understand that."

He leaned toward her on his forearms, his eyes dark and steady. *"You,"* he said with emphasis, "are becoming very important to *me,* and you have to understand *that."* He wanted to say more, but the waiter arrived, forestalling him. Dutifully, he ordered cheesecake and cappuccino.

"What do you think?" Britt asked, her blue eyes filled with eagerness as he rolled a bite on his tongue.

It was exquisite—impossible, as far as he could tell, to differentiate from the cow's-milk version. It was even lighter tasting without sacrificing that substantial texture that was cheesecake. He realized with simultaneous stabs of alarm and excitement that she probably did have something here. Whether she could truly get it off the ground and onto the shelves remained to be seen. Determination alone wouldn't do it.

But injecting a negative note in the face of her anticipation and excitement would be like smashing a daisy. He simply couldn't.

"It's delicious," he said, then analyzed the bite a little longer. "No, it's more than that," he said into her eyes. "It's something special."

She glowed. "And it's low in calories and fat! The consumer would have to be nuts not to love it."

He had to inject some practicality. "What kind of price can you offer it for?"

She looked momentarily troubled. She'd obviously been thinking about it. He should have known. "I'm not absolutely sure yet. On paper, the lower cost of raising goats as opposed to cows will make a big difference, but then I'm sure there'll be costs I haven't anticipated." She smiled, her eyes still gleaming. "Then, if it does take off, I'll need new milking equipment, and there's the problem of making sure you have milk all year round. Goats don't come into heat all year round like cows."

He shook his head with dramatic grimness. "Pity."

She swatted his arm. "This is a real problem. They breed from about August to November, and they have only a 305-day lactation cycle. If I don't carefully rotate the breeding, they'll all be dry the same two months of the year. That'd be great for business." She groaned and her broad grin slipped a little.

He closed a hand over hers and said gently but gravely, "You're sure there isn't an easier way? Like sell the herd, rent out all your pasture and still own your precious Bauer property?"

She placed her other hand over his and leaned forward with a look that told him she felt things and knew things he might never understand. "Renting pasture would probably carry the house, and selling the herd would solve my immediate problems, but I'd still have to find a way to make a living. Even more important, though, is the fact that I'm a farmer.'' She held up hands that had been carefully scrubbed and creamed for the evening, but still showed signs of hard work. ''I can't just sit on the land. I have to have fields planted and animals grazing.'' She smiled. ''Well, goats don't graze, they browse, but you know what I mean.'' She sobered, patted his hand again, then withdrew hers into her lap. ''But it's scary, you know? Jimmy's probably having a fit. He refused to take on anything iffy. He always said being a farmer was taking enough of a chance with life.''

Before a pall could settle over her excitement, Jake said bracingly, ''I'm sure you'll cope admirably. And if you come back from this trip with a few sales, or you make some positive contacts, the bank might change its mind about a loan.''

She gave him a skeptical look. ''I thought you were the realist.''

He smiled wryly. ''So did I. But I'm really beginning to think you can do this.''

THEY SAT IN THE DARK on a bench in the middle of the town square and watched the light evening traffic pass by. Street lamps lit up the brick facades of the bank, the post office, the city hall and all the shops that flanked the pretty patch of green preserved in the middle of commercial downtown.

Jake felt like a product of television's ''Quantum Leap''—as though he'd traveled through time and been dropped in a turn-of-the-century town created in Thornton Wilder's imagination.

''What are you thinking?'' Britt asked quietly.

The fragrance of cut grass and late-spring blossoms mingled with her floral perfume. He pulled her closer.

He could see one of the old globed streetlights reflected in her eyes.

"I'm not," he said. "I'm just feeling."

She smiled curiously. "Feeling what?"

"Comfortable," he replied. "Maybe a little out of tune with life as I've always known it."

A breeze spun around them and moved on. She reached up to brush a short lock of hair off his forehead. "It's Tyler," she said. "In Chicago you probably don't have time to think. Here, everywhere you turn there's something to remind you of all the people who came before you, of how lucky you are to be right here where we concentrate on every little moment."

Jake looked around him at the scene. He smiled, thinking it was like something you'd see around an electric train set up under a Christmas tree. Could this be real? He felt the tug of its appeal like a tangible thing. It came as a jolt to a hard-core product of the city.

"You aren't happy with your life in Chicago?" she asked.

"I don't know."

Shifting, she folded her elbow on his shoulder, looked into his eyes and frowned. "How can you not know if you're happy or unhappy?"

He considered that and grimaced thoughtfully. "I guess if happiness isn't the priority..."

She gasped. "How can happiness not be the priority?"

"Well, there's career, success, security...."

"What kind of success or security is there," she asked severely, "in unhappiness?"

"It's not exactly *un*happiness," he said with a wry grin. "It's more like *non*happiness."

In the evening shadows he saw her roll her eyes. "The absence of happiness is no happiness," she said, "no matter what prefix you attach to it. You'd better move to Tyler, Marshack, before it's too late."

He looked into her teasing gaze, his own challenging. "You think so?"

She felt herself slip into his eyes and for several seconds anchor there, like a tired little boat coming home. She had to drag her gaze from his to her watch. "Time to get my kids," she evaded.

Britt's children were high on the evening's excitement and revved to the point of combustion. She listened patiently as they interrupted one another, sharing details about the party. They laughed and giggled and poked each other as though the confinement of the Explorer after an evening of Star Wars adventures was wearing.

By the time they reached the house, Jake felt as though he'd spent the past ten minutes in a blender.

Britt sensed the change in him when she sent the kids into the house and turned to tell him goodbye. There was a tension in him that hadn't been present during dinner and their conversation in the square. Then she remembered the ride home, with the kids wired and loud. To the uninitiated, that could be a grisly experience.

She let out a ragged breath and accepted that while it was wonderfully stimulating to have him running in and out of her life, he could never be a serious part of it. They could care for each other and enjoy being together and even long for each other when they were apart. But there would always be four little bodies between them that would make any thought of permanence impossible.

"Thank you for dinner," she said, hearing the vaguely wistful sound of her voice. She cleared her throat. "Christy was thrilled with the brochures. It was kind of you to think of her."

"My pleasure," he said. "Will you call me collect every night and let me know how you are?"

She smiled and kissed his cheek. "Absolutely not," she said. "I'm going to be far too busy to think of anything but yogurt. But I'll tell you all about it when I come back and you come to collect."

It was a gentle set-down and he had no right to protest. She didn't owe him peace of mind. She was drawing a line—she and her children on one side and he on the other. For now, at least, he couldn't cross it.

But he had to let her know how he felt about her. He cupped her silky head in his hand and, leaning over her, kissed her soundly, emphatically. "Fine," he said. "I'll just check in with Judy. And I'll see you when you get back."

Breathless, her composure shaken, Britt watched Jake climb into his truck and back out of the driveway into the night.

CHAPTER EIGHT

DURING THE DAY, Britt found the solitude of the road stimulating. Behind the wheel of the refrigerated truck she opened her window, cranked the radio up and felt a little like a sixties pilgrim on her way to Woodstock.

Actually, she decided, that analogy wasn't at all appropriate. She wasn't on a search for self-enlightenment, she was on a quest for bucks—big bucks.

Her mind tried to hop to thoughts of Jake, but she refused to allow it to. She needed to think clearly and to observe every little detail without distraction. She turned the music up louder and began to sing.

The first day she called on all the little grocery stores on the way up to and along Interstate 94. She gave out samples of yogurt, and when those were well received, she distributed pieces of cheesecake and cream cheese Danish. She brought out celery sticks and dipped them in Yes! Yogurt salad dressing. The response was enthusiastic, but the sales were not, though she did sell two cheesecakes to a gourmet coffee shop in Lake Mills.

Undaunted, she stopped for the night at a campground just off the interstate. While munching on a ham-and-cheese sandwich, she made notes in a journal she'd brought to keep all her scattered ideas in. She was encouraged by the positive reactions she'd had to her product.

Tomorrow's schedule involved a craft fair at Portage, so she spent the evening folding the brochures she'd had printed, which touted the health advantages of goat's milk yogurt and the nutritive contents of her own particular products.

Then she climbed into the sleeping bag on the front seat of the truck and closed her eyes.

Solitude at night, Britt found two hours later, was as stimulating as solitude during the day, though for very different reasons. In the dark stillness she worried about her children, though Judy had assured her earlier that they were fine. She worried about her bills, her cows, Mildred. The darkness made her project's success seem like a pipe dream. There was too much against it, she had no capital, she was going to have to see to a million details by herself, she wasn't as strong as she pretended to be!

The urge to run screaming into the night was almost overwhelming. She sat up, poured a cup of coffee out of a thermos she'd had filled at her last stop and drank until the panic calmed.

SHE DIDN'T STAND a chance at the craft fair. The soft ice-cream booth was manned by the high school cheerleaders who, in derriere-skimming uniforms, served up beautiful smiles and a free bumper sticker with every cone.

By midmorning Britt was convinced the only thing she was going to be able to do there was make sure people tasted her product. She sampled out everything and forced thimble-size cups on everyone who passed by. She gave out hundreds of brochures and pointed out the nutritive value of her product.

The next day was better. She sold two cheesecakes and half a dozen Danishes to a hotel coffee shop, and a half carton of dressing to a little hole-in-the-wall salad bar somewhere between Westfield and Coloma.

The day after that, she set up at a street fair outside of Stevens Point and sold half of what she had in the

truck. Climbing into her sleeping bag after driving to
a campground, she lay awake again, too excited to
sleep. If she could do as well tomorrow at the flea
market in Merrill, then the following day at the Scandinavian fair in Rhinelander she'd be very close to
having enough money to pay Winnebago Dairy. That
brought thoughts of Jake to mind, but she refused to
concentrate on them. She missed home and her children and her kitchen abominably, and she'd decided
not to think about them, either—or at least as little as
possible. She had to concentrate on the pocket and not
the heart.

By midmorning the following day, she knew she'd
been foolish to have been so optimistic. She lifted the
hood on the truck, which for some unknown reason
had simply growled and shuddered to a stop, and
looked at the complex plumbing inside.

Unlike many farm women, who learned how machinery works out of necessity, she'd never acquired the
skill. She trusted in Providence—and the men in her
life who knew more about mechanics than she did. It
didn't help now to stare at all those parts and wires she
didn't understand. Doing so simply made them look
more foreign.

She looked up and down the bumpy little road she'd
chosen to explore off the highway. In a hopeful mood
that morning, she'd been certain there'd be an elegant
little gourmet shop that'd want to buy dozens of her
products. Now she saw no signs of life.

When she'd sat there for half an hour without another car passing, she consulted her map. It was eigh-
teen miles back to the interstate, but only four to the
next junction, a town called Goose Run. Britt tucked
her journal into her purse, slung her purse over her
shoulder, locked the truck and started hiking.

Exhausted from too many sleepless nights and too
many days of exuding charm and good cheer and en-

thusiasm, Britt felt worn out before she was halfway there. She buoyed herself up with thoughts of how beautiful the countryside was, how wonderful it smelled ... how many people were going to become addicted to Yes! Yogurt.

It was noon when she reached town. She presumed it was Goose Run; it was really hard to tell. There was a gas station, six run-down little cabins and two roads intersecting. One of them wasn't paved.

She approached a man sitting on a wooden bench outside the gas station. He had spread a checkered cloth and appeared to be setting out a veritable feast from a black lunch box. She put a hand to her stomach, thinking how silly it was that she'd been driving a truck full of food and it hadn't occurred to her to bring any of it with her to eat.

Quickly, calmly, she explained her problem.

The man nodded sympathetically, polishing a shiny red apple with a corner of his cloth.

"Motel across the street's neat and clean," he said.

"I'm sure it is," she agreed, "but my real problem at the moment is that the truck I was driving is filled with products I was supposed to sell today at the flea market in Merrill."

He picked up a three-inch-high sandwich and frowned at her. "Merrill's on the interstate. You're lost, young lady."

"I wasn't lost," she said calmly but firmly, finding it important to make the distinction. "I was exploring. But my truck died about four miles back. I was hoping you could fix it."

He nodded, took a bite of sandwich and chewed. "I'm sure I can. There's almost nothing doesn't get put to rights when August Cummings gets his hands on it."

That was reassuring. "It's right on the road," she said hopefully. "You can't miss it. But, please—" she indicated the spread of food before him "—finish your lunch first."

"Oh, I will, ma'am," he said, "'cause I don't have a wrecker. We'll have to call the wrecker at Lance Lake and I know for a fact he'll be tied up for the next couple-three hours. Eldorado in a ditch at Woodboro."

Britt's heart fell. Any thought she'd entertained of still making it to the fair today vanished. She tried to look desperate and found it wasn't hard. "Can't you drive out to my truck? Maybe it isn't anything major. Maybe you could just fix it on the spot."

He shook his head as he chewed another bite. "My wife just picked up my truck to go play bridge in Merrill."

Her shoulders fell and she couldn't suppress the groan. At least someone had gotten to Merrill.

With a smile, he offered her the apple. "Here. Won't seem so bad with something in your stomach."

BRITT STOOD beside the station owner—he'd asked her to call him Gus—and watched her rented truck being hauled into the shop by the wrecker. It had turned cloudy and she had to fight the early-evening melancholy peculiar to misfits and widows and anyone else separated from whom and what they needed in life.

Britt asked politely, "How long do you think it'll take you to assess the problem, Gus?"

He waved to the wrecker driver. "I'll get to it first thing in the morning."

Britt's heart sank further. "Morning?" She'd hoped to be on the road again by morning. She was supposed to set up at Rhinelander before ten o'clock.

"Granddaughter's birthday party tonight," he explained gently. "She wouldn't understand if her grandpa wasn't there. I'll come in early and get right to it, I promise." He pointed across the street to the motel. "Why don't you rent yourself a room and get some rest?"

Britt nodded dejectedly. She had little choice. She refused to spend any of the cash she'd made, but she did have a little room left on her credit card—very little. She'd get her sandwich makings from the back of the truck.

As soon as the wrecker driver removed the hook and went into the office with Gus, Britt opened the truck's back door. A blast of warm, ripe air hit her in the face. The refrigeration had failed. She stood there, the odorous air almost making her gag, and fought the urge to scream. No! It wasn't fair! She'd worked on the contents every night for weeks after the farm work was done. She'd pinned her hopes on them. Now she wouldn't have the money to pay Jake.

Jake. She remembered the business card in her purse with his home number on the back. She considered calling him, then quickly abandoned the idea. She'd drawn the line. She'd assured him she knew what she was doing, and had refused his suggestion that she call him to let him know how she was. She couldn't very well call him for help now. That would be using him unfairly.

Depressed and disillusioned, she asked Gus for some garbage bags and emptied out the contents of the truck while he locked up the shop. He carried the bags to his Dumpster, holding them at arm's length. The odor wafted back like a deadly fog.

He dusted off his hands and turned to smile at her. "You can clean the truck out in the morning while I'm working under the hood. Cheer up. Things'll look better with the sun."

Britt rented a room in the motel across the road and called Judy from an outside pay phone.

"You're late!" Judy said anxiously. "I was beginning to worry about you. Is everything okay?"

"I'm fine," she replied, forcing a note of cheer into her voice. "I've had a little trouble, though, and I'll be home a couple of days early."

Judy lowered her voice. "What happened?"

Britt explained.

"Oh, Britt," Judy moaned sympathetically. "What are you going to do tonight? Do you have somewhere to stay?"

She told her about the motel. "And I salvaged some chopped vegetables from the truck. I'll be fine. Soon as the truck's ready, I'll head for home. If I don't get too late a start, I should be there tomorrow night."

"Why don't I call Brick?"

"No."

"Jake?"

"No!" Britt said too loudly, then added more quietly, "No. I'm doing fine. How are the kids?"

Judy put Renee on, and one by one Britt spoke to her children, catching up on the end-of-school excitement. When she finally hung up, she was so lonely and so depressed she felt as though she carried an anvil on both shoulders.

At eight o'clock she was still sitting on the double bed in her dreary little room. Her stomach grumbled, but she'd put aside the vegetables long ago because she couldn't swallow them. Her throat had tightened in her effort to hold down her fear and disappointment.

Her feet hurt from the walk and her back ached from four nights of sleeping on the front seat of the truck. And she was so tired.

Some foray into commercial success, she thought, allowing self-pity to rear its ugly head. She'd gotten more compliments than sales, and now she was out of product and would probably be held responsible for the repair of the truck.

She lay back and tears slid from her eyes to the pillow. *I'm tired,* she thought again. *Tired of having to raise and support the children by myself, tired of the responsibility of a fifth-generation farm. I'm tired of work that's too difficult, bills I can't pay, responsibility that's too heavy and laughter that I have to force.*

That admission seemed to hang over her head like some terrible concession to weakness. She waited for it to make her feel better, but it didn't. All it seemed to do was make her feel guilty for not being made of stronger stuff. Great-Grandma Bauer would probably never have caved in like this.

She was pouring a glass of water in the bathroom an hour later when a knock sounded on the door.

She sniffed and tossed her braid over her shoulder as she went to answer it. It was probably Gus, she guessed, or the woman who ran the motel.

JAKE LOOKED into Britt's red, blotchy face and swollen eyes and felt the judicious I-told-you-so on the tip of his tongue evaporate. When she flew into his arms and began to sob, his mind emptied of everything but the need to hold her and offer comfort.

"I just wasn't—wasn't making the kind of—of sales I'd thought I would..." she was saying as he shifted the brown paper bag he held to press her closer. "But I just kept going and finally yesterday I—I had a really good day. I made half the money to pay you back. I was so excited."

She looked up at him with dark self-deprecation. He drew her with him into the room, dropped the bag on top of the television and closed the door.

"Ha!" she scoffed at herself, still clinging to him. "I don't know why I wasn't suspicious. Good things just don't happen to me. Well, they do, but not without a lot of effort and tribulation first." She sniffed and hiccuped as he looked around for somewhere to sit her down. Seeing the bed, he headed for it. "So this morning I went off the interstate just to—you know—

explore." She looked at him, expecting, he was sure, to have all his warnings of the weekend thrown in her face. He simply waited.

That little gesture of understanding seemed to destroy the little bit of composure she'd scraped together. Her face crumpled and she sobbed, "The truck died about four miles from here, then there was a Cadillac in a ditch and Gus's granddaughter had a birthday, and I opened the back of the truck and—and it smelled like bad beer!"

He held her and rocked her gently, wondering if the part about the Cadillac and Gus's granddaughter was important enough to the story that he had to understand their connection. Because he didn't.

She leaned away from him suddenly, wiped a tear from her cheek and asked in surprise, "What are you doing here?"

He continued to rub gently up and down her spine. "Judy told me what happened."

She made an indignant sound. "I told her not to call you!"

"She didn't," he said. "I called her and asked if she'd heard from you."

Her eyebrows rippled in a frown. "And you presumed I needed rescue."

He met her gaze intrepidly. "Yes."

Her pose collapsed and she leaned against him again. "You were right. Thank you. But how did you get here so fast? It's a six- or seven-hour drive."

"I didn't drive," he explained. "I flew to Rhinelander, rented a car—"

"At this hour?"

"A friend flew me up in his Cessna. The local Hertz rep was happy to accommodate me."

"For how much?" she asked.

"Please," he said with a grin. "Money's such a crass subject."

She sighed his name heavily and wrapped both arms around his waist.

He smiled to himself, enjoying her temporary dependence on him. He knew it wouldn't last long and chose to revel in it while he could.

She sniffed the air and raised her head from his shoulder. "What do I smell?" she asked.

"Fried chicken," he replied. "Fries, coleslaw and biscuits." Her stomach growled and he laughed softly, getting to his feet to retrieve the bag. "I knew you'd brought your own food along, so I figured if the refrigeration died, you probably missed dinner."

"Oh, Jake!" She scooted to the edge of the bed to make room for the bag between them. He handed her a carton of fries and she ate from it eagerly as he tore open the bag and, using it as a tablecloth, set out chicken, two containers of slaw, and rolls complete with pats of butter. "This is wonderful! I was starving."

He passed her a paper drink container and a straw. "Not exactly what the new guru of healthy goat yogurt should be caught eating, but for a nominal fee, I'll keep my mouth shut. So, did you learn any of the things you'd hoped to when you set out?"

Wiping her hands on a napkin. she stretched toward the bedstand for her purse and the journal it contained. She opened the book on her lap and, munching a french fry, reviewed her notes and began to relate her experiences.

He realized a little sadly that she was already changing. The tearful, clinging Britt who'd run into his arms at the door was already reverting to type. She'd recorded insightful observations, honestly noting bad as well as good reactions—though there seemed to be very few bad ones.

"The cheesecakes went very well. I had a little trouble getting people to taste the yogurt. I think they presumed it wouldn't be good, but once I got it into their mouths, they seemed to like it. I sold lots of it yesterday. And the dressing's going to be a real winner.''

"If you can produce more product,'' Jake said, pushing all the empty containers into the bag and lobbing it at the basket across the small room, "I can find a sales rep who'll take it around.''

Her eyes widened as she looked up from her notes. "Really? Where?''

"All over Wisconsin. If that goes well, all over the Midwest. The problem will be production. It's instant death to even really good products if the manufacturer can't produce it in enough quantity to fill orders.''

Britt sighed. "I've been thinking about that. I'll be selling the herd as soon as I get home, and buying goats. I'm pretty well set up for them already. I'll need some commercial equipment, though, and fairly quickly.''

Jake nodded. "If we can show the bank a big order, they might come through for us.''

There was a moment's silence.

"We?'' Britt asked. "Us?''

He nodded again and leaned back against the wall. "Okay. We come to the nominal fee I mentioned earlier.''

Excitement and trepidation rose in her side by side. "Oh?'' she asked calmly.

"I want to help you with this,'' he said. "My physical presence would be limited to weekends, but in Chicago, I can pull a few strings you wouldn't have access to.''

She liked the idea of an excuse to have him around. But there were some loose ends here she couldn't quite pin down but that seemed potentially troublesome. "Wouldn't Winnebago consider that a conflict of interest on your part?''

"I doubt they'd think of you as a threat. Anyway, we don't have a popular yogurt product. It was suggested we develop one, but the idea was squashed somewhere on the board. We still just put out the plain stuff bought by those who believe it induces good nerves, promotes sleep and wards off ulcers."

"Then..." She hesitated a moment, then looked him in the eye. "What about...us?"

He wasn't sure how to deal with this part of the equation, so he replied honestly, "I don't know. But I'd like to see you succeed in this, and I don't think you can get it off the ground all alone."

"My kids will be around," she warned. "I *like* them around."

He laughed. "I like your kids."

"They make you nervous," she corrected.

"I'm adjusting."

When she continued to look doubtful, he added, "*They* like *me.*"

That was a good point, she realized. But instead, she brought up a negative one. "If...this...between us becomes important, we're just asking for trouble."

He shrugged, acknowledging that with a grim smile. "It's already important, and we're already in trouble. It seems foolish to stop now when something good could result from it. Partners?"

His ready smile was like a glass of champagne at the end of what had been a very difficult day. She put her hand in his. "Partners."

CHAPTER NINE

JAKE LEANED back on an elbow and said amiably, "Our first mutual decision should be what to do about the bed."

Britt's smile was bland. "I rented the room. I get the bed. I've got a sleeping bag in the truck. You can use it."

"The truck's locked in the garage," he pointed out.

"Then you can sleep in the tub after I've had my bath."

"Okay," he said amiably. "You can walk behind the car when I drive home tomorrow."

She slanted him a wary look. "We can't share the bed."

"Why not? Aren't you to be trusted?" He sat up and leaned toward her, his grin broadening. "Does the widow Hansen harbor a lustful desire for Dudley Doright?"

She struggled valiantly to keep the truth from her eyes. She succeeded by narrowing them. "This is a small double bed," she said. "There is such a thing as stupidity prevention."

He shook his head. "I wish I'd been aware of that before I tried to find a private-plane pilot after hours, an all-night fast-food place in the boonies and a car to rent."

She laughed despite herself, realizing for the first time that it truly was amazing he was there. She folded her arms and asked, "And you think the widow Hansen's body should be your reward?"

He shook his head innocently. "No. Just the widow Hansen's bed." He smiled slowly, dangerously. "I'm a patient man. I can wait for your body."

She met his innocence with wide-eyed interest. "You're planning to live to be very old?"

He shook his head at her refusal to accept the inevitable. "It won't take that long," he said softly. "If you want your back scrubbed, just call."

She sighed, conceding defeat. She couldn't in all fairness consign him to the floor for the night when he'd gone to a great deal of trouble and expense to come to her rescue. "You'll stay on your side of the bed?"

"I promise to try," he said, getting to his feet. "But I'm a restless sleeper. I've got a bag in the car. Be right back."

He was in bed when she came out of the bathroom. His eyes were closed and he was as close to his side of the bed as it was possible to be. His nicely sculpted chest was bare, except for a light pelt of hair over his pectoral muscles.

She looked at the bed with trepidation, wondering if the bottom half of him was clothed. Then she bravely decided it didn't matter and got under the blankets without lifting them too far. He'd promised to stay on his side. She reached up to the lamp on the bedside table and turned it off.

As she leaned back into her pillow, she was grabbed in a pair of strong arms and gathered to the middle of the bed, where she was kissed senseless. The day's miseries vanished along with her concerns for tomorrow. Her mind seemed to short out as her body overloaded on sensation.

Jake's mouth opened and closed on hers, his hand swept gently, exploratively down the side of her cotton nightshirt. When it reached bare thigh, Britt inhaled, every system in her body stalling.

The gasp drew his tongue deeper into her mouth and he took shameless advantage. His questing hand did one slow sweep to her knee, then moved back up again as her heart rocketed hard enough to deafen her.

Then he released her, and she stared numbly into the darkness as she heard him settle back on his side.

"You promised!" she accused, like some enraged spinster.

"I promised to try to sleep on my side of the bed," he said, reaching back to manipulate his pillow into place. "I didn't say I wouldn't kiss you good-night. Good night, Britt."

"That was sneaky," she said, her voice low and righteous.

"I warned you the road was full of dangers you hadn't anticipated," he said. "You as much as told me to mind my own business."

She rolled onto her side, away from him. "You may consider the partnership dissolved."

"We shook on it. It's binding."

She turned halfway back to say icily, "There were no witnesses and no signed contracts."

"You'd welsh on a handshake?" His voice was filled with injured disbelief.

"I'd welsh on a hand that strokes my thigh."

"Because you liked it."

Britt's reply was to swing her pillow as hard as she could in the direction of his voice. She heard a satisfyingly startled "Ooof!" She resettled her pillow, punched it viciously, curled up into it and closed her eyes without refuting his statement. It would have been a lie.

BRITT AWOKE sprawled across Jake's body. Her face was nuzzled in his neck, her arm flung across his chest, her hand holding the sturdy angle of his shoulder. Her bent knee was hitched over him and her first coherent thought of the day was gratitude that her foot encountered cotton pajama bottoms on his leg.

She raised her head with a start to look down into his face. His eyes looked back at her lazily. "Maybe I should have extracted a promise from you," he said, "that *you'd* stay on *your* side."

Britt closed her eyes in embarrassment, accepting complete responsibility. She had a vague recollection of a dream that had felt all velvety and cozy—the way going to bed used to feel when Jimmy'd been alive. "You could have pushed me away," she said.

Doing so had never crossed his mind in the four hours since she'd stirred restlessly, then turned to him. Even when she'd said her husband's name, even when the deliciousness of having her against him, needing him, had turned to tightening tension and finally to pain, it hadn't occurred to him to put her back on her side.

Somewhere during that time he'd realized that he had no idea what to do about their different life-styles and her four children, but there was an inherent rightness in their being body to body in the middle of the night—a rightness from which he would not be able to walk away.

She ran into the bathroom. He pulled his clothes on.

Gus had the truck repaired bright and early. Jake paid him with a credit card, then added cash for him to see that the rental car was returned to Rhinelander. Britt and Jake wiped out the inside of the truck with a baking-soda solution.

"I don't understand why the truck motor and the refrigeration both failed." Britt frowned at Gus.

He wiped his hand on a rag. "Water in the diesel fuel last time you gassed up," he said. "Refrigeration probably stopped long before the motor died on you. Drive safely.''

"I'll pay you back," Britt promised Jake a little stiffly. She was having difficulty relaxing with him after having slept in his arms.

"You can just increase my partnership percentage," he said. It was her opportunity to remind him that she'd dissolved the partnership last night. She didn't take it.

"Fine," she said. "By the time I pay back all I owe you, *you'll* own Lakeside Farm."

She wasn't in the mood, but he made her think about business as they had breakfast on the interstate. He told her about a product rep he knew to be among the best in the business.

"You should think about packaging," he said. "How'd that photo of Mildred with the rose in her teeth turn out?"

She laughed. She'd had it blown up to poster size for her office. "It's wonderful. I was thinking that, for the yogurt, I'd like a waxed carton with a wooden or plastic spoon attached to it. Someone on the run will have everything he or she needs for a quick meal."

He nodded approval. "Good idea."

They talked through dinner in Waunakee and for the next five miles, until Britt fell sound asleep, her head bumping gently against the window.

Jake pulled into her drive at eight o'clock. Britt stirred awake as Judy and the children ran out to the truck. She was bombarded with hugs, kisses and questions.

Renee ran to Jake, her nightgown and robe flapping. "Hi, Jake!" she said with sincere delight. He lifted her up and was rewarded with a noisy hug. "I missed you."

"I missed you, too," he said, returning the hug, and realized almost to his surprise that it was true. She reminded him sharply of the vulnerable half of her mother.

Christy, Britt's controlled, efficient half, came to wrap his free arm in both of hers. "Hi. Judy says you rescued Mom."

He laughed lightly. "Well, maybe a little."

David held a small painted can up to him. It was covered with a haphazard array of stickers. "This is for you," he said.

Jake struggled valiantly to determine what it was.

"It's a pencil cup," David said proudly. "We made them for Father's Day, but... I don't have one—a father." He shrugged, frowning. "You know... I thought maybe you could put something in it."

Touched, Jake had to give himself a minute. "Thank you, David. I'll put it on my desk at work."

Daffy sat on his foot, whining for attention, and Jake reached down to pet her, grateful for the opportunity to swallow and draw a breath.

"Looks like he's won everyone over," Judy said quietly as Britt reached into the cab of the truck for her purse.

Britt glanced at her children, gathered in a tight little knot around Jake, and had to smile. He didn't look quite at ease, but he looked less uncomfortable than he had the first time they'd swarmed over him.

Then she noticed Matt hanging back. After a moment, he turned and went into the house.

Britt frowned at Judy. "Is Matt okay?"

Judy sighed, looking apologetic. "We have to talk about that before I leave." At Britt's frown of concern, she added quickly, "Now, don't get all upset. It wasn't anything really major. It's probably just boy stuff, but I think you should know about it."

The children followed closely as Jake went to Britt. Judy peeled the children from him and took them toward the house. They called goodbyes, and Jake waved until they disappeared inside. Then he turned to Britt. She looked upset suddenly, distracted, he realized.

"What is it?" he asked.

She shrugged and forced a smile. "I'm not sure. I think Judy had some kind of problem with Matt while I was gone. Anyway..." She dismissed that as being none of his concern and wrapped her arms quickly around him. "Thanks for coming for me."

He held her for just an instant, knowing any longer wouldn't be safe. "I'll be back Friday night to help you with the fences."

She had to add electric fence to what already existed or there'd be goats in downtown Tyler. "Great. Thanks again, Jake."

He climbed into the Explorer he'd left parked in her drive. He had to almost physically force himself to close the door. What he really wanted to do was carry her into the house and upstairs.

But he could see that she was worried about Matt, and it would be a dangerous thing to do anyway. He'd learned in the wee hours of the morning that simply holding her had a profound effect on him. He suspected making love to her would scramble his brain forever.

He waved and put the vehicle in reverse. Britt waved back, then ran toward the house.

"YOU MAY USE your bike to deliver your route," Britt said firmly. She was seated on the edge of Matt's bed and he was staring at the quilt drawn up to his waist. "Otherwise it's off limits. And you're grounded for the next two weeks."

He glanced up at her, his eyes angry and dark and troubled. "That's not fair," he said. "I didn't do anything awful. It was just one time."

"Coming home at ten and missing dinner while I was gone is more than being late," she said, trying desperately to maintain her reasonableness when she considered all the things that could happen to a young boy wandering in the woods at night. "You showed no respect for me or the rules of our house, and you frightened Judy, who was watching the four of you as a courtesy to me. I'm very disappointed in the way you behaved."

"I wasn't doing anything."

"Then why couldn't you have been home on time?"

"I wanted to be alone."

"I can understand your wanting privacy," Britt said, "but I'd have preferred you tried to find it in the basement, or even on the front porch. You are not allowed out that late and you know it. And you took advantage of Judy's being here."

His eyes filled with emotion and grew more hostile. "You gonna marry Jake?" he asked, pulling on the blanket and folding his arms over it.

The question so shocked her that for a moment all she could do was stare at Matt.

"Of course not," she said finally. "I won't be ready to marry anyone for a long time, if ever. Dad and I had something very special. It's hard to find that."

"But you need help," he said, his tone changing subtly, almost as though he understood how difficult the lonely struggle was for her. "You can't do everything by yourself. And he—he's always helping you."

"Because he's a kind person."

Matt's expression became startlingly adult and masculine. "I hope he doesn't come back anymore."

That surprised her. She tried to analyze the reason for it and couldn't. Men, she decided, even very young men, were confusing.

"Matt, I don't understand your attitude," she said gently. "Jake bought you that great bike when the fact that he ran over your old one was all your fault. You liked him well enough then."

He stared at the wall. "I didn't think he was going to try to move in then."

"He isn't trying to move in. He's going to be coming back to Tyler to help me with the goat pens and the new equipment we need, but he's just being a good friend." She knew that wasn't precisely accurate, but for the purposes of this discussion it was close enough.

She moved slightly forward until she could turn his chin toward her. "Are you afraid that I've forgotten your father?" she asked.

Raw emotion flared in his eyes, then he lowered them quickly. A tear escaped anyway. "He shouldn't have died," Matt said, his voice high and hurt.

Britt pulled him to her and wrapped him in her arms. For five minutes she cried with him. Guilt filled her as she realized that since the early months after Jimmy's loss, she'd had to concentrate so hard on handling her own grief and the overwhelming financial problems with which she'd been left, that she sometimes forgot how much her children must still be suffering.

Life went on somewhat normally; they played and laughed and did their chores, and she'd been grateful for that little bit of stability in a world grown almost too difficult for her to handle. But that didn't mean they'd adjusted, she realized. It just meant they were going on because she was going on and they didn't know what else to do.

"I know how much you loved him," she said, rocking Matt as though he were Renee's age. "We all did. It's okay to keep thinking about him and remembering him, but you have to realize that he isn't here to help us. And there are a lot of things I have to do to keep the farm together that Jake knows more about than I do. It's all right for us to have him as a friend. Dad wouldn't mind."

"It's okay for *you* to have him as a friend." Matt pulled out of her arms and wiped his pajama sleeve across his face.

"Why isn't it all right for you?" she asked.

He looked into her eyes for a moment, even opened his mouth to form an answer. If she could have reached into him and pulled it from him, she would have. But he finally shook his head and lowered his eyes. "'Cause it isn't," he said.

"All right." She felt the weight of his secret on her shoulders and knew that whatever it was somehow explained this sudden regression in his recovery from his father's death, this sudden hostility toward Jake. Britt stood, pulled his blankets up and leaned down to kiss him good-night.

"Tomorrow's the last day of school," he said grimly. "The guys'll all be biking to the lake every day to go fishing."

"That's the way it is," she said with far more sternness than she felt. "You can join them when your two weeks are up."

He turned his back to her and buried his face in his pillow.

Britt checked on David, who snored lightly in the other bed, then turned off the light and left the room. She headed for the coffeepot, wishing she could afford good brandy.

PERUSING the latest *Wall Street Journal,* Jake picked up his ringing telephone. "Sales," he said, still studying figures. "Marshack."

"Marshack?" a familiar feminine voice with an unfamiliar edge of anger said, "I asked to be connected with Doright."

The anger didn't register on him. Pleasure rippled up his spine. He allowed himself a private smile as he realized how pathetically besotted he was.

"Mrs. Hansen," he said, aware of Marlene looking up from her work. "What can I do for you?"

"I'm in the lobby of the building," she said sharply. "You can come down here and explain my account to me."

"Ah..." He tried to think fast. "I...got you another month's extension. I was going to give you a call and..."

"Really?" she asked coolly. "Well, I'm here now. Let's discuss this face-to-face, shall we?"

He didn't want her looking into his face; she'd see there what he'd done. But he wanted desperately to look into hers. It had been almost seventy-two hours.

"I know you're busy," she said while he hesitated. "But so am I. Still, I put my children in the station wagon and drove all the way down here to pay my bill, only to discover my account balance is zero. Can you explain that?"

"Ah, I..."

"To my face, please," she said and hung up the phone.

He cradled the receiver, realizing he was in for it. He couldn't wait. He pulled on his suit coat and headed for the elevator.

He found her standing near the elevator doors. She was dressed for the city in a lavender suit that exaggerated the angry color in her cheeks and confused the blue in her eyes to violet. Her hair was loose and a little wild and it was all he could do not to reach out and smooth it. A bone-colored high-heeled shoe tapped the terrazzo floor of the lobby.

"Hi, Jake!" "Jake!" "Hey, Jake!" From across the long lobby, a chorus of children's greetings pulled his eyes in their direction. Britt's kids were lined up on a bench, waving madly. Except for Matt, who just stared at him

He waved back. "Hi, guys. Visiting the big city, huh?"

"We're going shopping!" Christy said excitedly.

"And we..." Renee started toward him, but Britt stopped her with a pointing finger. The little girl went immediately back to the bench.

Britt turned to Jake, her finger still pointing. "You, Marshack," she said, jabbing him in the chest with it, "have some fast explaining to do."

He caught her finger in his fist and pulled her aside, behind an ornate Doric column. "You use real bullets in this thing?" he asked, shaking the finger he held, "or just blanks?"

She yanked it away, her eyes hectic with frustrated anger. He knew she wished she had him alone in a dark alley instead of a very public downtown-Chicago lobby. So did he.

"Don't get cute with me," she said.

He gave a helpless shrug. "I'm powerless to control it. You can't suppress cute, you know. It just—"

She grabbed his lapels. "You paid my bill, didn't you?" she asked, her deep whisper almost a growl.

"Yes," he whispered back in the same tone. "You took me in as a partner, remember?"

She tried to shake him by the lapels, but he was too firmly planted. She succeeded only in shaking herself. He didn't know when he'd enjoyed himself more.

"For ideas!" she whispered fiercely, "Know-how! Not to pay my bills!"

He raised an interested eyebrow. "What kind of know-how?"

"Food-business know-how."

"Damn."

"Jake!" She pulled his head down until they were eye to eye. "I'm serious. You're within a hairbreadth of being punched in the nose! Now..." She drew a deep breath, released him and smoothed his lapels. "I have a check in my purse that I am going to hand you. You are going to take it without giving me one word of flak.''

"Is it made out to the dairy?" he asked.

"Of course."

"Then I can't take it."

"Certainly the dairy has a cashier who can cash it for you."

"Then it would be common knowledge that I paid your bill. Why else would I take a check from you made out to the dairy and convert it to cash?"

Her ferocious glare returned. "I'll write you another one."

Jake saw not the glare, but the longing that lived at the bottom of her eyes and had been coming closer to the surface ever since he'd first met her. It was just under her anger now, even straining against it. It suddenly became a challenge to see if he could make it break through.

He pulled her farther behind the column. Out of the corner of his eye he saw Matt and Christy lean forward to try to keep their eyes on them.

"What are you doing in Chicago?" he asked, reaching up slowly to run his fingertips through her hair.

"I…well, uh…" She swallowed and he smiled. She slapped one of his hands away and struggled to regain her fierce expression. "I told you. I came to pay my bill."

He stroked again, undaunted. "You could have mailed it."

"It was due today."

"A telephone call would have let me know it was on its way."

She leaned subtly, unconsciously, forward. "Oh, sure," she said, the fierceness now a feeble pose. "The check is in the mail. You'd have believed that, I take it?''

"Of course," he whispered, leaning down to place the lightest kiss on her lips. "I know you to be impeccably honest. Very difficult, but honest."

Her eyelashes fluttered and she looked disoriented. "You do?"

"I do." He grinned. "Sounds matrimonial, doesn't it?"

She swallowed again. It seemed to be more difficult this time. "Will you please," she asked, sounding a little desperate, "let me sit down somewhere where I can write you another check?"

He flattened a hand against the small of her back and pulled her to him until they touched, her breasts to somewhere near his ribs, her hipbone to somewhere below his waist. The shock vibrated through him. "In a minute."

"Jake..." Her tone was high and quavery. The word was a threat, a warning, a plea.

He took a handful of her hair and kissed her. He felt her sigh in his mouth, felt the languid, accepting inclination of her body against his, the reluctant hand that rose to his shoulder, to his face, then around his neck to hold him with flattering strength.

He put into the kiss everything he felt—how he'd missed her, how she'd occupied his every thought, how sharply he remembered sleeping with her in his arms.

She gave the kiss everything he could have hoped for. He felt her confusion and her concern, but also her affection, her ardor, her gratitude despite her complaints, and the ingenuously blatant admission that she'd missed him, too.

"Oh, God." She dragged her mouth away from his to drop her forehead against the front of his coat. "Oh, God. What are we going to *do* about this?" She looked up at him, the longing leaping out to him, enfolding him—capturing him. "When I called you I had every intention of doing you bodily harm."

He grinned dryly. "You have," he said. "Probably not in the way you intended, but you have."

The elevator dinged, heralding the arrival of a full car. He dropped his arms and she took a step back. "What's this about shopping?"

She smiled, readjusting the purse that had fallen off her shoulder. "Got a check today from Chuck Stuart, the man who's renting my pasture. He bought my entire herd of Holsteins and is renting another twenty acres. I bought the prettiest Alpine goats you ever saw, but they're not arriving until tomorrow." She lifted both shoulders in girlish delight. "A whole day free. The kids need a few summer things and I wanted to deliver your check." She glowered teasingly and gave him a mock punch to the midsection. "Don't think you've heard the last of this. Can you come to lunch with us?"

"Sure. Let me make a quick call upstairs to let the office know I'm leaving." As Jake hung up the phone a few moments later, he realized two worrisome facts simultaneously. One, he was looking forward to having lunch with four children. Two, he wanted their mother more than he'd ever wanted anything in his life, and he was even considering permanent means by which to acquire her.

CHAPTER TEN

JAKE WANDERED SLOWLY back toward the office, Britt's arm tucked in his, the children running ahead of them gawking in shop windows and stopping in the middle of the sidewalk to look up at the tall buildings.

Britt laughed softly. "I hadn't realized what little rubes I've raised. Get them in the big city and they behave as though we live without electricity or running water."

Jake watched their excitement, a curious warmth filling him. "Life squashes that enthusiasm soon enough. It's kind of refreshing to see it."

"They certainly enjoyed lunch," Britt said. "The Hofbrau Haus will probably never be the same. Thank you." She tightened her grip on him when he ignored her gratitude. He looked from the children to her, an eyebrow raised in question.

"I said thank you. Please don't ignore me when I'm being grateful."

He pulled her against his shoulder, his attention returning to the children. "I wasn't. You're welcome. I was just wondering about Matt. Has he seemed different lately, or is it my imagination?"

She shook her head, her smile dimming. "No. Something is bothering him that he isn't sharing with me. I think it has something to do with his father. Unresolved grief, I suppose. He's vacillated between trying hard to help me and being a strong big brother to the other kids, and doing absolutely everything he can to aggravate and worry me.'' She told him about his staying out late when she was on the road. "He probably feels there's nowhere to turn to relieve the sense of loss.''

Jake remembered similar feelings from his own childhood all too clearly. His mother and his aunt had been struggling too hard to notice his raw grief, and his cousins had lived without a father for so long they didn't understand how he felt. It had taken him a long time to get over the frustrated anger that life had done such a thing to him when he thought he'd done nothing to deserve it. He'd been too young at the time to realize how indiscriminate life was in its distribution of anguish.

They stopped behind the children at a traffic light. He reached an arm out to pull Renee back from the curb, where she leaned out precariously, waiting for the light to change.

She turned around to grin up at him. "I was on the sidewalk," she said.

He caught her nose between the knuckles of his first two fingers, delighting her. "Your nose was in the street," he said.

The light changed and the children galloped across through the crush of people.

"Maybe," Britt said, looking up at him hopefully, "you could keep your ears open when you come out to help us put up the fence and the buck barn. As a man, maybe you'll see or hear something I'm not picking up on.''

He inclined his head, frowning. "Sure. But if I'm not mistaken, some of that moodiness seems to be directed at me.''

She glanced at him guiltily as she dodged a fast-moving baby stroller. "I think he believes you have plans to try to replace his father. Maybe you could reassure him that you haven't.''

They dropped hands as a woman wearing a power suit and carrying a briefcase burst between them, muttering to herself.

"Okay," he said when they joined up again, "but there's a subtlety here we have to iron out."

"What's that?"

He pulled her to a stop. Crowds of people broke around them. "I don't want to *replace* his father, but I'm getting pretty serious about his mother. I can't lie to him about that."

"Ah..." She looked pleased and frightened all at once. "My life is awfully busy now. I..."

"I know." He smiled at her, a smile she thought had a curiously sweet but predatory quality. "But that'll change. Or you'll decide to find time for me. One way or another I'm going to become part of your life. You might want to prepare the kids."

"Jake..."

"Until then—" he took her arm and led her on "—we'll talk business. Did I mention I've signed you up for a convention scheduled for the last weekend of the month?"

She was beginning to wonder about the wisdom of taking him on as a partner of any sort. "What kind of convention?"

"Products for the nineties consumer, with an emphasis on food. It's a natural. You up to it?"

The question was a direct challenge. She looked him in the eye. "Of course I'm up to it. Where is it?"

"Right here in Chicago."

"What does it cost?"

"I've paid your fees. We'll square up later."

"I'll have to find a place to stay."

"You can stay with me." He raised an eyebrow at her sudden flash of suspicion. "If you've got the guts. I'll come for you in a *dependable* refrigerated truck and help you set up. I'll even do your gofer work that weekend.''

''At a nominal fee?'' she asked sweetly.

''Speaking of nominal fees,'' he said, ignoring her baiting question, ''I can get you a good deal on a pasteurizing vat and some forty-quart stainless steel cans. Murphy's Dairy in Belton's going out of business. He's anxious to get rid of everything. He's got a filling machine, too, if you're ready for that.''

For a moment she was speechless with surprise. ''You have been busy.''

He shrugged a shoulder. ''You told me what you wanted. I did my best to see that you got it.'' He grinned and started on again toward the children, who were now waiting in front of the Winnebago building. ''See what you're missing,'' he said, looking down into her eyes, ''by keeping the partnership strictly business?''

LIFE WAS TAKING on a strong sense of unreality, Britt thought, as she scooped a coarse prepared mixture into the feed boxes. Just beyond the barn that housed the does and kids, Jake, Brick, Matt and David were putting up a buck barn.

For so long her world had been filled with the black-and-white Holstein cows her family had raised for generations. For the first few days of their absence she'd known a cold clutch of fear. Had she done the right thing? Could this possibly work? Had she destroyed Lakeside Farm forever?

Then she'd discovered that the goats, from whom she could make twice the money in half the space, required twice as much of her time. But what they cost her in time, they repaid quickly in personality and cleverness.

Britt had grown up loving cows, but she'd never quite had the heart-to-heart connection with them the goats were already inspiring. They made her feel as though she were surrounded by a horned, cud-chewing band of particularly precocious children.

"When are they gonna have babies?" Renee, helping with the feed, reached into the pen to pat a sleeping kid.

"Not until spring," Britt said.

"Why?"

"Because it takes about five months."

Renee counted on her fingers. "But there could be babies by Christmas."

Britt shook her head. "No, the does can't get pregnant yet."

"Why? No daddies?"

"No, because goats are in an anestrous cycle at this time of the year." At Renee's predictable frown, she simplified the explanation. "They don't want any daddies around. They just want to do girl stuff."

"Color and go shopping?"

Britt laughed, moving to the next stall. "Something like that. In August or September they'll be ready."

Renee stood on the slats of the stall and leaned her weight back on her hands. "Will you?"

"What?" Britt asked absently.

"Be ready to get pregnant?" Sun slanted into the barn, gilding her daughter's enthusiastic smile as Britt looked at her in surprise. "I think we should have another girl, so there'll be less boys."

"We can't have another anything," Britt said calmly but emphatically, "until we have another daddy."

Renee pointed in the direction of the hammering. "We have Jake."

Britt moved to the next stall. "But I'm not married to Jake."

"Sally Hermann's mom isn't married to the man who lives with them. And she's gonna have a baby."

Britt longed for the days when a mother could tell her inquisitive child that a woman had to be married to have a baby. Of course, she knew even in Great-Grandma Bauer's day a smart child would have questioned the statement.

"It works out better for everyone," Britt said, "if mommies and daddies are married when babies are born."

"Then you could marry Jake."

"I have to make lots and lots of yogurt, Renee," Britt explained patiently. "I don't have time to have a husband."

Renee followed her sulkily to the next stall. "Well, aren't we ever gonna have a baby?"

For an instant Britt's mind filled with memories of fragrant skin and toothless smiles and uncomplicated, unquestioning love. Her gaze lost its focus and a smile formed on her lips. "Oh, maybe... Some day..."

With a whoop, Renee ran from the barn.

"WE'RE GONNA HAVE a baby!"

There was a loud rattle as Jake lost his grip on the corrugated sheet metal he held in place while Brick hammered. Brick, hammer raised, stopped midstroke and turned to him, an eyebrow raised.

"You're nuts, Renee!" Matt, inside the five-foot-tall structure, appeared in what would eventually be the doorway.

Renee stuck her tongue out at him. "Mom said!"

"When?" Matt demanded.

"Just now."

"When," Brick asked calmly, "is she going to have the baby?"

Renee walked into the structure, then leaned out around the side to answer the question. "One day," she quoted, "when there's time and she doesn't have to make yogurt."

Jake felt his pulse dribble back to normal. Brick tossed the hammer in his hand to restore his grip on it. He grinned at Jake. "Did you see your life pass before your eyes?"

Jake expelled a strained laugh and shook his head. "For one awful minute I thought Britt might have someone else."

"You mean you've never . . . ?"

"No."

Brick struck a nail home, then frowned at him. "Why not? She's not ready, or you're not up to four kids and a woman with more acres of stubborn than pasture?"

Jake answered intrepidly but kept his eye on the hammer. "A little bit of both."

"But you love her."

Jake didn't even have to think about that. "Yeah."

Brick grinned and hammered in another nail. "Then don't worry about it."

"Why not?"

"'Cause you're already sunk. Doesn't matter what you do, you're hers. Believe me. I know what I'm talking about."

"I'LL CLEAN UP," Jake said to Matt. Brick had left and Matt was helping pile the odds and ends of lumber and sheet metal into the wheelbarrow. "I heard your mom give you permission to ride to the park to watch the baseball game."

Matt shook his head, his grim expression unchanging. "Thanks, but I can do my share."

"You did more than your share today," Jake said. "You're pretty good at carpentry."

"I helped my dad a lot."

"Mine was great with cars," Jake said, helping the boy with the long end of a two-by-four. "He was working on a '57 Chevy when he died."

Matt looked up, a spark of interest in his eyes. "I can't wait until I can have a car."

Jake smiled. "You won't have to remember to leave it up on the front porch."

Matt laughed, then, as though disappointed in himself, resumed the frown. He struggled with a large piece of sheet metal, telling Jake firmly, "I've got it!" when he tried to help.

Matt struggled to roll the metal. Finally getting it under control, he glanced at Jake as he placed it on top of the pile in the wheelbarrow. "When did your dad die?"

Jake wheeled the debris toward the shed behind the barn. Matt ran alongside with a hand on the metal to steady it. "When I was ten," Jake replied. "Pretty much like you. It took a long time before I got over it. I still miss him sometimes when I'm riding in the Chevy."

The dinner bell clanged as Jake and Matt separated the odds and ends into piles. "I miss my dad all the time," Matt said, his voice heavy in the room lit by one bare bulb. His eyes were dark and anguished as they focused on Jake. "I don't want another one."

Jake nodded. "I understand that. I felt the same way."

"Did your mom get married again?"

"No."

"Then you don't understand," Matt said aggressively. "Mom wants to marry you, doesn't she?"

Jake had acquired enough experience in the time he'd spent with Britt's children to know they missed nothing. "Actually, she doesn't. All she wants to do right now is get her yogurt on the market."

"But that'll change," Matt said, leaning against the doorway and staring at the dusky sky. "She doesn't cry as much anymore. She doesn't miss Dad like she used to."

Jake leaned against the other side, both touched and frustrated by something he felt swelling in Matt, something he didn't understand and couldn't seem to reach. "I don't think that's true. I think she still misses him very much, but she had to find a way to keep the farm and pay her bills, and give you kids all the things you need. That isn't easy, Matt. She doesn't have much time to think about herself."

Matt turned to look up at him, a challenging man-to-man expression in his eyes. "She thinks about you. I can tell. She said she's going to Chicago with you for a weekend."

"Yes, but that's business."

"She's going to stay at your house. I know all about that stuff."

Jake had little difficulty interpreting "that stuff." "We don't have that kind of relationship yet," he said honestly.

"Matthew!" Britt shouted across the yard. "Jake! Dinner!"

Matt waved a hand and pushed away from the door. Britt disappeared inside the house.

"All right," Jake said levelly as they started toward the back door, side by side but with a wide space between them. "I care about your mom. I don't know if she'd ever want to marry me or not, but I think that would be between her and me. She's a very devoted mother, but she has a right to do some things for herself—whether or not you like it. It's hard to keep going forward, and sometimes the past has been so difficult that we don't even want to move ahead, but that's what life does—it just keeps moving. You have to keep moving, too, or you get stuck in a place that just doesn't exist anymore."

At the bottom of the back-porch steps, Matt stopped, his eyes filling. "I'm stuck, anyway. I—I..."

He looked into Jake's eyes for a long moment, then shook his head and ran up the steps into the house.

Jake watched him go, startled by the depth of misery he'd glimpsed in the boy's eyes. He suspected it was more than simple grief. But what?

"IS THAT CENTERED?" Jake held up the enlargement of the artist's rendering of Mildred with the rose in her teeth. He stood on newspapers on the counter of her booth in the Chicago Convention Hall and held the Yes! Yogurt logo up against the crosspiece at the top with one hand, the other holding an industrial stapler.

"Slightly to the right," Britt directed from down below.

He moved it slightly.

"A hair to the left. Perfect!"

Jake stapled the artboard in place and leaped down to stand beside Britt and look up at it. The booth did look pretty good, he thought, for a business that didn't have unlimited resources. They'd assembled it on the spot with materials Jake had had precut to her specifications. They'd painted it Scandinavian blue and yellow to match the yogurt packaging, and decorated the front with a collage of photographs of her and the children in yogurt production.

Britt frowned thoughtfully. "Do you think it's too folksy?"

"The consumer loves folksy. And once they taste your stuff, they won't care what the booth looks like. Everything out of the truck?"

Britt indicated the giant refrigerated case that held yogurt, dressing, cheesecake and Danishes. "Everything." She looked around. She was one of just a few exhibitors still working in the hall. "I guess we're finally done."

"Great." Jake packed up his tools and hefted his tool bag over his shoulder. "I'm starved for a cheeseburger and fries."

Britt glanced at her watch as she shouldered her purse. "It's 11:00 p.m., Jake. Everything'll be closed."

He put an arm around her shoulders and led her toward the doors. "This is Chicago. We can find anything you want to eat, and we can dance all night if you want to."

She smiled up at him. "Nice thought, but we have to chop vegetables all night."

He grinned and kissed her temple. "How romantic. A weekend tryst in Chicago over goat's milk yogurt and green pepper rings."

Britt was fascinated by how alive the Windy City was at midnight. When she and Jake had sat in Tyler's town square after dinner at the lodge several weeks earlier, everything but the police station had been closed, and they had joked about the streets being rolled up after eight o'clock.

In Chicago it felt as though the city was just getting its second wind. Theaters and restaurants were full, the streets were crowded with people and the glow of neon lights made it almost as bright as day.

Britt sat up straighter in the cab of the truck as Jake turned into an older neighborhood where ancient oaks lined the streets. The trees had been strung with fairy lights. She smiled, thinking how dark the Wisconsin countryside was at night.

"I expected you to live in a posh, modern lakefront neighborhood," she said as he pulled into the driveway of an old brick building that took up almost an entire block and had obviously seen a recent restoration. After he'd picked her up in the truck that morning, they'd gone straight to the convention hall to set up. This was her first glimpse of his home.

He glanced at her as he pulled into a spot that had been stenciled with his name. "I wasn't really interested in a view when I moved into this place," he said, "although there's a wonderful panorama of downtown from almost every room. I just wanted to be close to work so I didn't waste a lot of time traveling. I'd done enough of that as a sales rep to last me a lifetime."

"I don't blame you," she said as he took her overnight bag from her and helped her down. "I hate driving in the city. With a carful of children arguing and teasing it turns me into a wild woman."

"Mmm," he said speculatively, fitting a key into the lock on the back of the rented truck. "A wild woman, you say? I think I'd like to see that."

She reached in for the two grocery bags and handed him one. "I don't mean wild in any way even remotely exciting. I mean wild as in screaming for quiet and being completely unreasonable with anyone who doesn't cooperate."

He smiled down at her as he locked the door again. It was difficult for him to imagine her that way. She'd always seemed such a paragon of control.

"I'll believe that when I see it for myself," he said, tucking the grocery bag in his arm and wrapping the other around her shoulders. "Come on. I'll make you a great cup of coffee and we'll chop vegetables till the cows come home."

"The goats," she corrected.

"Whatever."

Jake's condo was spacious, an easy flow of one bone-and-brown room into another—living room, library alcove, dining room, kitchen. He led her down a corridor off the living room to a bone-and-beige bedroom whose drapes were open to the brightly lit vista of busy Chicago. The view glittered with life.

Jake indicated the bathroom off the corner of the room. "Freshen up," he said, "and I'll put on the coffee and get started on the vegetables. You want everything in sticks?"

She nodded. "That seems to be more manageable."

"Okay." He waggled his eyebrows. "Feel free to change into something more comfortable."

She looked down at her jeans and sweatshirt, then up at him. "More comfortable than this?"

He pretended disappointment. "You mean you didn't bring a slinky nightgown?"

With a roll of her eyes, she closed the bedroom door on him.

THEY CHOPPED vegetables until 2:00 a.m., while sipping coffee and talking about everything from baseball to business.

Jake finally yawned and glanced at his watch. Then he looked at Britt, her hair beautifully disheveled around a face that looked as fresh to him now as it had when he'd picked her up at ten that morning.

He put down his knife and took a sip of coffee. "How can you still be functioning and beautiful?" he asked over the rim of his cup. "It's two-fifteen."

She glanced up at the kitchen clock in surprise. "Really?" Then she gave him one of those warm, sweet smiles that seemed to be his reason for living lately. "Oh…" She sliced a red pepper into neat strips. "I'm a mother—I'm used to being up at 2:00 a.m."

He folded his arms on the kitchen table and leaned toward her. "But your kids are at an age where they don't get you up in the middle of the night anymore, aren't they?"

She nodded as she dropped the pepper strips into a gallon-size plastic bag and sealed it closed. "But they're great for telling you when you're tucking them in at nine o'clock about the eight dozen cookies they promised their teacher you'd make for the next day's party, or the assignment they can't do without your help. They're great for *forgetting* to tell you until the last minute that they need a blue dress for the next day's program, or to have their patches sewn on for the next day's after-school game." She smiled and stretched. "Arsenio Hall and I are on pretty intimate terms."

The remark had been playful, innocent, but the bright, colorless room suddenly filled with heat and tension. Desire stronger than anything he'd ever known rose in Jake like fire up a draft. He put down his cup carefully and looked her in the eye. "Lucky Arsenio," he said.

Britt understood precisely what he was feeling. Her cheeks flushed with her own responding heat. It would be so right to make love with him. For a blessed few days she was free of all responsibility to anyone but herself and the dream that would gain her what she wanted. It would be such a comfort to lie in his arms tonight and for once in her life think only of herself.

But she'd once loved a good and honest man who'd been everything to her, as she'd been everything to him. She knew what lovemaking could be when a man and woman were committed to each other heart and soul, rather than simply providing a night's solace or entertainment.

It would be more than that with Jake, but it wouldn't be everything. She smiled at him sadly, and began busily to pack up vegetables and put them in his refrigerator. He helped, then took the sponge from her when she went to clean off the table.

"I'll do that," he said. "You'd better get some sleep. We have to be on the spot early to make sure you're ready when they open at ten."

"Right." She kissed his cheek and headed for her room without looking back.

Jake wiped off the table and cleaned up the kitchen, then turned off the lights and went to sit in the chair near the window and look out at the darkness. Small sounds came from the room where Britt was preparing for bed. He sighed and propped his feet on the windowsill, feeling frustrated, depressed and all kinds of other things he didn't have names for. It was going to be a long night.

CHAPTER ELEVEN

"GOAT'S MILK YOGURT? You're kidding, right?"

Jake smiled at the doubtful expression on Mike Buchanan's face. "No, I'm serious," he replied. "As the president of Favorite Foods, you owe yourself a taste of Yes! Yogurt."

Jake and his longtime friend wandered together through the convention hall. "In fact, you're lucky I spotted you before I noticed Charlie Bonaventure. You'll have first crack at the product that's going to wow the nineties."

Buchanan's famous competitive nose rose to sniff the air. "Where is he?"

Coolly, Jake pointed across the hall to an ice-cream exhibit, where the small, thin man leaned over a display of flavors. Buchanan and Bonaventure had embarked on a fast-foods partnership twenty years earlier. After a falling-out three years later, each had dedicated his career in the food industry to finding more exciting products and making more money than his competitor, Buchanan with a string of elegant gourmet shops, Bonaventure as a distributor of the unusual, sophisticated treat.

Mike fixed narrowed dark eyes on Jake. "Where is this goat's milk yogurt booth?"

Jake turned him forty-five degrees and pointed again. "The blue-and-yellow one with the pretty redhead in the white apron. She also makes frozen yogurt, cheesecakes and salad dressing."

"And you're sure you're right about this?"

"Go taste it for yourself."

"You coming?"

"No, I've got to make a few more contacts."

Buchanan raised a suspicious eyebrow. "Not Bonny?"

Jake put an arm around Buchanan's shoulders and started him across the floor in Britt's direction. "No. I won't say a word to Bonaventure unless you decide against carrying Yes! Yogurt, or if you offer her a flimsy deal."

Buchanan looked affronted as Jake gave him a gentle shove toward the blue-and-yellow booth.

Good start, Jake told himself as he looked around, trying to spot the Dutton brothers. While he'd been talking to Mike, he'd seen them wandering near the New Age aisle, poring over the program's list of exhibitors. As owners of the finest catering business in the Midwest, they were his next target.

He glanced toward Britt's booth and saw Mike peeling the lid off a cup of yogurt while Britt talked excitedly. She'd be filling him full of nutritive data, telling him about the pristine conditions under which the yogurt was made and, if she was smart, about her four children and the dog. Buchanan was a pushover for a pretty face.

Jake headed off in search of the Dutton brothers.

"MR. BUCHANAN from Favorite Foods wants to have dinner with me!" Britt whispered fiercely as Jake returned to the booth at lunchtime with Nutri-burger sandwiches from one of the booths across the aisle. She had a grip on both his arms and the two Saintly Sodas in his left hand clinked together dangerously.

"Really?" He didn't know whether to pretend surprise or indulge the suspicions he harbored toward his handsome friend. "A date?" he asked.

She yanked the bottles out of his hand and set them down, missing the innuendo. "To talk business!" she said, getting a grip on him again and shaking him. "I think he's considering taking on some of my products!"

"All *right*."

"You said this could happen but I don't think I believed you."

He raised a censorious eyebrow. "Well, I hope you've seen the error of your ways. Sit down. The burgers are getting cold."

"Will you come with me?" she asked, too excited to sit.

He pulled the second folding chair toward the back of the booth. "Of course. One of the burgers is mine."

"No, I mean to meet Mr. Buchanan for dinner." She took the wrapped sandwich he offered her and put it aside. "Please? I'd feel better if you were with me."

He liked that. He'd have to find Mike this afternoon and warn him not to mention his part in sending him to see her.

"Sure. If you like." He reached a long arm out for one of the bottles of soda. "Sit down and eat something. You hardly had any breakfast."

"I know." She grinned ingenuously. "I'm too excited to eat. I guess I can't believe my scheme just might work."

"It won't if you expire from starvation. You still have a long afternoon ahead of you, a business dinner tonight and six hours tomorrow. Eat!"

She unwrapped her sandwich and took a bite. She chewed, then frowned. "What is it?"

"It's called Nutri-burger. Made with all kinds of healthy stuff and just a little bit of very lean beef."

She took a long swallow of her soda, then made a soft sound of approval. "What's this?"

"Ah..." He read from the label he held. "Saintly Soda. Quenches your thirst without filling you full of phosphate buffers and artificial coloring. Contains carbonated carrot, celery, beet juices, and..."

"Carbonated beet juice?" she asked weakly. "Tell me you're making that up."

He laughed softly. "I'm making it up. It's just a soda with fruit juice and sparkling mineral water."

She pretended to glower. "You're going to pay for that, Marshack."

He smiled across the small space that separated them. "How soon?"

"I'll let it be a surprise," she threatened with a sultry look that was almost his undoing. "Just keep watching over your shoulder."

As she turned away to tend to two giggling young girls wearing paper dresses from one of the clothing booths at the other end of the exhibition, he decided to ignore her advice and let her sneak up on him. He would live in anticipation.

BRITT SPENT the afternoon in a state of almost painful excitement. Everyone was stopping at her booth, because word was getting around. Not only visitors in the food industry flocked to her, but other exhibitors, who claimed to have heard from *other* exhibitors how delicious the cheesecake and frozen yogurt were, did too. As they sampled those, she urged them to try a small carton of yogurt, explaining while they tasted about its unique low-fat, low-calorie makeup. She distributed leaflets, vegetables dipped in salad dressing, and smiles.

By closing time, she was almost shaking with an exhaustion that demanded she lie down, and a warring excitement that would have made doing so impossible.

She was so nervous about her meeting with Buchanan that she ran through the open door of Jake's bedroom in her slip, her blue dress draped over one arm, the sedate lavender suit on the other.

Jake, in T-shirt and slacks, took a step back out of the wardrobe closet, a white shirt hanging from his hand by the collar. She held up first the dress, then the suit. "Which one?" she asked, looking distressed. "I hate them both."

He needed a moment to compose himself. He saw creamy white shoulders bare but for two thin silky straps. His eyes followed the lace molded over her softly rounded breasts, then the silky fabric that clung to her flat stomach and thighs. It occurred to him that he could have it all off of her in an instant.

"Feminine?" she asked. "Or businesslike?"

He looked into her worried blue eyes and admitted to himself reluctantly that he was the only one having fantasies. Her mind was on business.

Jake put the shirt on and turned to the wardrobe mirror as a self-protective measure. "The dress," he said.

Her reflection nodded from behind him as she left the room. "Too late in the day for a suit," she said.

And the fabric of the dress was clingier. He kept that detail to himself as he reached into the closet to yank out a tie.

SEVERAL HOURS LATER Britt followed Jake into the elevator in his building in a kind of trance. He had to keep reaching back to tug her along, because she didn't seem able to walk and at the same time cope with the fact that she'd just made her first major business deal.

Jake pushed ten and smiled down at her indulgently. "You going to be okay?"

She blinked, unable to focus. "I'm not sure." Other things were beginning to occur to her, things she'd been too nervous to think about during the dinner meeting, but that were beginning to form a pattern now. Things that were even taking precedence over the deal.

"You're going to be doing a lot more of this," Jake said, rubbing a hand gently between her shoulder blades. "You'll have to develop more of a poker face."

The elevator bounced lightly to a stop and the doors parted. "Like you," she said as he took her arm and led her toward his apartment, "when you put your napkin on the table halfway through the meal and told the waiter to bring the check."

He unlocked his door and ushered her inside. "His offer wasn't nearly good enough."

She shed the little bolero she'd worn over her dress and went to the window that looked over the city. Excitement was finally quieting in her and something else was taking its place—something she'd never thought to feel again, something quite remarkable.

"I thought it was a pretty good deal," she said.

Jake tossed his jacket beside hers and went into the kitchen. "He was able to do much better. And he did. Champagne to celebrate?"

She smiled at the darkness and the city. "Please."

Jake wasn't quite sure what to make of her reaction. They had made a good deal, and he'd expected her to be excited, even a little shocked. But that wasn't what he read in her eyes. Oh, that was there, but it lay under a kind of dreamy surprise, a startled perception of something he apparently couldn't see. He wondered if it was something as simple as seeing her dream begin to come true—of knowing what she was truly capable of.

He smiled to himself as he popped the cork and poured the bubbly wine into flutes. He couldn't wait until she realized this was just the beginning. The Dutton brothers would talk to her tomorrow, and Talbot's Treats wanted to meet with her in the afternoon.

He found her sitting on the sofa, her shoes kicked off, her knees tucked under her. She accepted the flute from him with a smile that touched him with mild alarm. Though he hadn't put a light on, there was a glow from the kitchen, and he could see that the dreamy quality was gone from her eyes. There was something startlingly astute in them, barely hidden under a flirtatious flutter of eyelashes.

She touched the rim of her glass to his as he sat beside her, his elbow on the back of the sofa.

"To beginnings," he toasted.

Her knowing eyes looked into his as she smiled. "To beginnings," she said.

Jake felt snared in her gaze, and momentarily lost all awareness of where he was. The persistent longing that always came and went when she looked at him rose along with the flirtatious excitement and caught him as completely as though she'd physically taken hold of him. He sipped the champagne, hoping to steady himself.

Britt felt like the busy effervescence in her glass, as though she were filled with bubbles and everything in her life was finally rising to the top. She placed an arm on the back of the sofa and reached out a hand to toy with Jake's ear.

He raised an eyebrow, but didn't move.

"How long have you and Michael Buchanan been friends?" she asked softly.

She was tracing the rim of his ear with a fingernail. Everything inside him sparked. But he had to concentrate on her question. He knew it was loaded.

"Friends?" he asked innocently.

Her fingers moved to his hair and her nails combed it back slowly, over and over. "Friends," she repeated.

She leaned sideways to put her glass on the table, took his from him and placed it beside her own. "This morning I thought it was just a fateful coincidence that he *happened* to stop at my booth, *happened* to notice and want to sample all my products, *happened* to have the most successful gourmet chain in the area.''

Her smile softened and she ran a thumb lightly over his cheekbone. ''Then I realized fate must have had a little help.''

His control shorted out. ''Well . . . you're just presuming that I—''

''Sent Buchanan to me?'' she suggested in a whisper, framing his face in her hands and giving him one long, slow kiss. ''Probably threatened him with physical harm if he didn't offer me a deal?''

She raised her head only slightly to look into his eyes and went on, her lips just torturous inches from his, ''I'll bet you even made him pretend he'd never met you before so I wouldn't suspect.'' She kissed him again, invading his mouth with her tongue.

He held on to a bare minimum of control, but she was running the tip of her tongue lightly over his teeth, and that minimum, too, began to slip away from him.

''I got suspicious,'' she said huskily as she drew back again, one of her knees folded on top of his as she leaned even closer, ''when you called him Mike.''

''That's . . . his name,'' he whispered drunkenly.

''No, it's Michael. You wouldn't have been that familiar on a first meeting. You called me Mrs. Hansen for days.''

''Well . . .''

''Did you know the Dutton brothers talked to me late this afternoon?'' she asked.

His thought processes were definitely dimmed, but he was sure he'd scheduled them for Sunday.

''They weren't supposed to come until tomorrow.'' He realized too late the light in his brain had not only dimmed, it was out.

She nibbled punitively on his bottom lip, then along his jaw to his ear.

"They came this afternoon," she said, working her way back to his mouth, "to make sure the appointment was secure. I think word was getting out...." She followed the other side of his jaw, then back again. "And they wanted to be sure they had first shot. They pointed out the rep from Talbot's Treats who was hanging around and watching reactions. I suppose he'll be by tomorrow, too?"

Jake nodded, accepting defeat. He'd never imagined being vanquished could be so delicious.

She stopped at his lips, ran her fingers through both sides of his hair in a move that raised goose bumps all the way to the soles of his feet, then held his face in her hands and looked him in the eye.

"I have just one question," she said.

Oh, God. A test. He didn't have it together sufficiently at the moment for a test. "Yeah?" he asked hesitantly.

Her face was inches from his. "Try to be absolutely honest, Jake. Why did you do it?"

That was easy. He smiled, it was so easy. "Because it's a great product and you deserve to succeed," he replied. "Because I want you to keep the farm and honor all those former generations of Bauers. Because I want your kids to have every little thing they want and go to college."

That was all true, every last word. But the *real* reason, the fact that was turning his life around, that was making things he'd never considered before more important to him than things he'd worked for all his life, followed in a simple declaration.

"And because I love you. I have no idea how we can make this work, but deep down, with every breath in me, I'm driven to do for you because..." He paused on a laugh, at a loss to explain. "I don't know why. It started when I caught you falling from a roof and got my first look into your eyes. I can't explain it because it's new to me. I just know I'm not happy unless I'm with you, and even then, I feel so much better when I'm doing something I know will make you happy."

"Oh, Jake." She sank against him, her arms wrapped around his neck, her face against his throat. She planted a kiss there, then lifted her head to look into his eyes. Hers brimmed with tears. "It finally came to me as we drove home tonight. I created a good product, I know I did. But you're making it happen. Ever since I met you, you've been doing things for me when there was nothing in it for you."

He had to clear his throat. "I am your partner in this venture," he reminded her nobly. "I do stand to profit if you succeed."

She smiled and nodded slowly. "Some partnership. All you've done so far is shell out money and put up fences and sheds, and make all the contacts I know nothing about." She taunted him with a tender kiss. "But profit wasn't your motive, was it?"

Now he was frightened. He was completely under her control, powerless to resist, powerless to want to. But he tried valiantly.

"No," he said, kissing her back as gently. "I was hoping you'd think I was so clever and wonderful you'd let me make love to you."

She leaned slightly away from him to give him a scolding look. "I do think you're clever and wonderful, but that's not why I'm going to make love with you."

He lost air and just barely held on to comprehension.

"I'm going to make love with you because everything you've done for me and my children has been completely unselfish, and because I know what genuine love is all about." She smiled and got to her feet, offering him a hand up. As he stood in front of her, a tear slid down her cheek and her mouth quivered.

Worried, he put a hand to her face. She held it there with her own and leaned into it. "Love is all about a man like you, Jake."

The shreds of his control tore loose and he swept her up into his arms. He carried her to his room, banking desire, fighting passion, trying to concentrate on the tenderness with which she filled him.

But she made it difficult. As he placed her in the middle of his bed, she refused to relinquish her hold on his neck, bringing him down with her, on top of her, so that all the heat raging inside him fanned hotter and higher.

Britt felt as though a wall had fallen, a dam had broken, a mist had cleared. This was right. This was love.

Feeling swelled in her. Thoughts of Jimmy rose, then receded to become part of her past. She was consumed with awareness of Jake's touch.

The skirt of her dress was up around her waist and the small covered buttons in the front had all been opened. His strong, smooth hands swept her from knee to thigh, up then down, then up again. His lips kissed and nibbled at the swell of breasts above her lacy bra.

Britt had to work at unfastening his shirt. The shudder beginning to invade her body was making its way to her extremities. The job finally done, she tugged at his T-shirt, finally freeing it from his belt and slipping her hands up under it to stroke his warm, muscled back.

The touch of her fingers against his flesh paralyzed him for a moment. She pressed her advantage, running her hands in wide circles from his right to his left shoulder, than skimming his waist with her fingernails at the line of his belt. He felt himself slip over the edge of madness.

He tore off the shirt and T-shirt, then lifted her off the bedspread with one hand while pulling the dress off her with the other. The slip that had so tantalized him earlier was dispensed with in an instant—he'd been right about that.

Confronted with the vision of her in white lace and panty hose, he divested himself of the rest of his clothing first, letting his eyes feast a moment longer. Then he splayed a hand under her back, lifted her to him and unhooked her bra. Her breasts spilled out against his chest, small but round and swollen, her nipples tightly beaded. She expelled a little sigh and leaned her weight against him.

She said his name with a gusty little breath. He felt the flutter of her eyelashes against his collarbone. He thought he could probably die now and feel as though his life had been very full.

Britt had long since stopped struggling for a grip on reality. For the moment the past was in the past and the future was too distant to be of concern. This small space of hours was so immediate. The love she took and the love she gave were all that mattered.

She kissed the warm flesh under her lips, the strong pulse beating there in time with hers. She tilted her head back and looked into his eyes in the darkness. She could see them clearly, as though she had a personal key to the night.

"I love you, Jake," she said. "I love you so much."

He laid her down again, leaning over her on an elbow as he swept her disheveled hair from her face. "I love you, Britt." He drew his hand back to touch his chest. "It's like a light and a fire...right here."

She smiled, looped her arms around his neck and pulled him down to her. "Then share it with me," she whispered.

He did. Everything he felt for her, all the tenderness and passion, every protective instinct and every possessive urge concentrated in his fingertips as he ran them over and over her, learning every little secret her body held.

He discovered that his lips at her throat made her hunch a shoulder and giggle, his hands on her breasts drew out a moan, his hand moving up the inside of her thigh made her lean into him and wait, her body taut and trembling. His fingers invading inside, teasing, pleasing, made her gasp and cling to him.

And what she did to him taught him things about himself he hadn't known before. He'd always thought himself a man of considerable control, but when she rained kisses down his chest, then paused to nibble at the jut of his ribs, he felt that control slip.

He'd always been steady, unshakable, but her nails skimming down his side, along his thigh then up again, caused a tremor inside that was more than physical. She made him feel as though the whole world shook.

Striving to be patient, to draw out this deliciously agonizing foreplay for her benefit, he took a fistful of her hair and gently pulled her up, removing her hand from his thigh. He lowered his head and closed his mouth over the tip of a breast, seeking to distract her. But her artful hand closed over him and he was lost.

Giving in to her again, he entered her. Her warmth closed around him, drawing him deeper. And that was when he finally understood that he'd never known himself at all. Who was this man full of quaking emotions? What had taken over his body that a simple biological function had become a vast emotional experience?

Pleasure rolled over and over Britt. First the sweetness of being filled with a man—a good man. Then the indescribable exhilaration of sensation torturing her on the brink of fulfillment, then bursting inside her like the sudden flight of a bird, taking her higher, faster, nearer to the mysteries of the heavens. Then dropping in free-fall for long perilous moments, until she became aware of Jake's arms enfolding her, pulling her close against the solidity of his body until her world stabilized.

"God," she whispered, shaken.

"I know," Jake replied. His own voice was ragged, his body and his emotions feeling strange and new.

Britt twined her fingers in Jake's hair and kissed his collarbone, afraid to tell him what she felt. She was changed. She was still the mother to her children, still a Bauer tied to the land, still the moving force behind her small company. But the woman she was had a new life force, a stronger heartbeat.

Jake felt completely disoriented, but curiously on the right track. His life had taken a strange turn the day he met Britt, but now at least she was on the road beside him. He had no idea where they were going, but they were going together.

"Jake?" she whispered. "Did I mention that I love you?"

He squeezed her tighter and kissed the top of her head, wondering what had become of him that a few simple words could reduce him to jelly. "Only once," he said. "I'd love to hear it again."

She raised her head to look at him. Her eyes were lazy, her hair rumpled and wild. "I think I said it twice," she scolded gently, crossing her hands on his chest and resting her chin on them. "Weren't you paying attention?"

He grinned. "The second time I think you had your hand on my thigh. That part of my memory's a little scrambled."

She seemed pleased with his answer. "I love you," she said again. "In fact, it's probably uncool but I think I even adore you."

He brushed her tumbled hair back. "I don't think it's uncool, I think it's wonderful. And it's reciprocated."

She sobered suddenly. "Do you find it a little scary?"

He thought about it. "No. But you do?"

She shrugged a silky shoulder. "Well, you've got only you. I've got four children." She rubbed her index finger thoughtfully over his bottom lip. "That hasn't slipped your mind, has it?"

He had to pull her finger away to think. "No, it hasn't."

"And you still adore me?"

"Absolutely. It's even part of *why* I adore you."

"Really?" She didn't entirely understand that, but at the moment it was enough that he could admit he loved her while understanding fully what they were up against. She could now deal with other problems. "Do you have anything in the refrigerator? I was too excited to eat at dinner."

He blinked and decided a predictable woman would have been dull company. "Ah...ice cubes, canola oil margarine, a bottle of Tía María mix and lots and lots of chopped vegetables."

She made a face at him that made her look about ten years old. "I'm starving," she complained, "and all you can do for me is sauté Tía María mix and serve it over ice?"

"I can put chopped vegetables in it."

"I'm very tired of chopped vegetables. No ice cream?"

"Well, of course not," he replied dramatically. "I have the doyenne of frozen yogurt as a houseguest. I doubt we'd be here at this very moment if you'd discovered Dove bars in my freezer."

She laughed. The sound filled him with a delicious sense of well-being. "You're right, of course. How about bread. Do you have bread?"

"I have bagels."

She sat up, interested. In the darkness she was all ivory breasts and billowing hair. "Cream cheese?"

"Sorry."

"But you have butter," she said, swinging her legs over the side of the bed.

Jake hooked an arm around her waist and pulled her back to him. Her hair had fallen over her face and he pulled her astride him, losing himself in the silken strands. "I'm hungry, too," he said.

She wriggled against him. "And I'll bet you won't be happy with a bagel."

He swept her hair back to look into her eyes, his own suddenly dark and serious. "I don't think I'll ever be happy again if you're not within reach."

She shook her head, her light eyes as grave as his. "Neither will I, Jake."

There were practical considerations to that fact neither could consider at the moment. But that was a problem for Monday morning. It was only Saturday night.

Jake grasped her hips and positioned her, and when she came down on him he knew the same all-consuming sense of wonder he'd experienced earlier. Amazed that it could happen again with the same force, he gave himself over to it.

Britt felt herself filled with him and knew the same comfort, the same awe. Fingers locked with his, she began the slow, inevitable cycle and lost herself in its rhythm.

CHAPTER TWELVE

SUNDAY BROUGHT a contract with the Dutton brothers, and with Talbot's Treats. A salad-bar chain ordered dressings by the case, and a posh Chicago restaurant signed for a dozen cheesecakes a week for the next six months. Britt consulted Jake worriedly.

"It's a good deal," she said, "but I'd have to travel to Chicago probably twice a week with the cheesecakes. That'll take time I won't have, with all the orders I'm getting."

"Take it," he advised. "I know an LTL hauler who'll take those along with the Favorite Foods order."

She stared at him. "A what?"

"A hauler that deals in small volumes—less-than-truckload amounts. It's something new and just what you need."

"I thought I'd have to deliver."

He shook his head. "You'll be far more valuable keeping production moving." He gave her a steady, sober look. "You've got a strong grip on your market," he said. "Now you have to produce the product. And look at the numbers you've agreed on. You're sure you want to work this hard?"

She was suddenly, sharply, terrified. But of paramount importance was saving Lakeside Farm for her children. "Of course I am," she said, and went back to her customer to make the deal.

THE BOOTH disassembled and packed in plastic in the back of the truck, Britt stood in the middle of the convention hall, a strange melancholy taking hold of her.

The gaiety and excitement of the exhibition was over. Brightly colored booths, posters and banners had all been taken down. Weary exhibitors spoke quietly as they packed up their wares and carried them out to the parking lot. Several maintenance people pushed wide brooms across the littered floor.

Change was always unsettling, she knew, particularly for a woman who'd lived in the same town on the same property all her life, and whose biological makeup echoed an ancestry that had occupied the same space for the past 150 years. But she felt more than unsettled. She felt . . . different.

She had just embarked on a way of life that would be very different from the farming she'd always done and loved. She was becoming an entrepreneur of sorts out of dire necessity. She needed to succeed in a big way. But she could also fail in a big way. That was a sobering thought. If that happened, she would lose not only the farm and her children's heritage, but all the money, time and energy Jake had invested as well.

Jake. A little quiver of excitement raced through her blood. Jake. She closed her eyes, able to conjure up vivid memories of the night in an instant. Talk about change! She'd had so little time for her physical self during the past year, but now she was sharply in touch with herself. Every nerve ending had come to life and now craved what it had lived so long without.

Probably, she guessed with a little sigh, because the experience had been so much more than physical. She wrapped her arms around herself as she remembered every wonderful attention he'd accorded her, every touch of his mouth and his hands, every little word he'd whispered to her that had kept her so absorbed she'd completely forgotten the bagel she'd thought she wanted.

She laughed softly, hugging herself.

Long, strong arms came around her. "I think I'd better take you home," Jake said, kissing her ear. "It isn't a good sign when you stand alone in an almost empty room and giggle to yourself."

She leaned her head back into the hollow of his shoulder. "I was thinking of you," she said.

"And that made you laugh?" he asked dryly. "Thank you, Brittany."

"No," she said, turning in his arms. "It made me feel good. And because only a moment before I'd been terrified, it made me laugh."

"I see." He turned her toward the doors. "And what were you terrified about?"

She wrapped an arm around his waist and leaned in to his shoulder as they walked to the truck. "My life has changed. I'm excited and encouraged by the wonderful response and delighted with the orders, but it's kind of scary."

He squeezed her close. "You can do it. I don't have a single doubt."

She sighed. "I'd better do it. If I blow it, I won't be able to get back what I had before. I guess that's what's most frightening."

"What you had was a mountain of debt. You'd have lost the farm if you hadn't launched Yes! Yogurt. You could still lose it, but at least you'd know you'd done everything you could."

She frowned as he opened the truck door. "I guess. I just wish it was a little more certain than that."

He surprised her by lifting her bodily into the truck. "You want a sure thing?" he asked.

She sat on the seat, her legs dangling, his wicked grin inspiring her smile despite her concerns. "Like what?"

"Like we're going to pick up Chinese food and I'm going to take you home and make such outrageous love to you you'll be so high on life there won't be room in your mind for problems of any sort for weeks. By then Yes! Yogurt will be the talk of the industry."

She folded her arms and feigned a considering look. "Are you going to let me *eat* the Chinese food first? I never did get my bagel this morning."

"One helping," he said, swinging her legs into the truck. "Seconds will have to wait until later."

"With you there is no later."

He reached a hand up into her hair to pull her down and kissed her soundly. His eyes smoky, he said, "But there'll be happily ever after. It's my Dudley Doright pledge."

When she was thinking practically, she didn't see how there could be a happily ever after. But when he looked into her eyes like that, his own dark with desire and bright with love, she couldn't think practically, she could only feel. And she felt wonderful.

For the first time in her personal history, Britt wasn't anxious to get home. She missed her children, but the intimate two days with Jake had been like reaching an oasis after a long stretch of desert. It was hard to make herself leave the sanctuary and continue on her own— even though Jake had smoothed the way for her.

On the way to Tyler Monday morning, they picked up the forty-quart stainless steel cans she needed and packed them in the back of the truck.

"You'll have to hire help," Jake said. "Do you have enough left from the sale of the herd to pay a few people for a couple of weeks until money starts coming in?"

She nodded. "If it doesn't take too long." She turned to him worriedly. "What if my customers don't pay?"

He gave her a grinning glance as he checked the mirror to change lanes. "They'll pay. Favorite Foods and the Duttons have good, solid reputations. If you have trouble with the smaller accounts, you've got me to collect for you. That's what I do, remember?"

"Mmm, sure," she said, rubbing her shoulder against his. "You tried to collect from me and ended up lending me money. What's wrong with this picture?"

He swatted her knee. "You were special."

"How come?"

"Because the first thing you did was fall into my arms. I knew right away you had a thing for me."

"You pulled me into your arms," she corrected.

He pinned her with a glance, half teasing, half serious. "But you liked it there."

She remembered clearly the touch of his hand on her thigh. She leaned her head onto his shoulder. "Yes, I did. I'm going to miss you this week."

"I'll be back Friday night to help you over the weekend."

Britt closed her eyes and let herself absorb his delicious embrace. Though she would be working night and day, Monday to Friday would seem interminable without him.

"WHAT ABOUT PLATES? Should we have everyone bring their own plates and utensils?" Amanda Baron, taking notes for the loosely organized but extremely efficient committee to prepare food for Tyler's Fourth of July picnic, looked up from her legal pad. She turned to her mother. "Did you donate those last year, Mom?"

Alyssa Baron, in whose kitchen the group had collected, walked around the large table topping up coffee cups. "Marge did." She patted Marge Peterson's shoulder as she moved on to fill Anna Kelsey's cup.

"Your grandfather and I donated two hundred pounds of hamburger and Kuhn's Market gave free hot dogs."

"You can count on the plates again," Marge said.

"If you want to use tongue depressors for spoons," Cece quipped, "I might be able to get a deal on those."

Everyone laughed. "Now that she's a nursing supervisor at Worthington House," Anna said, "we can all look to her for choice rooms and special treatment in our old age."

Alyssa frowned teasingly at Anna. "As though any respectable convalescence home would admit us. All they'd have to hear is that we play whist for money while watching Mickey Rourke movies and we'd be blackballed."

Laughter filled the room again. Britt watched the action from the kitchen counter, where she served her cheesecake onto Limoges plates and spooned blueberry topping onto it. This particular collection of women always made her feel as though all was right with the world.

She had admired Anna, Alyssa and Marge for as long as she could remember. Her Aunt Anna, still attractive at fifty, was always so warm and kind. A Bauer herself, she was the true heart of her branch of the family. She'd never met a stranger or failed to lend a helping hand in a crisis.

Alyssa Baron, Judson Ingalls's daughter, had her father's dedication to the community and her own unique openhearted approach to everyone and everything. The same age as Anna, she had a face and figure Britt would have appreciated right now.

Marge, who'd been a friend of Britt's family for ages and a business associate of Britt for the past year, had proved her affection and her loyalty on more than one occasion.

Amanda, an attorney, had helped Britt with an impatient creditor when Jimmy died. Amanda had provided comfort as well as a very charming but lethal legal expertise at a time when Britt had desperately needed both.

And Cece... Britt winked back as Cece laughed from across the table, where an argument had developed between Anna and Alyssa about whose potato salad was better. Cece was like having a sister.

"Who's organizing the ice-cream social?" Amanda asked over her mother's argument.

Cece raised her hand. "I am." She withdrew a list from her purse. "The Rotary Club is donating the ice cream—three flavors. And I have about fifty commitments for cakes and pies already."

"All *right*," Amanda said, taking notes.

"And Britt's promised three cheesecakes."

Britt raised an eyebrow as she carried plates to the table. "Three?"

"One for the social," Cece explained seriously, "and two for me."

Britt rolled her eyes at her. "Ha, ha. If you want one, you have to line up at the park pavilion like everybody else."

Amanda passed a proof around the room. "This is what our ad will look like. It has all the what, when and where stuff for the parade, the games and the potluck picnic. Right?"

The proof, with its border of stars and fireworks, was passed around and approved.

"Janice and David will be home for the picnic," Anna said, studying the proof and passing it to Alyssa. "She called me last night from Chicago."

Everyone leaned eagerly forward for news. Until fairly recently, Janice Eber Markus had been part of this group, always interested in community activities and fun to be with. A new marriage meant spending a lot of time in Chicago, where David was a financial adviser, and occasional weekends and holidays at home in Tyler.

"How is she?" Alyssa asked, passing the ad on.

Anna widened her eyes expressively. "Disgustingly happy."

"Wonderful!" Marge expressed what they all felt. Then she picked up her last bite of cheesecake by squashing it with the tines of her fork. "Does that take care of it?" she asked. "I've got to get back to the diner."

Amanda tapped the tip of her pen on her pad, a sly smile on her face. "Before you go, Mom has an announcement."

Alyssa gave her daughter a scolding look from the head of the table. "That would be premature. I haven't made up my mind."

Marge pushed her plate away and leaned toward her eagerly. "Tell us anyway. What?"

"It isn't a certainty," Alyssa said reluctantly, hooking her index finger in the handle of her cup and twisting the elegant china back and forth. "I . . ."

"You're getting married?" Anna guessed.

Alyssa frowned. "Be serious."

"You're having breast augmentation surgery," Marge offered.

Alyssa laughed. "Good idea, but no."

"She's having an affair," Amanda said.

A collective gasp ran around the table.

"Amanda Baron!" Alyssa said, obviously caught between shock and laughter. "Go to your room, or take that back this instant!"

Mischief in her eyes, Amanda leaned toward her mother. "Then *tell* them."

Cheeks pink, Alyssa admitted reluctantly, "I'm thinking of taking over Ingalls F and M. There! Isn't that anticlimactic?"

Amanda patted her on the shoulder. "Way to go, Mom." She turned to their companions. "Isn't that great? Don't you think she'd make a brilliant chairman of the board?"

The congratulations were instantaneous and unanimous, then silence fell and frowns collected around the table.

"Is Judson stepping down?" Anna asked cautiously. "Because of..."

"He's thinking about it," Alyssa said, pouring another cup of coffee, her hand shaking just a little. "The goings-on at the lodge have certainly preyed on his mind." Then she smiled and let the suggestion of scandal drop. Everyone at the table did also. "I don't think he ever considered that I'd want to take over the business. But it's been in the family so long. I feel a responsibility to hold on to it."

"I think you could do it," Anna said, apparently choosing her words carefully, "but do you really want to? I mean, this is a stage of your life when you should be enjoying your family and traveling and—and taking art classes or something."

"Traveling doesn't appeal to me," Alyssa replied, "and I'll always be available to my family, but I feel as though this could be...interesting." She raised a noncommittal shoulder. "We'll see."

Britt put a hand on her arm. "I think so, too. You've been organizing and administrating community projects for years. We all know how capable you are."

"I am a little scared," Alyssa admitted.

Cece leaned toward her with an encouraging smile. "That's probably healthy. Life is frightening, but even failure is better than never trying anything."

"That's right," Marge said, pushing away from the table. "I think you should go for it." She grinned as she tucked a battered straw purse under her arm. "But an affair would probably be more fun. You want a lift to work, Anna?"

"Please." Anna hurried along after her as Alyssa walked Marge to the door.

"Thank you for encouraging her," Amanda said to Britt and Cece. "I think this would be great for Mom, but she's not so sure. She wants to help Granddad. She's lived for us kids for so long, she needs to do something for herself." She tucked her pad into her tapestry briefcase, then leaned it against the edge of the table as she smiled at Britt. "Like you did. We're all so proud of you. Grandfather brags about you to anyone who'll listen."

Britt shrugged a little uncomfortably. She was still frightened enough herself to find congratulations a little premature. "It's a long shot. The outcome remains to be seen."

"Now you're being modest," Cece teased. "I saw your cheesecake on the menu at a restaurant in Milwaukee."

Britt looked surprised. "What were you doing there?"

"Uniform shopping." She sat a little straighter and pretended propriety. "Nursing supervisors have to look spiffy, you know." She glanced at her watch and sprang to her feet. "I've got to get going. See you two at the picnic. What time are we setting up?"

"Ten," Amanda replied.

She waved at Britt and Amanda and headed for the door, where Alyssa was still chatting with Marge and Anna.

Amanda gathered up her briefcase, Britt shouldered her purse, and there was laughter and a honking of horns in front of the house when everyone drove off.

It was interesting how much life remained the same in Tyler, Britt thought as she drove home along the dusty, sun-dappled road, yet how much things had

changed. She'd just spent a cozy hour and a half with
a group of women she'd known since childhood. Yet
who'd have guessed twenty years before that pretty little Amanda would become a lawyer, that idealistic
Cece would travel to Nicaragua on a medical mission
of mercy and return a widow, that attractive, accomplished Alyssa would consider running the business
that had been in her family for generations, or that she,
Britt, would trade cows for goats and go into food
production?

Life in Tyler certainly wasn't dull, she decided
philosophically. Sometimes scary, often frustrating,
always unpredictable, but never dull.

"OKAY, NOW I DON'T WANT to put pressure on you or
anything," Brick said to Jake as they watched the last
batter walk to first base. "But we've got two men on,
two men out, and it's the bottom of the ninth. We're
down two points."

Across Tyler's city park, a swarm of women were
organizing the food tables. On the playground equipment, small children played under the supervision of
teenagers. On the ball field, it was civil servants against
the downtown merchants. Jake, without an affilia-
tion, had been drafted by Brick when one of Brick's
fellow officers sprained an ankle on the monkey bars.

Jake turned to him with a bland smile. "Thank you.
Now I can take my turn at bat with an easy mind."

"Just try to remember," Brick said, his eyes bright
under the bill of his baseball cap, "that what you do
now will probably make or break you in this town. But,
you know, don't let it get to you. Just go out there and
have fun."

Jake tried to push him on ahead. "Let's just break
batting order. You're the one with the jock history. You
hit the plate."

Brick shook his head. "My game's football. I'm nothing special with a bat." He patted Jake on the back and pushed him toward the plate. "But I've got faith in you, son. Go. Make us proud."

Jake's teammates whistled and applauded him as he hefted the bat, eased into his grip, got comfortable and took his position. Then silence fell.

Brick had been teasing, Jake knew, but there was a curious grain of truth to what he'd said. Britt's friends and relatives had been watching him when he came to Tyler the past few weekends. He was being measured and judged. Britt was special to her friends and family, and they were protective and possessive of her. He'd scored a few points by gaining her time on payment of her bill, and helping her with yogurt production. But they didn't give their trust or approval easily. He was still the rep from the monster dairy they'd all come to equate with the demise of their life-styles. He was being tolerated, but he hadn't been accepted.

Santori pitched a fastball Jake was too nervous to swing at. He let it go. There was a gasp, then silence.

He firmed his grip and his stance. Another hard and fast one. He swung and missed by a hairbreadth.

Calm, he told himself. *Keep calm. You can do this. It's like the first time you found yourself alone with Britt's kids. You just followed instinct, took charge. Think that the ball is yours, the game is yours, their trust is yours—Britt is yours.*

He saw it coming as though in slow motion, spinning like a very steady top. He held his breath, swung and connected. The crack was as loud and sharp as a shot. There was a collective cry and everyone stood as he started to run. The ball was still arcing when he hit first. By the time he hit second it was going down—way beyond the fence.

"GO, JAKE!" Britt was screaming. Brick's wife, Karen, stood beside her, both fists clenched as she watched the action.

Britt's heart tripped and her eyes filled as the ball fell beyond the fence and the screams and applause became deafening—even in the wide-open park.

She watched Jake round third, slow his pace and finally cross home plate to the welcoming cheers of his teammates and Brick leaping into his arms.

Britt laughed in the hope that no one would notice she'd been crying. "Brick's certainly excited," she said.

"He had twenty bucks on the game," Karen said, offering her a tissue. "Mop up. This isn't *Carmen*, you know. It's just a ball game."

Britt gave her a casual look. "Maybe I had money on the game, too."

Karen smiled and put an arm around her shoulders. "I know who your money's on. Come on, we're supposed to be slicing hamburger buns."

BRITT STUDIED the last bite of potato salad on her plate and groaned. "I can't eat that," she said.

Before the words were out of her mouth, David, sitting beside her, reached over and speared the salad with his plastic fork. Then he dropped his empty plate in the litter bag Britt had provided and sprang to his feet. "Goin' to the monkey bars. See ya."

"Where does he put it?" Jake asked in amazement, watching the scrawny boy race toward the playground equipment. In one hand Jake held a diet cola; in the curve of his other arm, Renee snored softly. "He ate more than I did."

"Growing spurt," Britt said calmly as she settled back with a hand to her stomach. "By September all his school pants will be high-waters and I'll have to buy new everything. The way we've eaten today, I may have to let out the seams on a few of my own things."

Jake leaned against the old maple tree under which they'd spread their blanket. The park was rimmed with trees and there were now colorful square patches of blankets and towels everywhere as families ate and relaxed. Only the children still moved around restlessly, impervious to weariness.

All the young girls, Christy included, had gathered near the bleachers, where a group of cheerleaders had taken the opportunity of being together to practice.

On the field, boys Matt's age played touch football. Britt turned her head to watch him in vague concern. The group he was with had been strutting rowdily since lunch. Though she knew they weren't bad, simply adolescent, she wished Matt would align himself with the boys gathered around the fire truck, listening intently as the chief, in Bermuda shorts and a fuchsia polo shirt, explained the equipment.

Jake looked down at Britt, trying to concentrate on her face rather than on the small but perfect jut of her breasts in the yellow cotton sweater, and the long expanse of tanned leg beneath her cuffed khaki shorts.

She looked tired, and not just postpicnic tired. He knew the kind of hours she'd been keeping, because he kept them with her on weekends. And at every turn she had a child needing something, a phone to be answered, a problem of one kind or another to solve. She'd been heroic. But he didn't know how long she could continue the pace.

Britt turned her head to find Jake watching her with a look in his eyes that warmed her blood and speeded her pulse. And the sight of him with her child in his arms somehow added to his sex appeal. A short six weeks ago he'd been uncomfortable around her children. Now he was completely at ease with them—at least the three younger ones. Matt had made a point of being remote or difficult or both, but Jake had taken it in his stride. She loved him so much for that.

Renee got her second wind later in the afternoon and they all participated in the three-legged race, the water-balloon relay and the tug-of-war. They stuffed themselves at the ice-cream social, then settled down for the band concert.

"Where's Matt?" Britt asked Christy as she finally ushered the children into the back seat of the station wagon after the fireworks display. "Did you tell him I said it was time to go?"

"Yes," Christy said, apparently pleased to be able to relate Matt's answer. "He said he wasn't ready."

With a sense of fatalism, Britt marched off to the ball field. One day without altercation with Matt would have been nice, but she'd been foolish to think it might happen. Something was driving him, something he wouldn't share and she couldn't quite understand—except that it seemed to involve pushing them to a confrontation.

Four boys ran in close formation in the summer uniform of cut-off sweats and T-shirts. Matt carried the ball in a game that seemed to have been reduced to a kind of keep-away because of their small number. Two of the boys she recognized as the Monroe brothers. They lived with their mom, a single mother who entertained a steady stream of men—who seemed to be her only visible means of support. The boys were continually in trouble. The third boy, Danny Peterson, smoked a cigarette as he ran, though he was no older than Matt.

Britt tried diplomacy first. "Matt, we're ready to go," she called.

He ignored her completely.

"Matt!" she shouted more firmly. "We're leaving *now*."

He was tackled and fell as the other boys piled on. They all rose, laughing. Matt looked in her direction and waved. "Bye!" he said. The other boys laughed, then squared off for another play.

Britt felt her temper snap and her fear rise. She'd known this day would come. Matt would flex his budding male muscles and push against her because his father wasn't around to explain that manhood wasn't simply in the biceps.

She'd dreaded this moment because she'd never before reacted in anger—at least not physically. She'd always counted on being smart enough to avoid having to get physical.

Adolescent boys, however, operated on a different level.

She went to the group, grabbed the back of Matt's T-shirt and yanked him around. She looked into surprised blue eyes so much like Jimmy's that her anger was momentarily interrupted by a spark of grief. The other three boys held their ground.

"We're leaving," she said quietly, clearly. "And you're coming with us."

She saw the war in his eyes, saw him glance back at his friends. This had probably gone further than he'd intended, but he was trapped now. His status was at stake. "I'm playing ball," he said. "I'll be home later."

"You're coming now."

"No."

She reached for him but he blocked her grip, slapping her arm up and out of his way. His eyes blazed with something she couldn't identify except to know that it wasn't simple anger. She saw fear there, distress, guilt.

Fear deepened in her even as determination strengthened. Suddenly he seemed almost as tall as she was, and she saw not a trace of the love and respect she'd earned and built in all her children over the years. What if she couldn't be stronger than he was? What if she simply didn't have the muscle to make him come?

She reached for him again, determined that nothing else was going to be taken from her. Then a strong hand grabbed her arm and pulled her back. Jake pushed her behind him, and she saw him take a fistful of Matt's shirt. He held him briefly while they measured each other, Jake's eyes dark with a menace she'd never seen there before, Matt trying valiantly to retain dignity while he very obviously dealt with trepidation.

Then Jake moved so that his back was to the other boys. Retaining his grip on Matt's shirt, he spoke too quietly for them to hear. "We're leaving," he said, "and your mother wants you to come with us. Now you can head off to the car right now, or I can carry you there in front of your friends. The choice is yours."

Matt glowered at him. "You're not my father!"

"The way you're acting," Jake replied, "I'm glad of that right now. Which is it?"

Matt pulled back a fist. Jake didn't move a muscle, but said ominously, "Make it count, Matt, because that's the last thing you'll ever do with that arm."

The anger in both of them, the suggestion of violence, made Britt feel physically sick. But apparently it was a level of communication Matt understood, because when Jake released him, he ran to the car.

The ride home was silent, the day's fun completely eclipsed by Matt's behavior. And Britt felt a strange resentment she didn't understand. She hadn't had control of that moment with Matt. She was surprised to find herself annoyed that Jake had.

At home, Jake kept Matt on the porch while Britt went inside with the other children. He sat him down on the top step, wondering what in the hell had happened to the nice kid with whom he'd made the bike deal.

"I don't have to listen to you," Matt said belligerently.

"No, you don't." Jake leaned back against the porch post, looking into Matt's eyes, trying desperately to read what he saw there. It was more than anger and resentment. "Except about one thing. If you ever raise your hand to your mother again, I'll make you regret the day you were born, so help me."

Matt's stiff expression collapsed and Jake saw him swallow with difficulty. "I didn't mean to do that," he said, his voice heavy and strained. "I just—I . . . didn't mean it." Then he looked into Jake's eyes and admitted, as though it gave him some small relief, "I already do regret the day I was born."

"Why?" Jake leaned toward him, softening at the boy's obvious regret. "Why, Matt? What's wrong?"

Matt struggled manfully against tears and finally just shook his head, looking away.

"Nobody blames you for missing your dad," he said, trying to open a door in the wall the boy had put up. "But it won't help anything to wish you were gone, too. Your mom needs you."

"No, she doesn't," he said bitterly. His eyes welled and he sniffed, dashing a hand at his face. "Christy's the smart one, David's the nice one, Renee's the cute one."

"You're the oldest one," Jake said urgently. "The man of the family."

Matt looked at him evenly. "Isn't that you?"

Was that it? Jake wondered. By loving Britt, he'd challenged the boy's position? "Right now I'm just a friend of the family," he said. "I'm sure your mom would never think seriously about a man her children didn't like."

"They all like you," Matt said grudgingly. "Renee thinks having you around is just like when Dad was here."

"Why did you change your mind about me, Matt?"

Matt looked startled, even horrified by the question.

"You can tell me. I can take it."

Matt drew in his breath in a gulp. "Because you are like him," he said hurriedly.

"Your father?" Jake asked, confused. "But you loved him."

Matt's next breath ended on a sob. He opened his mouth to speak, his eyes pouring out what he couldn't form into words. Jake struggled to read it, but couldn't quite put it together. Matt sprang to his feet and ran into the house.

BRITT WAS curiously remote as she walked Jake to the truck. He thought he understood; he'd interfered where he had no right. It left him feeling frustrated, demoralized, vaguely in the way.

"I was just thinking," he said, "that it might be better if I stayed away next weekend. Let Matt loosen up and relax. Maybe he'll tell you what's bothering him."

He needed the rest, too, she knew. For weeks he'd worked all weekend with her, helping her install the new equipment and get it working. He'd helped with the cooking and the children, then had slept on the sofa because she wanted to be discreet in front of the children. He'd accepted that without needing an explanation. Her resentment disappeared as she thought about all he'd done.

She hated the thought of not seeing him for two weeks—or possibly longer. Given enough time in Chicago, he might remember how free and easy his life had been, how much he had in the big city that Tyler could never give him, how much he could experience with a single woman that she, Britt, could never offer.

"That's probably best," Britt made herself say, but the lie was audible in her voice.

He turned to look into her eyes and saw her carefully closed expression. He leaned down to give her a perfunctory kiss, climbed into the Explorer and drove away.

He turned to look into her eyes and saw her completely relaxed expression. She leaned down to give her a perfunctory kiss, carried her to the bassinet, and drove away.

CHAPTER THIRTEEN

"MARSHACK!"

Jake looked up from a salesman's report to see Foreman standing halfway across the office. He beckoned to Jake, then disappeared beyond his heavy, corporate door.

Jake went, suspecting what was coming. He'd expected it long before this. He'd been pretty high profile at the Products for the Nineties Exhibition, and though Winnebago hadn't participated, his support of Britt's product probably could be construed as conflict of interest despite all his assurances to the contrary.

"Close the door," Foreman said.

Jake went over his resignation speech in his mind. It occurred to him wryly as he watched his boss adjust the beige miniblinds against the morning sun that he seemed suddenly to have lost all ambition. Only two short months ago the promotion to vice president had been all he thought about. Now office scuttlebutt said he had it in his pocket, but it didn't seem to matter. The only thought on his mind was of Britt and how much he missed her and the children.

Foreman sat behind his desk and leaned back in his chair, swiveling sideways so that he looked at Jake over his shoulder. "Seems the issue of the widow Hansen's come up again," he said.

Jake raised a nonchalant eyebrow. "Really? Her account's current. I went over the receivables just this morning."

The vice president pinned him with the paternal look. "I'm not talking about receivables."

The exhibition. Jake waited.

"You have a thing for her?" Foreman asked.

Jake felt his temper flare. But then he'd had a lot of trouble with it in the past two weeks. He'd had a lot of trouble with everything.

"That's personal, Mr. Foreman."

"I'm afraid your getting personal with her becomes a business matter. Did you know Chicago Kitchens signed her up this week?"

Jake had heard from one of the Duttons. He'd been thrilled for Britt and a little disappointed when she hadn't called to tell him. He'd wondered if she'd been discovering, now that Yes! Yogurt had been well and truly launched, that she didn't need him anymore—particularly if he was going to interfere with her children.

"Yes, I did," he said.

"I also learned that you helped set her up with Favorite, the Duttons and Talbot."

"That's true," Jake admitted.

"That's cause for dismissal." Foreman turned so that he faced Jake, could give him the full power of his vice-presidential stare.

Jake gave him the full power of his I-don't-give-a-damn, lackey-in-charge-of-sales-and-collections stare. "I can be gone in an hour," he said.

Foreman studied him a moment, then shook his head paternally. "The trouble with you, Marshack, is that you're too good to stay where you are, but you won't kiss enough butt to go anywhere else."

Jake nodded. "It's a fastidious thing."

Foreman let that go. "I like you. In fact, I quoted you to the board when it was recommended you be fired for supporting Mrs. Hansen. I told them you told me Winnebago should be getting involved in the food-for-the-nineties trend, that we should stop living on past glory and start going aggressively after new products."

Jake was a little surprised by what he saw coming.

"I told them I thought you'd be willing to redeem yourself. Since we couldn't convince Mrs. Hansen to part with that prime lakefront property, maybe we can get that cherry little yogurt business from her." He smiled, apparently expecting Jake to be thrilled with the proposal. "That way we can start with an established product but do far more with it than she could ever hope to."

"What's your offer?" Jake asked calmly.

Foreman named a price. It took all Jake's poker-face conditioning to hold back the "Hot damn!" on the tip of his tongue. He'd expected the offer to be measly, paltry, insulting—to anyone but what they presumed would be a tired little woman bored by now with the tyrannies of business and its exhausting demands.

But the offer was good—even generous, for a product just off the ground and not really cruising yet at a bankable altitude. She'd be able to do everything she wanted to do and more.

He nodded consideringly. "You want me to take the proposal to her?"

"I want you to *sell* it to her. I want you to come back here with a signed contract. I want to be able to take it to Chancellor and put it in front of him as a done deal."

"I see." And he thought he did. The board had discussed developing and launching a new product, but Foreman had been against it saying it risked capital at a time when they were in a comfortable space. Then every other dairy had come up with a new product and Winnebago had held steady and safe—but unnoticed. Everyone else had the publicity, the applause. Yes! Yogurt would save Foreman's face.

But Jake didn't care about his motives. It was the deal of a lifetime. Britt could pay off her debts, remodel the house, start four college funds and finally have time to think about herself—and him.

SHE WAS AT HER DESK in the small room they'd wallboarded off in the storage shed now used for shipping. She was frowning over a six-foot-long calculator tape she held in one hand, while with the other she stroked the white kitten, curled into a tight ball in the middle of her paperwork.

As Jake walked in quietly, his eyes went over her hair, caught back in a saucy ponytail, her delicate shoulders in a pastel plaid shirt hunched over her work, her long fingers petting the white fur, her elegant profile puckered in thought. His heart swelled and filled so much it hurt. God, he'd missed her.

Britt looked up and saw Jake coming toward her. Joy flared in her chest. The pervading loneliness she'd suffered since the night of the picnic was swept away with the intimacy of his smile. Happiness flowed over her as she leaped out of her chair and into his arms.

They closed around her with the strength and tenderness she'd remembered during every interminable night. Nostrils filled with his comfortable Old Spice scent, she rubbed her cheek against the excitingly scratchy beginnings of his beard. Then he wove his fingers under the ribbon that held her ponytail in place and pulled her head back. She smiled into his eyes, passion blossoming in her along with the happiness.

She'd missed him, too, Jake saw. And she wanted him as much as he wanted her. His eyes devoured her sweeping eyelashes, her flushed cheeks, the little tremor of her bottom lip as her mouth opened, waiting.

He closed his mouth over hers and made no attempt to be tender or understanding. He wanted her to know the depth of his feelings, the heat of his desire, the ferocity of his hunger.

Britt welcomed the possessive quality of his kiss, of his arms. Any shred of doubt left in her about whether they should be together was decimated by a pair of hands that were everywhere—convincing her that nothing in her life would matter without him.

"Jake, I've missed you so much," she gasped when he released her long enough to let her catch her breath."

"And I didn't think of you once," he said, nibbling along the cord in her neck and into the vee of her blouse.

"You didn't?" She didn't sound worried.

"No," he said, finding the swell of a breast and rubbing his lips against it. "I thought of you a million times, every moment of every day. At night you were like an image painted behind my eyes. I could feel you in my arms." He raised his head and said with a frown, "Britt, we've got to do something about this."

Her grin gleamed. "Can you stay for dinner?"

He gave her a wry look. The last thing on his mind at the moment was food.

"Because," she explained, running a tantalizing fingertip along his bottom lip, "the Kiwanis are having a carnival in town and Brick's picking up the kids at seven."

His grin spread slowly. "I'll stay."

BRICK WAS PROMPT. Matt treated him to a cold shoulder, too, Jake noted with a guilty sense of satisfaction as Brick ushered the children out to the car. At least it wasn't just him.

As he and Britt walked back into the kitchen, Jake decided that he would tell her about Winnebago's offer, then take her up to her room to celebrate.

But she apparently had a schedule of her own. With a look in her eyes he'd have been a fool to question, she tugged him up the stairs and into the green-and-apricot bedroom.

With the waning sun streaming through the windows, they pulled clothes off each other, touched and stroked and murmured endearments and promises. Jake tugged Britt down with him to the middle of the bed, swept his hands and his mouth from the tip of her nose to the soles of her feet and back again. He ran a hand along the inside of her thigh and she opened herself to him, wrapping her arms around his neck as he rose over her.

"Jake," she whispered, her eyes brimming, her voice grave, "I love you. I've been waiting for you."

He entered her with the same confident possessiveness he'd kissed her with in her office. He no longer had doubts about whether or not she could be his. She was. He saw it in the eager arch of her body as she took him inside her. In the little pleat of emotion between her closed eyes as her body enclosed him. In the deliciously surprised look in her eyes that mirrored what he, too, felt at finding that making love now was just like it had been in Chicago—again! Miracles just didn't happen over and over.

But there it was—snaring him, tossing him round and round until he could barely remember his name, sending him into realms of pleasure he'd never known before.

Britt experienced the perfection of their lovemaking to the very core of her being. Her physical self shuddered and gasped, her spiritual self knew a oneness with Jake she'd never expected to find with a man a second time. She'd thought her love for Jimmy had been a once-in-a-lifetime thing. But a very generous God had blessed her again. She held fast to Jake and followed him into the sunset.

BRITT SURFACED from a velvet dream and reached instinctively for Jake. Her hand found an empty expanse of sheet and she propped herself up on an elbow, startled awake.

She saw him sitting in the chair. He had pulled on jeans and was watching her with a lazily possessive expression that brought vividly to mind the delicious hour they'd just spent together.

"Hi," she said softly. "Why don't you come back to bed?"

The invitation was almost more than he could resist. But he had a point to make. And he had to remember why he was here.

"Two reasons," he said, propping a bare foot on the edge of the bed and resting his arm on his bent knee. "One, I believe I belong here."

"Oh?" She smiled. She'd already granted him that at some point during the long, lonely two weeks.

"Yes," he said, his eyes running over her bare shoulders in a way that made her stomach flutter. "I'm moving into your life, Britt."

She sat up, clutching the blanket to her bosom, her eyes wide with confusion, her lips parting. She looked into his eyes, trying to read precisely what he meant.

"Marriage," he clarified. "As soon as we can arrange it."

"Jake, I—"

"I'll respect your memories of Jimmy, I promise. I know it'll be hard with Matt, but I think I can work that out eventually."

Emotion choked her. He meant every word. She could have it again—everything she wanted. After the dark and difficult year it was so hard to believe that could be possible.

"Jake, think!" she said forcefully. She scooted closer to the edge of the bed, bringing the blankets with her. "Four children! Four." She held up her right hand and folded in the thumb. "The younger ones have been so good because they adore you, but they can be stubborn and naughty and absolutely exasperating."

He leaned forward and scooped her up, blankets and all. "I wonder where those traits could have come from?" he asked, settling her in his lap as he leaned back in the chair. "Their father, no doubt."

She looped her arms around his neck and tried to look severe. "All right, you'd have five of us with those qualities. Is that really what you want?"

"Yeah." He kissed her long and lingeringly as proof. "Must be an aberration in my makeup."

"Oh, Jake." She ran her fingers through his hair in a way that raised gooseflesh on his arms. She tilted her head apologetically. "I barely have time to breathe with the business doing so well. I signed with Chicago Kitchens this week."

He swatted her hip where his hand rested. "I heard about that. I thought you might have called me to share the good news."

She lowered her lashes. "I thought this was kind of a wait-and-see time for you. I was afraid calling you even with good news would break the distance you were trying to establish."

He frowned at her. "I thought *you* needed the time."

She looked surprised. "Why?"

"Because I was pressing and you still weren't sure you were over Jimmy."

She rubbed the nape of his neck absently while tears pooled in her eyes. "I'll never be *over* Jimmy. We shared so much and loved so hard...." She swallowed audibly. "But I need you. And I love you with the same..." She groped frustratedly for the word. "The same—I don't know—totality, I guess, with which I loved Jimmy. Can you live with the fact that there'll always be another man tucked in my heart?"

He glanced at the photo of Jimmy and Britt on the dresser, and thought of the children stamped with his features and the basic good cheer in his face. It would be awfully hard to resent a man who'd loved so well.

He pulled her head to his shoulder and kissed her hair. "Of course, Britt. I don't want to take anything from you. I just want to give to you."

"But..." She lifted her head, her eyes clear but serious. "There'll be so little I can give you, at least until I get this business under control. It's turned into a mustang on me. This afternoon Mike Buchanan called me—he wants to talk about picking up more products. I'm going to have to build an industrial park pretty soon."

"That's the second reason I couldn't come back to bed," he said.

She narrowed one eye, obviously losing the thread of the conversation.

"When you asked me to come back to bed," he reminded her, "I told you there were two reasons I couldn't."

"Right. And the second?"

"Winnebago sent me with an offer to buy Yes! Yogurt from you."

He waited with anticipation for the delight, the excitement to flash in her eyes, the smile to light her face. But she just looked at him, her eyes blank. She looked at him so long that he frowned and began to ask worriedly, "Britt, what...?"

She clutched the blanket around her and stood up stiffly. "Winnebago sent you?" she asked.

He guessed that question had some significance, but for the life of him he couldn't find any. "Yes," he answered cautiously, still sitting, still trying to understand her reaction. "They're offering . . ." And he told her, let the large figure roll off his tongue with all the satisfaction he felt for what she'd accomplished despite formidable odds.

The blank look on her face vanished and ripe anger took its place. He sighed and stood, mentally girding himself for battle. It would have been nice to know what the hell they were going to fight about, but—hey! Why should life take a reasonable turn now?

CHAPTER FOURTEEN

BRITT FELT FURY and hurt struggle for supremacy inside her. He hadn't come because he'd wanted to, because he'd missed her. He'd come because Winnebago had sent him. Now that they couldn't take her farm, they wanted her business.

And she'd made love to him—wild, eager, passionate love that had made her feel so alive, so wanted, so... God! Shame washed over and over her. She should have known better. She should have realized that dreams were only that. Reality was that you worked hard for what you got, lived with comfortable tedium from day to day and were lonely a lot of the time because trusting was just too chancy. Men like Jimmy were rare.

She glowered up at Jake, the blanket clutched around her.

He folded his arms and guessed wryly, "You're not pleased."

"Did you expect I would be?" she demanded icily.

"Yeah, I did," he replied. "It's more than generous. You can pay off all your debts, put money away for the kids' education and relax a little. What's so deplorable about that?"

"If you don't see it," she said, turning away from him, "then I can't explain it to you." She had to kick the train of her blanket aside to avoid falling over it.

Jake rolled his eyes, and finally impatient, grabbed her arm and turned her around. This time he had to kick the blanket.

"Come on," he scolded sharply. "Don't argue like a woman. Tell me what you're talking about."

Anger bubbled up in her and spilled over. "All right! I'll explain it to you very carefully!" She strained up at him in her bare feet, his quiet calm as he waited for her to explain further infuriating her. "Your intention from the very beginning was to wrap up the widow Hansen and her prime lakefront farm and hand it over to your employers. What were you going to get for it, incidentally? We never did discuss that."

He was just angry enough at her hurtful implication to hurt her back. "A vice presidency," he replied evenly.

He saw the shock register in her eyes, the pink of temper in her cheeks turn to pallor. It felt good for about two seconds, then he regretted it. She pulled herself together in an instant and the anger was back.

"Well," she said, "at least I was a pretty high step up the ladder. Anyway..." She tossed her head and he watched the pink-gold of her hair undulate in the dying light. The scorn in her eyes distracted him from the dull ache beginning in his gut. "You were really very clever, Marshack. Earn the lady's trust, support her every move, work with her until she's completely convinced that you want her to succeed every bit as much as *she* wants to, begin to tighten the noose with lucrative deals and big money, then reel her in when it all gets to be too much. What's your commission on this? Thirty percent? Isn't that what the big finders get?"

They stared at each other for a long moment, her pale blue eyes scornful and accusing, his brown gaze filled with a quiet but smoking anger. Then he grabbed her, yanking her from her imperious stance. She bounced into the barrel chair with a little scream of surprise. He held her in it with a hand on either side of her, the anger in him catching fire.

She tried to stand, but his hand on her shoulder kept her in the chair. "Stay there," he said, his voice ominously quiet. "Now I have a few things to say."

Mad enough to chew briars, she held her shielding blanket in place and looked him in the eye. It was hard. She'd never seen him like this—all the sweetness, understanding and tolerance that had once defined him for her gone. She angled her chin so that he wouldn't see she was just a little bit afraid of his sudden, dangerous unpredictability.

"Go ahead," she challenged. "Explain yourself if you can."

"I don't have to explain myself," he said, sitting on the edge of the bed, facing her. "But maybe someone should explain you to you."

"You aren't suggesting," she asked, "that a man like you could know what a woman like me is all about?"

He shrugged a broad, bare shoulder. A small grim smile came and went. "Cowardice isn't all that complex."

Britt gave herself less credit than anyone else did, but if she knew anything about the woman she was it was that she never rolled over and gave up. Never. She stared at him, at a loss for words.

He nodded. "Yes, you're a heroic farmer, mother, survivor of all life's dirty little tricks. You've put your brain to work when a lot of other people would have given up, you marshaled all your resources, and it looks like you're going to win in a big way." He reached for his shirt at the foot of the bed, and she tried to get to her feet again, deciding the conversation wasn't making sense and she didn't have to sit around and—

He put a foot to the side of her chair, blocking her between the wall and his long, jeans-clad leg. "I'm not finished," he said, his eyes pinning her.

He slipped casually into the shirt, buttoned the buttons. "You have wonderful children," he went on, "and you're there for them every minute. I admire that. But it's the woman in you that's chicken. You've been running away from me from the first moment you realized you loved me."

She gasped indignantly and pointed to the expanse of bed behind him. "I just made love with you! You call that running?"

He gave her a fatalistic shake of his head as he stood and tucked the shirt into his jeans. "That was just because you missed me. You miss the physical side of being with a man you love. But the minute I get close to tapping you inside, where you live, you put every obstacle you can think of between us. The kids, the farm, the business—"

"Those are potentially—"

"Problematic. I know." He sat again and reached to the bedside table for the watch he'd pulled off when they'd rolled together in the bed and the expansion band had caught in her hair. "But what isn't? The real problem is that you're clinging to this place because you're comfortable here and you're not sure you could cope anywhere else, and you're clinging to Jimmy because you know you succeeded with him—he loved you and you loved him and every one of the children reinforces that."

He put on his socks and running shoes. "With me, you'd have to start all over. You'd have to find a place for me in your relationship with the kids."

"They love you. I . . ."

He looked at her levelly as he bent his leg and tied his shoe. "You don't know how to share them anymore. I saw it in your eyes the night of the picnic. You couldn't

have forced Matt to come with you, but you resented
the fact that I could. You have quite a dynasty here. I
almost messed that up.''

Britt trembled with anger and guilt and confusion.
"How dare you suggest that I'm manipulating—"

He let out a long breath and pushed himself to his
feet. "If the day ever comes," he said, looking down
at her, "that Matt or Christy or one of the little ones
wants to make his or her life somewhere else, I just
hope that you'll let him go without loading past generations of Bauers on him. Your children aren't clones,
you know. They're separate beings with needs and
dreams that might be completely different from
yours.''

She stood, her eyes blazing. "You just don't understand family because you didn't have one! You don't
understand people whose lives are rooted in the earth.
You're angry because I won't sell out for money like
you did!''

His temper strained against the tight hold he had on
it. "You won't sell," he said, "because that would give
you time for me, and you wouldn't know what to do
with it. Goodbye, Britt." He went to the door and
turned the knob.

She followed him halfway across the room, then
stopped. Standing on the braided carpet at the foot of
her bed, she said shrilly, "There's more to life than
money and sex!''

He half turned to her. "There's love," he said, "but
you're afraid of it.''

She made a scornful sound. "As though you know
all about it.''

He was making a mistake, he knew, walking back
into the room. Leaving her was hard enough already.
But he closed the space that separated them in three
long strides, wrapped her in one arm, making her de-

fenseless in her cocoon of blanket, then took a fistful of her hair and pulled her head back.

The kiss began in lieu of the swat he would have liked to give her. He opened his mouth over hers and delved deep with his tongue, holding her immobile while he took every liberty to which he felt entitled.

Then he gentled the kiss, his tongue now coaxing, teasing, tantalizing, his hands roving and possessive, so that in the darkness of the night she would remember every little touch they'd shared. Then he took a handful of her bottom through the blanket and pressed her intimately against him. He felt her fidget and heard her moan, and the action only served to underline his motive as his body reacted to hers.

She was limp and gasping when he let her go. He put a hand behind her head and tipped her backward onto the bed. "Don't tell me I don't know how to love you," he said, and left the room.

BRITT PULLED her shirt and jeans on and smoothed the bed. She heard Brick's car arrive and the Explorer depart. When David and Renee ran upstairs to tell her about the house of mirrors and the Ferris wheel and the bear Brick won at the ring toss, she had a smile ready for them.

She listened attentively and took them down to the kitchen to make cocoa and found Brick and Christy already had it in production. Snapping off half an oatmeal-raisin bar, Brick took one look at her face and frowned.

"Look, Mom!" Christy stuffed a very large, very frowsy pink bear into her face. "Brick won it for you. He got one of those rubber ring things on six bottles in a row!"

Britt forced a grin his way. "You had an unfair advantage."

"Oh, yeah?"

"All that experience handling donuts."

He pointed her to a kitchen chair. "Overused cop joke. Sit. I'll have you know I had no advantages." He struck a dramatic pose. "It was just me and row after row of deadly pop bottles."

"Where's Matt?" Britt asked.

"Went upstairs," Christy replied. "He's mad 'cause Brick wouldn't let him stay at the carnival with Danny Peterson and Stevie Monroe."

Concern for her oldest slapped her anew, but she felt so battered at the moment it didn't hurt. It just thickened the wall between her and her peace of mind.

"How's Karen?" Britt asked as Brick brought her a cup of cocoa.

"Beautiful. Bossy." He sat opposite her with his own cup, adding with a grin, "Damn near perfect."

She could see that he had questions of his own he was holding back for an appropriate time. The children told her more about their exciting evening and she listened, taking pleasure in their bright-eyed enjoyment. That would never change, she thought stubbornly. Nothing could diminish her love and pride in her children. How dare Jake consider that selfish?

When their cocoa was finished, Britt urged the children up to bed. They hugged Brick and went without complaint, still talking and laughing about what they'd seen and done.

Britt had hoped Brick would leave, but he simply rinsed out his cup and helped himself to coffee from the carafe on the counter. "Want some?"

She held out her cup. If he was sticking around, she had a feeling she was going to need the caffeine. As he went back to his chair, she tried to steer him away from what she suspected he'd hung around to discuss.

"Karen tells me you're about ready to start building on your Timber Lake property," she said brightly. "It's such a perfect—"

"I stayed to talk to you," he interrupted.

She fluttered her eyelashes teasingly, still trying to divert him. "How flattering."

His grave expression didn't change. "So, what happened tonight?"

She tried to look forbidding. "Brick, my personal life is my own business."

"When you're ruining it," he said, "it becomes the concern of those of us who care about you. Come on. I'm not moving until I hear the whole story."

She swallowed a lump burning in her throat. "He's just not what I thought he was."

He raised an eyebrow. "What did you think he was?"

"Trustworthy. Sincere."

He frowned. "He is. Working with the other side of those traits most of the time, I pride myself on being able to identify honesty and reliability when I see it." He studied her a moment, then took a sip of coffee. "He crossed you, didn't he?"

She dropped her cup to the table with a bang. "Why are you on his side before you even know what happened?"

"Because I like him," Brick replied. "Everybody likes him. I know how he feels about you. He was leaving when I pulled up and he was not a happy man. What'd you do to him?"

"Maybe he did something to me!" she said a little too loudly. "Maybe he finally came back after being away for two weeks only because Winnebago Dairy sent him with a very large offer to buy Yes! Yogurt."

"How large?"

She told him.

He looked into her eyes, obviously trying to decide why that amount of money should have upset her.

"Horrors," he said finally. "How dare he try to relieve you of a terrible burden while making you an enormous profit? What was he thinking? The man should be horse—''

"Will you shut up!" Britt snapped, scraping back her chair and crossing the room to stare at the darkness beyond the window. "Will you just go home to Karen and leave me alone?"

"Karen's working tonight," he said, his voice filled with grim amusement. "I'm free to spend hours making you see the error of your ways."

"Lucky me."

"Come and sit down."

"Go away."

Strong, gentle arms came around her and squeezed. "Are you more upset about the offer or about the fact that that's what brought him back to you?"

She started to cry, deep, gulping sobs that tore at her throat. He turned her to him and wrapped his arms around her.

"He called me a coward!" she wept. "Me! Because I won't sell. Well, I told him what I thought of him!"

"And what is that?"

"That all I ever was to him was a way for him to secure a promotion, first through my property and now through my business."

"Britt, that's absurd. He hired a plane to come to you when you were stuck in the boonies, he used all his contacts to help you, and he came out here every spare moment he had to do all the building dirty work for you."

She backed out of his arms to insist aggressively, "Because by helping me he was helping himself. I was a direct route to a vice presidency."

Brick folded his arms and leaned back against the counter. "Bridget Chancellor would probably have been a far more direct route."

Britt snatched a paper towel and dabbed at her eyes. "Who?" she asked in confusion.

"Bridget Chancellor. The daughter of Winnebago's president. Jake was dating her before he met you."

"How do you know?"

"I know people who know people. When it looked like it was getting serious between you two I sort of...looked into it."

She shook her head. "Brick, I can't believe—"

"The point is, if all he wanted was a vice presidency, he could have saved himself a lot of effort, frustration and probably verbal abuse by smiling on the beautiful Miss Chancellor. She'd have married him in a minute. I'm sure his future after that would have been guaranteed."

The discomfort of hindsight began to grow in Britt. She went back to the table and fell into her chair, frowning into space. "Then why did he come here with that offer?"

Brick resumed his chair across from her. "I'm sure the dairy sent him because they thought he'd have some influence with you." He leaned slightly sideways until he intercepted her empty gaze. She came out of her thoughts and focused on his gently censorious eyes. "I imagine he agreed to do it because he considered it a truly good offer. You're working like a dog, Britt, and you're beginning to look a little the worse for wear. I've noticed. I'm sure he has, too. And if he loves you like I think he does, it's hard for him to watch. He probably thought he was helping you."

"But he knows my whole heart and soul are in it," she said, still unwilling to absolve him of guilt. Her own was prickling and she felt grumpy and grim.

Brick studied her a moment. "To distract you from wondering what to do about him?"

She gave him an impatient look. "To save my farm. To gain some security for my children."

He shrugged a shoulder. "You've done that."

"I've also acquired more debt in the process. I can't just stop."

"You could take on help."

"Brick, you know I've done that. I've got three kids from the high school, the Simonson girl working full—"

"I mean administrative help," he interrupted. "Someone at your level. You've got a bonanza on your hands, Britt. Will you admit to me that you're just a little afraid of it?"

She rested her chin on the heel of her hand, feeling suddenly exhausted. "Now you think I'm a coward, too."

"Need isn't cowardice," he said, pushing away from the table and standing. "You've had to depend on yourself so completely this past year, you've forgotten that you're only human." He bent to kiss the top of her head. "But you are. Don't get up. I'll see myself out."

"Please," she said with a dry smile as she got to her feet, "allow me the pleasure of pushing you."

At the door, Brick gave her a grin, then stepped out onto the porch. The night was warm and fragrant and reminded her sharply of another night not too long ago when she'd stood in the doorway of a strange little motel feeling lost and depressed and lonely, and had found Jake standing there. She fought the little thrill of pleasure that tried to return.

"He came back because he was sent," she said, leaning a shoulder against the doorframe. "Not because he wanted to come."

"You read minds now, do you?"

Grudgingly, she gave him a hug. What she really wanted to do was gut-punch him. "Thanks for taking the kids to the carnival. Now, get out before I call a cop."

"Ooh." He made a low suggestive sound. "Maybe Karen'll answer the call personally. She'd know what to do with a beautiful night. See ya."

Britt locked up and turned off the downstairs lights. Then she headed for the stairs to check on the children and take a shower. She found Matt sitting on the stairs, half his body in the downstairs shadow and the other half in the light from the upstairs hall. The image was strangely profound, she thought; he seemed trapped somewhere between night and day, darkness and light.

"Can't sleep?" she asked, sitting beside him.

He looked a little fragile tonight, but more accessible than he had in weeks. His eyes looked into hers, dark and frank. "I thought I heard you crying," he said.

She put an arm around him and smiled. "I was. Even mothers can lose it sometimes, you know. But I'm fine now."

"It's Jake, isn't it?" he asked. "He isn't coming back."

"I'm not sure," she said honestly. "We had a quarrel and he was pretty angry when he left."

She felt him lean into her. "Because of me?"

"Absolutely not." She took advantage of his momentary dependence and hugged him close. "Because of a lot of things we disagree on. He said things that hurt me, and I said things to him I wish I hadn't."

A little gasp of pain erupted from him, part sob, part cry. She held him even closer, her heart aching for him and the burden he carried that he couldn't share.

"Honey, please tell me what's wrong. I promise not to shout at you or scold you. Just tell me."

He was silent a long moment and she closed her eyes, praying he'd finally trust her enough to tell her. But he simply turned his head into her shoulder and sighed heavily. "It isn't anything, Mom. I just know what it's like to say things you wish you hadn't said.'' He hugged her hard, then said good-night and ran to his room.

Britt lowered her head to her knees, a dark sense of loss rolling over the guilt and weariness that already filled her. She'd saved the farm, but somehow she'd lost Jake in the process, and she felt as though she were losing Matt.

She tried to conjure up images of Jimmy in her mind, but he no longer lived there. He was in a little corner of her heart, but no longer available to give her reason to go on. Jake had taken that place in the past month. And now he, too, was gone.

She checked on the girls. Renee was asleep, one leg thrown over the side of the bed. Britt pushed it gently under the covers. Across the room, Christy read in the shallow glow of a book light attached to a library copy of *Anne of Green Gables*.

Britt leaned down to kiss her forehead. ''Don't read too long, sweetie.''

Christy replied without taking her eyes from the page, ''I just want to finish this chapter. Good night, Mom.''

Britt went into her bedroom and closed the door without putting the light on. A bright moon picked out the side of the bed closest to the window and the barrel chair. She could see Jake sitting in it, bare-chested, eyes dark and dangerous.

She determined to shed the image as she shed her clothes and put on a pair of tailored pajamas she'd bought when she took the children to Chicago. She'd thought they suited her new executive image.

He hadn't come to her because he wanted to, she reminded herself as she crawled into bed. He'd come because they'd sent him. So she didn't need him. Even if he had broken up with Bridget What's-her name. Britt already missed him like fury, but she would adjust.

She lay back into her pillow and made a mental list of all the things she had to do the following day and for the rest of the week. A million details crowded her mind. She had several appointments with buyers next week, on top of a very full work schedule. And it was almost August. She had to start giving thought to school clothes for the children. And Daffy needed her tetanus booster.

She smiled at the ceiling, pleased at how well she'd reestablished control. Then she closed her eyes and rolled over. The scent of Old Spice filled her nostrils, filled the darkness, filled her being. She buried her face in the pillow and wept.

CHAPTER FIFTEEN

"WHAT DO YOU MEAN, she wouldn't sell?" Stan Foreman demanded.

Jake faced Foreman and Chancellor across a marble table in a top-floor meeting room. The paternal treatment he'd grown used to in his dealings with Foreman was absent this morning, Jake had noticed. In the presence of *his* boss, Chancellor, Foreman was all hard-nosed bluster. It was precisely what Jake had expected.

There was a certain comfort in having known how this meeting would develop. It was nice to know there were some things in his life he still understood.

"I mean," he said mildly, "that she's determined to build it on her own. It's important to her. It means more than the money you offered."

Chancellor leaned back in his chair. "Our research showed her in a poor situation, productively and financially. She's operating on a shoestring after just surfacing from a great deal of debt, and she's running this single-handedly. What's your feeling? Does she want more money?"

"No."

Chancellor looked down at the file on the table. "Well, she's getting it off the ground, all right, but one day soon she's bound to encounter a slip in quality control, a shipping delay, a client who simply changes his mind." He closed the file, as though the next course of action was clear in his mind. "I think we should send you back with a slightly bigger offer and a warning of all the dangers she might encounter. Tell her that according to every source and all our experience, she'll be down for the count in no time. Advise her to sell now while she can."

Jake smiled wryly. It amazed him how easy it was to watch everything that had once been so important go down the tubes. "I won't do that, Mr. Chancellor. She's very determined."

Foreman huffed indignantly, a show for the president's benefit, Jake knew.

Chancellor simply met his gaze across the table. "Marshack, you've been an important part of our team. But you seem to be losing the team spirit." He frowned in dramatic concern. "If we hadn't thought so highly of you, you'd have been gone when word got back to us about the support you're giving this little lady. If Bridget had had her way, you'd have been maimed as well as fired."

Foreman turned to his boss in a moment of stunned surprise that something personal should enter into a business discussion. Then, remembering which side his bread was buttered on, he looked back at Jake with judicious severity.

"But I'm a reasonable man," Chancellor went on. "And this doesn't seem like an unreasonable request. I'm sure if you explain to the young lady what we've discussed, make it clear that your job is at stake, she'll be inclined to see things our way."

Jake placed his hands against the cold, flat marble, let himself enjoy the feel of status and success one last time, then pushed himself to his feet. "The lady thinks for herself, gentlemen. She won't be influenced by me. And if the day ever came when I let my career turn on a threat or a bribe, I wouldn't be able to live with myself." He narrowed his glance to focus on the vice president. "How do you do it, Foreman? You know where to send my check. Goodbye."

Out on the busy Chicago street, Jake took a deep gulp of fresh air. He drew in bus exhaust and perfume, and the faint fragrance of midsummer blooms. It was exhilarating. In a day or two he'd have to decide how and where to get another job, when and how to enter Britt's life again, because having to was a given. But for now, he just walked and let the freedom wash over him.

BRITT WORKED like a fiend. No part of the yogurt-making process, from milking the goat to slapping shipping labels on cartons, escaped her scrutiny or her possessive touch. She'd always been up at dawn, but now she seldom got to bed before midnight, after keeping paperwork current and running a watchful eye over the figures. Under the exciting glow of success was the horrible fear that it could all go wrong at any moment, that someone would discover someday that she didn't really know what she was doing, that though she'd developed an exceptional recipe, the contacts and the business advice had all been Jake's, and without him it would all fall apart.

She should have called him and apologized, or at least called and simply talked. Her accusation had been unfounded, born out of hurt feelings and extreme exhaustion. But the longer he stayed away, the harder it became for her to take the first step. What would a bright, successful single man want with a widow and four children anyway—particularly one with a bad temper who was stubbornly devoting every moment of her life to the children and a demanding business? She couldn't imagine.

So she bravely, regretfully, considered her relationship with Jake over and wearily tried to keep control of her business and everything that entailed, while seeing that Christy still got to piano lessons, Renee to ballet and David to t'ai chi. She hugged Matt, told him jokes and tried to keep him busy, because she didn't know what else to do for him. Quiet and remote, he'd gone on the Boy Scout trip and returned unchanged.

The crisis began the third week in August when Britt, about to lose patience with a recalcitrant Renee, who'd whined and quarreled all day, noted the flush in her daughter's cheeks and the overbright light in her eyes.

"Summer flu," the doctor diagnosed the following afternoon, when her feverish symptoms hadn't diminished. "Just keep her quiet. It'll run its course."

And it had. It went from child to child, choosing discriminately not to infect two at once, so that instead of Britt being done with sick children in three days, the time stretched to nine days, to eleven.

Christy was the last to come down with it, and the most troublesome patient because her headache wouldn't allow her to read.

"*Please* let me get up and watch television," she pleaded pathetically. "I'm bored, Mom."

Britt, who'd been up with retching children almost every night for the past two weeks, was hot and headachy herself. *No,* she thought. *I don't have time. Not me.*

"In a little while," she said, fluffing pillows and pouring more orange juice. "Let me get some blankets and pillows set up on the sofa."

Christy sat back impatiently as Britt took away her lunch tray and went downstairs.

"You do not have to get sick," Britt told herself firmly. "You held financial destitution at bay by simply refusing to let it happen. You can stay well. You can."

But economics and germs, she soon discovered, did not operate in the same way. Her headache was getting worse, she could barely swallow and her muscles felt as though she'd just spent two hours with a personal trainer after thirty-three years as a couch potato.

On an emergency run to the market for Jell-O, the only thing she could digest, she ran into Cece.

Horrified gray eyes went over her diagnostically in the rice, pasta and beans aisle. "I give you twelve hours to live," Cece said, taking Britt's chin in her hand and turning her face from side to side. "Flu?"

Britt gently but firmly removed Cece's hand. "No. The kids have all had it, but I'm not going to get it. I don't have time. See ya. The kids are alone and I have to get home."

"Britt—"

"Bye, Cece."

JAKE MET Caleb Dutton at a party to promote a new product. Still invited to food-industry functions, he went, thinking he might meet the right contact with the right job.

Dutton, sipping champagne from a plastic glass, cornered him near the buffet table. "I hear you're unemployed."

Jake toasted him. "It was time for a change. How are you?"

Dutton grinned. "The change wouldn't be shapely and redhead, would it?"

Jake returned his grin, while conflicting emotions churned in him. He'd forgiven Britt's accusations, even though he understood where they'd sprung from, but he'd hoped to retain a little pride by making her call first. She hadn't.

"How's Yes! Yogurt doing for you?" he asked, trying to keep the conversation on business.

"Great," Dutton replied. "I owe you for putting us on to it. What have they got, anyway? I'm not going to get it standing here talking to you, am I?"

Jake sipped his champagne. "Got? What do you mean?"

"Mrs. Hansen had an appointment with me yesterday morning that she had to cancel. Said the kids were sick."

Jake's attention sharpened. "Which one? Sick with what?"

Dutton frowned. "That's what I'm asking you. I figured it must be fairly serious for her to cancel the appointment. We were going to talk about upping our order and adding salad dressing. Jake?"

Jake had slapped his glass onto the table and was already halfway to the door.

"YOU'RE GOING TO DROP in your tracks!" Cece warned, following Britt around the kitchen as she nibbled on a triangle of dry toast and heated chicken soup for Christy. "Then what good will you be to your children?"

"They need me," Britt said, her voice hoarse, her face white. She scuffed across the tile in baggy gray sweats and slippers. "I have to keep going. The business . . ."

Cece picked up the spoon Britt dropped on the floor and tossed it into the sink. Britt watched the movement, her eyes glazed, then took another from the tall cup of utensils on the counter.

"The kids need you," Cece shouted, "the farm needs you, the goats need you, your accounts need you! Don't *you* need anybody?"

Britt turned a slow, painful gaze on her. Her eyes hurt abominably. "I could use a friend," she said, "so stop yelling at me."

"As your friend and your medical professional," Cece said with desperate patience, "I'm telling you to get some rest before you do irreparable damage to yourself. If you don't stop right now, I'm calling Brick.''

"He's on duty today. Don't you dare bother him.''

"Well, I'm going to bother *somebody* if you..."

JAKE HEARD the argument from the other side of the screen door. He didn't bother knocking.

Britt and Cece turned as the door slammed closed behind him. Cece groaned in relief and went to him. "Thank God!" she said. "Maybe you can do something with her. The kids have been sick with the flu for more than a week, now she's got it and she won't stop. She should be in bed, but she won't listen to me.''

Britt stared at him. Her immediate reaction at the sight of him was joy. In jeans and a Northwestern sweatshirt, he looked large and fit and strong, and she felt weak enough herself at the moment to enjoy the notion of falling against him and letting him hold her.

But the joy was exhausting and short-lived. He hadn't called once. Even if it had all been her fault, he could have called. Something about that didn't compute, even in her befuddled state, but she wasn't sharp enough to sort it out.

She tried to square her sagging shoulders in the ratty old sweatshirt and ran a hand over her disheveled braid. She looked down her nose at him. "What brings you this time? Did Winnebago up the offer?''

He'd never seen her look so pathetic. Even the night he'd picked her up in Goose Run there'd been a spark in her eyes. Now illness and exhaustion had snuffed it. In oversize sweats, with her hair in a dull tangle, she made his heart contract painfully. But she still had enough sass to be sarcastic. He supposed that was a good sign.

He crossed the room to her, took the wooden spoon she was using to fend him off and dropped it in the saucepan on the stove. Then, resisting her fists easily, he lifted her in his arms.

Cece led the way upstairs.

"Jake Marshack," Britt said, pushing against his chest and bucking. "You put me down this minute! I am not a feed delivery!"

"Alfalfa isn't usually this noisy," he said, proceeding as though she were heavily sedated instead of struggling in his arms.

"I don't want you here," she said, pushing the heel of her hand against his pectoral muscle. He didn't seem to notice. She had to stop when the effort made her head spin.

"That's too bad," he said.

"I don't *need* you."

Cece swept back the spread and blankets and stepped aside to allow Jake to place Britt in the middle of the bed. "That," he said, pulling her slippers off, "is a lie."

The moment he straightened, she sat up and tried to swing her legs over the bed. He pinned them down with one hand and pushed her shoulder back to the pillow with the other.

"You stay there," he said, a threatening quality in his tone that stopped her on her elbows. "Or I'll forget that you're an invalid."

"Christy is sick," she said anxiously. "I have to get David to—"

"I'll take care of it," he said, his voice gentling as he put both hands under her to dislodge her elbow, and laid her back against the pillows. "You are not to worry about a thing, do you hear me? Or I'll have Cece give you something to knock you out."

"Cece wouldn't do that."

"Oh, yeah?" Cece, rooting through Britt's dresser drawer, looked up with a wicked grin.

Britt wheedled wearily, "Cece, how is he going to know the routine, the ... ?"

"It's all on your kitchen calendar." Cece produced a cotton nightgown and went to sit on the edge of the bed. "I'm off today and tomorrow. I'll take the kids wherever they need to go, and he'll be free to stay here and look after you and Christy."

"You have a job," Britt said crossly to Jake. "You can't spend your time here."

"I'll call in sick," he said from the foot of the bed.

"That would be a lie."

"Not," he replied, studying the carpet, "if I'm not specific about who is sick."

Britt folded her arms and stared out the window, betrayed. "Thank you," she said stiffly.

"Oh, don't pout," Cece scolded, "and show a little gratitude." She looked over her shoulder at Jake. "Why don't you check on that soup while I make her comfortable?"

Jake headed for the kitchen, detouring into the living room, where Christy was watching television. She was propped against a bank of pillows, her face pale but her eyes gleaming with interest. "Hi, Jake!" she called, flatteringly pleased to see him. "Did you come to take care of us?"

"Yes, I did." He leaned over her to kiss her forehead. "How you doin'?"

"I'm getting better, but my head still hurts so Mom won't let me go outside yet." She turned the smile to a pout that reminded him of her mother. "Mom promised I could sit on the porch today if it was sunny. And it is."

"I'll see if I can negotiate a deal for you. Ready for some soup?"

"Yeah." Christy reached up an arm to circle his neck and hug him. "I'm glad you're here."

"I'm glad, too. Now lie back, and I'll bring you some soup in a minute."

"CECE, I don't want him here," Britt said stubbornly as her friend helped her into the clean, cool nightie.

Cece's gray eyes scolded as Britt's head emerged from the neck of the gown. "Will you stop fighting? It must have become a reflex with you or something. He's here to help and you need help. Shut up and accept it gracefully."

Britt subsided, certain now there would be no help from any quarter.

JAKE BROUGHT soup on a tray and placed it on Britt's bedside table. Then he looked down at her, hands on his hips. "I'm going to carry Christy out to the porch swing after lunch," he said. "She's craving fresh air, and she really looks pretty good. What do you think?"

"What I think hasn't seemed to matter since you arrived," she said. "Do as you please."

The truth was she'd planned on letting Christy go outside in the afternoon, anyway, because she *had* looked improved that morning. But he didn't have to know that.

He sat beside her, pulled her toward him with one hand at her back and propped up her pillows. With both hands under her arms, he lifted her to a sitting position, then put the tray on her lap.

"Eat," he advised. "Maybe it'll improve your disposition."

She did. It didn't.

She heard the younger children come in from a trek to the lake with Judy and squeal excitedly because Jake was there.

Judy ran upstairs to say hello to Britt. "I'm glad to see you've finally given up and admitted you're sick," she said.

"I didn't admit anything. *He* brought me up here."

Judy waggled her eyebrows. "Lucky you. If you'd get rid of that long face, he might join you."

Britt sighed and closed her eyes. "You'd better leave before you catch something."

Wasn't anyone on her side?

BRITT SLEPT FITFULLY, tossing and turning with the increasing discomfort of sore throat and headache. Jake gave her a couple of pills during the night and bathed her face and throat with a cool washcloth. It felt so wonderful she couldn't even pretend animosity.

"Thank you," she said hoarsely. "How's Christy?"

"Fast asleep," Jake replied. "All the kids are. I just checked on them."

"You'd better get some sleep," she whispered. "I'll be fine."

She felt him lie down beside her and take her hand. She leaned her head against his upper arm and finally fell into a deep sleep.

When she awoke, it was raining. The clock read one o'clock. She propped herself on an elbow and stared. Judging by the fact that it was daylight and not dark, it must be one o'clock in the afternoon. She sat up and swung her legs over the side of the bed, determined to get up, but quickly changed her mind when stars snapped behind her eyes and her spinal column seemed to go limp.

She fell back against the pillows with a groan and felt herself drift off to sleep again.

BY THE EVENING of his second day on the job as Britt's nurse and nanny, Jake was beginning to feel as though he had things under control. Cooking was a skill he'd acquired to make his bachelor fare more interesting; cooking with three children crowded around him and asking questions God Himself might have had to think twice about was another matter entirely. But he was getting into it. They wanted only honesty, he was discovering, not brilliance.

He also did laundry, kept the toys and kitten debris to a minimum and kept a watchful eye on the yogurt operation, all with three children moving around him like little moons in eccentric orbits. It occurred to him during one particularly mellow moment—when he'd delivered popcorn to the kids on the living-room sofa and discovered they'd left a place for him—that he could have pulled in six figures a year and not felt as important, as vital to the progress of the world as they made him feel.

Matt remained remote, but Jake made a special point of talking to him, asking him things about the routine of the house and the foods the children preferred, trying to draw him into the tight little circle they were forming. Matt looked at him with that desperate need in his eyes, but resisted being drawn any closer than mere coexistence required.

BRITT WOULD SURFACE to awareness from time to time and hear laughter emanating from downstairs, or the low hum of earnest conversation. Occasionally the children would come upstairs, bright-eyed and full of stories about Jake—how he made pigs-in-a-blanket for breakfast, rescued David's balsa-wood glider from the big oak at the end of the drive, fixed Renee's broken doll with Krazy Glue, then pretended his thumbs were stuck together.

She'd grown superfluous, Britt decided, in a maudlin mood as the children raced downstairs for yet another adventure with Wonder Nanny. Everything was running fine without her. No one needed her—not her children, not her business, not Jake.

She found herself wishing he had to go back to work, then she'd entertain a vague memory of him lying beside her during the night, present but not intrusive. He'd never made a move toward her, but apparently neither had he made a move away when she turned to him, because she'd awakened once in the middle of the night sprawled over him. She'd whispered his name but he hadn't answered. Too tired to move, she'd let herself drift back to sleep, enjoying the solace of his arms.

Superfluous *and* pathetic, she decided. Maybe he'd been right. Maybe she was nothing more than a coward, after all. Still too headachy to examine the possibility too closely, she turned her face into the pillow and went back to sleep.

JAKE SWEPT the lace curtain aside without regard for its delicacy and frowned into the darkness. Matt hadn't come home after his paper route, hadn't appeared for dinner, and at close to nine o'clock there was still no sign of him. Christy had helped him call Matt's friends, and no one had seen him.

Worry chewed at his insides. He'd promised Britt he would handle everything. He'd never have a chance with her if he let anything happen to one of her kids.

Making the children promise not to say anything about Matt's absence, he'd sent them to bed, and had spent the past fifteen minutes trying to decide what to do.

He was about to dial Brick when headlights swept a ghostly pattern into the drive as a police car pulled up behind his Explorer.

He was outside and off the porch in one leap, his heart pounding. Brick appeared in the shallow wedge of light from the porch, pulling Matt out of the passenger side of his cruiser with a firm grip on his arm.

Even in the dim light, it was obvious the boy was green. He was huddled into himself, for the light shirt that had been adequate earlier had left him chilled when the sun went down. Jake guessed his subdued expression also had something to do with the grim look on Brick's face.

"What happened?" Jake demanded.

Matt stared at the ground while Brick turned him over to Jake. "Found him and the Monroe brothers in the park with a six-pack of beer and some cigarettes. I didn't think Britt'd be crazy about that, so I brought him home."

As Brick's eyes met his over the boy's head, Jake read a plea for compassion under the sternness.

Jake took hold of Matt's arm and felt him tremble. Feeling guilty and responsible, he looked at the boy in helpless frustration.

Matt glanced up at him, defiance warring with nausea and that nameless need always visible in his eyes. Jake made an instant decision.

"Thanks, Brick," he said. "I'll take it from here."

Brick assessed him for a moment, then nodded. "All right." As Jake turned the boy toward the house, Brick asked, "How's Britt doing?"

"She's slept for two days," Jake replied. "Cece wants to keep her down for the rest of the week. I think that would require bricks and mortar on her bedroom door."

Brick laughed lightly, then sobered. "Look, if you need backup with Matt—or with anything—call me."

"Thanks. I appreciate it.

Matt waited just inside the kitchen, leaning heavily on the back of a chair, his face alternately white and chartreuse. Jake closed and locked the door behind him.

"I want to talk to my mom," Matt said, his manner defiant, though his eyes sent a different message.

Jake approached him, arms folded. "She's asleep," he said. "I don't think she'd want to know how many rules you broke tonight. You want to tell me about it?"

Matt's eyes brimmed with misery. Jake waited patiently, trying to copy a look he'd seen Britt use successfully over and over again—a look that said she was open to discussion, but she wasn't taking any crap. Matt opened his mouth and Jake could almost see the words form on the tip of his tongue. Resisting the urge to grab him and shake them out of him once and for all was the hardest thing he'd ever done.

"No," Matt said finally.

Jake felt bitter disappointment. He remembered at that moment why he'd spent so many years avoiding the responsibility of family. It asked so much of you and you found yourself so completely unprepared.

"Okay," he said quietly. "I'm sure this must be getting old for you, but you're grounded again. The bike's off limits except for your route. You pull anything like this on me again, Matt, and you'll regret it."

The misery in Matt's eyes brimmed and spilled over. "I don't have to listen to you!" he shouted. "You're not my father!"

Jake grabbed the boy's shoulders and gave him a small shake. "Matt, your father is gone, and at the moment I'm what you've got. I took over for your mom until she's well again, and that means it's my job to *make* you do what I say, whether you want to or not."

"I can take care of myself!"

"Really? Well, how smart was it to sit out in the park without a jacket four days after having had the flu?" He put a hand to Matt's cheek and found it cold and clammy. "How smart was it to be caught with beer when you know I'm going to come down on you for it?"

"I don't...!" Matt's angry reply was suddenly derailed by a dry heave, a look of horror in his eyes, a desperate hand over his mouth.

Jake got him to the small bathroom off the kitchen just in time for him to rid himself of a novice's reaction to alcohol and nicotine. Matt retched and cried. Afraid he would choke, Jake ran a gentling hand over his back as he soaked a washcloth under the cold-water faucet with the other. "Take it easy," he coaxed quietly. "Just relax. Relax."

Finally finished, Matt flushed the john, closed the lid, then fell on top of it, all defiance gone as he cried his heart out.

Jake sat on the floor and leaned against the wall, pulling Matt on his knee and running the washcloth over his face. Tears streamed down the boy's cheeks faster than Jake could mop them up.

"Today..." Matt sobbed, his thin shoulders heaving against Jake's grip, "was his birthday."

Jake rinsed the cloth again and reapplied it. "Whose birthday?"

"My dad's!" The words exploded in anguish.

Jake tossed the cloth into the sink and pulled Matt into his arms, finding little difficulty in relating the boy he held to the grieving boy he'd been when his own father died all those years ago. Matt offered no resistance, just wrapped his arms around him and held on, trapped in his grief.

"I know how much you miss him," Jake said gently. "I wish I could do something to make it hurt a little less, but I can't. It just has to burn, then one day it'll be a little better."

"Nobody even thought about him today," Matt wept on. "Not even Mom."

"She hasn't forgotten him," Jake assured him, rubbing his back, his hunched shoulders. "She's feeling pretty sick right now. The flu hit her hard because she was tired from working such long hours to pay all the bills.''

Matt nodded, sobs quieting, his body leaning against Jake's. "I know. It's all my fault, anyway.''

Jake frowned down at him. "What's your fault?''

Matt straightened away from him, a pleat forming between his brows as he concentrated on some thought or image visible only to himself. "That my father died.'' He said the words calmly, quietly, but they rang strangely in the little room.

Jake was sure he'd misunderstood him for a moment, then Matt looked into his eyes and guilt shone there, hot and barbed and excruciating.

"What do you mean?'' Jake asked.

Matt expelled a ragged sigh. "Mom and Judy had gone to Chicago, and I was supposed to come home right after school to help Dad with the chores, because he had to take the other kids to all their lessons. But me and Stinky stopped to shoot a few hoops and took the later bus: I got home late.'' He shook his head as though he wanted to stop, but Jake rubbed his back and urged him to go on.

"He took my bike away, and he said if I couldn't learn to do the things I was asked to do, then I'd have to learn to do without the things I like.'' His face contorted and his breathing grew shallow. Jake held him close, knowing something that had festered for a year was about to come out. "I was walking away, and I said under my breath—'' a sob scraped his throat ''—I said, 'I'd like to do without *you.*' He didn't hear me, and I—I didn't mean it, but I said it and then…he died!''

"Oh, Matt!'' Jake held the boy as he fell into a new paroxysm of weeping. He could only imagine how that misplaced guilt had hurt and infected everything Matt had done since his father's death. "That wasn't your fault,'' he said firmly. "Everybody backtalks like that.

It isn't right, but it's a natural reaction to being deprived of something you like to do, even when you deserve it. But what you said didn't cause your father to die. He had an accident that had nothing to do with you!"

"No," Matt insisted. "I said—"

Jake pushed him back and made him look at him. "You are not responsible for your father's death," he said, trying to speak with the absolute conviction he knew the boy needed to hear. "I'll bet you every kid in this world has reacted the same way to his parents at one time or another. Do you think they're responsible for all the accidents that happen, for all the parents who die before their time?"

Jake could see in Matt's eyes how desperately he wanted to believe. "But it happened right after—"

"That doesn't matter. He was hurrying to get done because he had extra things to do. Maybe he got careless, or maybe an edge of the ditch gave way. I don't know what happened. What I do know is that it wasn't your fault."

"But I—"

"It wasn't your fault!"

Matt's eyes brightened just a little. "You don't think so?"

"I *know* it wasn't your fault. When someone we love dies, we tend to take the blame one way or another because it helps explain something that seems so wrong to us. But there comes a time when you just have to understand that that's the way life works. People are born, and people die, sometimes before they've really had a chance to live. Sometimes when there are a lot of people around who'll really miss them—like your dad had. But it's the way life is, and it's something we can't change. Blaming yourself doesn't change it. It just prevents you from doing the things you have to do."

Matt leaned against Jake as tears continued to spill over. Jake wet the washcloth one last time and handed it to him. ''Now, wash your face and let's get you to bed. We've got a big shipment going out tomorrow. It's going to take all of us to get it out on time.''

Jake got to his feet, pulling Matt up with him. Then he noticed Britt standing in the doorway in her bathrobe. Her face was pale, her eyes huge and spilling tears, her hair freshly brushed and braided.

Matt ran to her and she wrapped him in her arms. As they cried together, Jake left the room.

CHAPTER SIXTEEN

BRITT TUCKED Matt into bed as though he were three years old. He looked familiar again after a year of looking a little like a stranger, and she felt as if she'd regained her firstborn through some long-awaited miracle.

She leaned down to hug him fiercely. "I don't want you to think about being to blame ever again," she said urgently. "Do you understand me?"

"Yes." He hugged her back, then looked at her in a kind of wonder. "You don't think I did it, either?"

"No. You heard Jake. Life does unfair things and you just have to accept that. Your father loved you very much, Matt. He loved all of you, but you were his first son and he was very, very proud of you. He loves you now, so think about him, but pick out your favorite time with him and use that to remember him."

Matt nodded, his smile open and free. "Are you feeling better?" he asked. "You still look pretty awful."

She gave him a mocking frown. "Thank you very much. Now, go to sleep. Sounds like Jake has lots for you to do tomorrow."

"He was nice to me," Matt said, leaning wearily into his pillow. "Even when I wasn't very nice to him."

She stood and turned off the light. "I guess because he knows a good kid when he sees one, even if the kid isn't acting like it at the time. Good night."

"I think it's because he loves us." Matt's voice followed Britt to the door. She paused, about to argue with that suggestion, but heard Matt's soft even breathing and knew he'd be asleep in a moment. She closed the door instead.

WHEN SHE GOT DOWNSTAIRS, Jake had straightened the kitchen and was making his bed on the sofa. She went as far as the coffee table, leaving it as a barrier between them as he turned, pillow in his arms, to see what she wanted.

His eyes were carefully remote, she noted, a little like Matt's had been until a short hour ago. She had caused that, she knew. She and her accusations. Still not completely sure they were unfounded, she was now more confused than ever.

"Are you . . . comfortable down here?" she asked.

Comfortable, he thought. Interesting question. No, he hadn't been comfortable, he'd been miserable. Having lain with her in his arms one night to help her finally get some sleep, he'd discovered he didn't have the fortitude he'd thought he had. He'd wanted her desperately, continually.

But all she did was look at him with those uncertain, doubtful eyes. It made him want to lay her in the middle of the sofa and make such love to her that there wouldn't be room for a sliver of doubt in her brain or in her heart.

He studied the dark smudges under her eyes, the stunned emotion in them from the episode with Matt, and had to remember that she was still an invalid, still considered him suspect.

"Sure," he replied, giving the pillow in his hands a heartfelt punch before tossing it to one end of the sofa. "I'm comfortable. You need anything before lights-out?"

"Yes, I need something," she replied, pursing her lips impatiently. He had to look up at her eyes; her puckered mouth was too inviting. "I need to thank you for helping Matt. I couldn't have handled that better and I'm his mother."

Hands resting loosely on his hips, he shrugged. "You're also a woman. Psychologists can teach us intergender communication and all the other stuff that's supposed to help us get along more smoothly in the nineties, but under it all, it takes a man to fully understand another man. We feel responsible for everything, even for the things we can't do anything about. He assumed the blame for his father's death, probably because he didn't know how else to explain it, and I'll wager that the destructive behavior that's been driving you crazy was his way of earning the punishment he thought he deserved. Hopefully that's over now." He gave her a grim smile. "Until he meets a special girl and discovers that he can have patience with the working of a woman's mind, but he'll never understand it—not really."

It was a carefully worded accusation. She didn't know how to respond, so she ignored it. She did feel that his assessment of Matt was on target. "I appreciate that you took time with him. Thank you."

"Sure." He nodded. "Now, hop into bed before you get chilled."

"Ja-a-ke?" A child's plaintive cry came from the top of the stairs. Renee's voice.

Britt followed him to the foot of the stairs, where he stopped to look up at Renee. She wore yellow cotton pajamas, the too-long legs rolled up. "Yeah?" he asked.

Renee rubbed her eyes, gave her mother a cursory wave, then said plaintively, "The closet door's open."

"Why don't you close it?" he asked.

" 'Cause there could be something in it," she said, her voice whiny with fear. "I want you to close it."

Britt started up the stairs. "I'll do it, Renee," she said.

Renee shook her head. "I want Jake to do it."

Jake loped up the stairs, giving Britt a faintly superior lift of his eyebrow as he passed her. He swung Renee onto his hip and spoke quietly to her as he took her back to the room she shared with Christy.

Britt leaned against the railing and pulled herself up the stairs, vaguely jealous at having been replaced as monster-buster. In a very short time Jake had given her children that little extra edge of security that came with size and muscle—something she just couldn't provide.

When she passed the girls' room, Renee was giggling. Britt climbed into bed, feeling dejected, *rejected*.

"You need your closet door closed?"

Britt lifted her head off the pillow as Jake moved like a shadow to the side of her bed.

"I'm fine," she said a little stiffly, then dropped her head back.

He pulled at the blankets she'd disarranged. "Now don't get huffy," he said, his voice quiet and amused, "just because the kids are sharp enough to trust me."

"I'm not huffy."

"You're pouting."

"I'm not. I'm trying to go to sleep."

She jumped when she felt his hand caress her cheek, his thumb run across her lips. Sensation ran riot inside her.

"Your bottom lip's hanging out three inches," he said. "I can feel it."

She caught his wrist to yank it away and immediately regretted the action. She had hold of warm, tensile muscle that lay passive in her grip one moment, then turned on her the next, catching her hand and drawing it to his lips. He kissed her knuckles.

"You're feeling stronger," he said. "I don't suppose you need me anymore."

A sharp "I don't suppose I do!" poised on the tip of her tongue, but a long family tradition of honesty prevented her from saying it.

"Good night," she said instead.

His hand stroked her hair, tucked the blankets in around her shoulder. "Good night," he replied, and left the room.

JAKE WAS expertly flipping pancakes when Britt wandered downstairs the following morning, determined to resume control of her day and her family. The girls were setting the table while David poured food into Daffy's dish in a corner of the kitchen; the kittens were lapping milk from a communal bowl and Matt was pouring juice into a lineup of glasses.

"Good morning," she said, already feeling control slipping away from her.

The children interrupted a spirited argument about going back to school to give her hugs and welcome her once again to the living. Matt was clear-eyed and smiling, she noted with a renewed sense of wonder and gratitude.

As they went back to their chores, she looked over Jake's shoulder. "You've got to stop spoiling them like this," she said. Then, seeing the blueberries in the plump cakes, she felt her long-dormant appetite suddenly sharpen. "I love blueberry pancakes," she confessed, forgetting she'd planned to be aloof this morning.

"The kids told me," he said, paying more attention to his cooking than to her. "I thought this might encourage you to eat a little today. Sit down. Want tea instead of coffee?"

"Please." She went to her chair, feeling disgustingly malleable.

Britt was chewing slowly to accustom her stomach to the prospect of food, and savoring every delicious bite, when the telephone rang.

Matt went to answer it as Jake brought Britt a cup of tea.

"Mom!" Matt whispered sharply, holding the phone against his chest and making frantic beckoning motions with his free hand.

"Who is it?" she whispered, going to him and reaching for the receiver.

His eyes wide, he said softly, "The 'Oprah Winfrey Show.'" Everyone at the breakfast table, Jake included, looked up.

Britt rolled her eyes at his joke and snatched the phone from him. "Cute," she said. "Just for that I get your second helping of pancakes. Hello?"

She reached to the counter for support when a sparkling young voice identified herself as representing the producer of the "Oprah Winfrey Show." Jake placed a chair under Britt and eased her into it, putting a pad and a pen in her lap.

Everyone was talking about her yogurt, the young woman said. Oprah, on a new, less-radical diet, had picked up a carton at a Favorite Foods outlet the previous week and had had one for lunch ever since. Would Britt consider appearing on the show the day after tomorrow, and would she bring some of the other products Michael Buchanan had told Oprah about when she'd called him to find out how to reach her?

"Me?" Britt asked dumbly, her saucer-size eyes automatically turning to Jake and her children. "On television?" Her voice came out high and broken.

"The twenty-seventh of August," the young woman said. "The day after tomorrow. Is that too short notice? We know we're rushing you, but we thought you might be able to fit us in since you're so close to Chicago, and we'd like to schedule you before Phil or Sally find out about you.''

Her eyes widened further and her jaw dropped. Sally or Phil...?

Jake and the children were now clustered around her, Jake encouraging her to accept with a deep nod, the children whispering frantically, ''Do it, Mom! Say yes!''

Terror grabbed her by the throat. She opened her mouth to reply and nothing came out. She cleared her throat and dug deep inside herself for coherence and control.

''Yes, of course,'' she replied evenly. Was that her voice? ''I'd love to. Where do I go and what time...?''

While she scribbled notes, Jake and the children tightened into a knotted hug. Renee jumped up and down and Jake had to put a hand over her mouth to muffle the squeals until Britt hung up the telephone.

She stood and turned to them in a kind of trance, the little bit of color she'd regained that morning gone completely, her eyes still filled with disbelief.

''I'm going to be the featured guest,'' she said, her voice flat with numbness, ''on the 'Oprah Winfrey Show.' Day after tomorrow. I—I can't... believe it.''

Jake eased her back into the chair and sent Christy to the table for her tea. ''Take a deep breath,'' he said, ''then tell us everything.''

''I'm going to be on the 'Oprah...''' she began again, her eyes unfocused.

''You told us that, Mom,'' Matt said. ''How did she find out about you?''

''I don't know...'' Then she remembered about Oprah's fateful purchase at a Favorite Foods store. She related what she could recall, took a sip of the tea Christy brought, then looked up at Jake and said, her eyes brightening a little, "I'm going to be on television."

"What else, Mom?" Christy knelt beside her, her cheeks flushed. "What else did she say?"

In a state of mild hysteria, Britt laughed, then put a hand over her mouth and said with an affected tilt of her eyebrow, "They know they're rushing me, having me on the show the day after tomorrow, but they wanted to get me before Phil and Sally discover me."

Christy screeched. "Phil Donahue and Sally Jesse Raphael?"

Britt put her hands over her face and stomped her feet on the floor. "Do you believe it?" she squealed.

As the children giggled with her and dragged more details from her, Jake cleared the table, smiling to himself. There'd be no stopping her now. It paid to have connections. All he could do was hope he hadn't connected himself right out of her life.

He was mulling over that possibility when he was suddenly grabbed by both arms and yanked around to face her. She was certainly regaining her strength, he thought.

"You've got to come with me!" she said. The desperation, the need, was in her voice, in her grip, in her eyes. "Please! Tell the dairy you're still sick. Tell them you *died,* but you've got to come with me!"

He played it cool. "Who's going to stay with the kids?"

"I want to bring them with us."

There was pandemonium as the children squealed and cheered and danced around the kitchen. When the chaos had abated, Jake pretended to consider her request—or rather, her demand.

"I suppose we could go up tomorrow," he said. "Buy you something to wear, stay overnight at my place...."

More shouts and dancing, more chaos.

Britt threw her arms around him. "Oh, God," she groaned. "I should have said no. I don't think I can do this. Do you think I can do this? What if I say something stupid? What if I freeze? God, what if I trip walking on camera? You *have* to come with me."

"I'll come with you as far as the greenroom. After that, it's your baby."

She frowned. "The greenroom? What's that?"

"Where you wait to go on. Kind of a quiet room where you can watch what's happening on a monitor and pull yourself together."

She put a hand to her stomach. "I'm going to be sick."

"You've *been* sick," he reminded her. "But you're well now. I know this is scary, but you can do it. Just pretend you're telling a new client about your product."

"Instead of forty million people."

"Right."

"I'm going to be sick."

JAKE KEPT his patience and his sanity in the days that followed by gripping them with both hands. Between the children running through his apartment, trying the garbage disposal, the trash compactor, the Jacuzzi and his Nautilus equipment, and Britt vacillating between almost catatonic hysteria and raving good cheer that involved nonstop talking and an endless collection of corny jokes, he was afraid he'd have to have himself committed before she made her TV appearance.

Taking them shopping was no less harrowing. Keeping four children from harm and within reach in a big city with all its attendant dangers was almost as character-building as helping Britt select a dress. The only benefit to the four hours she required to make a decision was that by that time the children were exhausted and all sitting at his feet against the chair in which he waited. Renee had climbed into his lap, collapsed like fifty pounds of elbows and knees and gone to sleep.

The department buyer kept smiling at him indulgently and bringing him cups of coffee. He prayed for a robbery, a fire, a bomb threat—anything that would finally get him out of that lavender-carpeted stronghold of sequins, lace and triple mirrors.

Then Britt came out in this mauve thing that was the last style he'd have chosen but did dynamite things to her body. V-necked in the front, suggesting without revealing, it had long sleeves and skimmed her thighs about an inch above her knees. It was completely unadorned except for large buttons down the front to the hemline. It made her breasts look larger and her legs longer, yet the whole effect was seductively demure. He knew instinctively it would sell anything.

Sometime in the course of trying things on, she'd pulled the fastener out of her hair and it now lay around her bare throat and softly molded shoulders like a glimpse of dawn. The color of the dress turned her eyes lavender. He felt weak with love and admiration. He also felt a vague trepidation.

It was one thing to know what she was capable of, but it was quite another to see her transformed before him. Everything she'd been through in the past year, all she'd endured since he'd known her—the hard work, the struggle, the desperate attempt to keep the threads of her children's world together—was wrapped up in those few yards of mauve crepe.

She presented the image of woman—softness, strength, sincerity, sunshine.

He realized with a sharp glimpse of truth that she'd be just fine on her own. She didn't need him. How, he wondered, had he come to need her so desperately?

BRITT LAY on her back in Jake's bed and stared into the darkness. The boys slept in one of the condo's two spare bedrooms, the girls in the other. Jake had left his bedroom to her and was sleeping on the sofa. She wondered if the arrangement was out of a wish to be responsible and discreet in front of the children, or a cooling of interest in her.

In just a few hours she was going to appear before millions of people on national television, and she wanted nothing more at the moment than to be held in Jake's arms and reassured that she would not make an idiot of herself.

She rose on her elbows as she realized she just needed to be held in Jake's arms—she didn't particularly care whether she had a reason or not. He'd become such a vital part of her life—such an important part of her children's lives—that she couldn't imagine the future without him.

On a business level, she was approaching some scary decisions. She'd prefer to make them with his advice. But he had his own career to consider. She couldn't tie his corporate dreams to a fledgling company that seemed to be headed for miraculous success, but was still prone to the hundreds of pitfalls that lay in wait for any new business.

She curled into her pillow and smiled into the dark at the images that had run through her mind most of the night. Jake in jeans and a T-shirt, hauling lumber with Brick, or moving a heavy piece of equipment into place, shoulder and back muscles rippling, strong biceps and ready laughter making it look easy. Jake at the stove in her kitchen, children crowded around him, flipping pancakes, French toast, and bacon and eggs all at once and with the same competence with which he'd built a buck barn. Jake watching television with Renee asleep in his arms and Christy leaning lazily against his shoulder; Jake on the back-porch steps with Matt and David on either side of him, talking about girls.

Then, unbidden, the memory of the ugly accusations she'd thrown at him the day he'd come to the farm to extend Winnebago's offer crowded in around her, haunted her. With the wisdom of hindsight, she knew Brick had been right. Jake had simply brought to her what he'd thought to be a good offer, and she'd reacted like a shrew because it had been the offer that had brought him back and not her dynamic attraction. She shook her head ruefully over her own ego.

Dawn crept around the edges of the curtains as she swung her legs out of bed and pulled on her robe, determined to apologize, to tell him how much she needed him, to ask him to take her on as a partner in life and in business.

As she walked stealthily into the shadowy living room, she discovered she wasn't the only one with insomnia. Jake was propped on an elbow on the sofa, Renee and David sprawled over and beside him, talking about what it would be like in the television studio and whether or not their mother would end up on "Knots Landing."

Television studio. Terror developed anew, erased the thought of making peace with Jake and brought back the fist that had lived in her stomach since the telephone call two days ago.

"I'll fix breakfast," she said at Jake's assessing glance. "I need something to do."

The children chattered excitedly while they ate breakfast. Britt nibbled on a piece of toast and thought how different the apartment looked this morning. Its usually pristine, monochromatic decor had been rearranged by her children. There were splashes of color everywhere—Renee's Barbie doll on the sofa, Matt's red-and-gold sweatshirt in a chair, David's favorite yellow fire engine in the middle of the carpet, the flowered tights Christy had bought with her allowance the day before draped over a lamp table.

She glanced at Jake, wondering if he'd noticed the disorder. He was leaning back in his chair watching her, his eyes quiet and unreadable.

"Getting nervous?" he asked.

She drew in a slow breath and let it out. "I've been on the brink of a breakdown since the call came. I hope I don't blow this."

He shook his head as though that possibility didn't exist. "I'm sure America will love you. You've got everything you need? We can run out this morning for any last minute—"

"No." She smiled into his carefully detached expression. "We got everything yesterday."

"Then why don't you take a long, slow bath while I clean up?"

She put a hand on his arm, stopping him as he reached for her cup and saucer to stack them with his. "I've got a better idea," she countered. "The kids and I will clean up while you take a shower."

At a look from her, the children began gathering plates and cups. She shooed Jake toward the bathroom.

The children were watching television and Britt was wiping off counters when it occurred to her to check through the condo for dishes. After the busy day yesterday, they'd collapsed early and gone to bed without tidying up.

She found popcorn bowls in the den where Matt and Christy had played video games, a cup near the sofa where someone had had cocoa, and a glimpse into Jake's room revealed a pottery mug on the dresser.

As she snatched it up, her glance fell on the document under it. It was the stub of a check with the Winnebago Dairy logo in the corner. It showed a pay-off figure on company stock, a profit-sharing plan, a quarterly bonus and a monthly salary prorated to a date a week or two before.

It took her a moment to comprehend what she saw. This was the stub of a severance check. No wonder Jake had been free to nurse her through the flu and bring her to Chicago. He'd quit his job. Or been fired.

She carried the cups and bowls into the kitchen, then, sure the children were still occupied, went to the bathroom door and rapped sharply.

"Yeah?" Jake asked.

"Are you decent?"

There was an instant's hesitation. "Somewhat," he replied finally.

She opened the door to find him standing in front of the sink, wearing a towel around his hips. He was shaving with a straight razor. One side of his face was still lathered. His hair was wet and uncombed, his eyes wary as she closed the door behind her and leaned against it.

"What's the matter? The kids okay?"

"The kids are fine," she said. "I'm the one who's upset."

He studied her another moment, then went back to the job at hand. "So what's new?" he said amiably. "Lately, you're always upset about something. You're going to get old before your time, Britt, if you don't loosen up."

She pushed shaving cream, deodorant and hair tonic aside and hiked herself up onto the bathroom counter. She looked into his eyes while they concentrated on the mirror.

"Did you get fired because of me?"

The barest blink was his only reaction to her question. He shook the razor into the little pool of water in the sink and made a long, smooth stroke from chin to cheekbone. "No. Why?"

"Because I found this on your dresser." She waved the check stub.

He glanced at it in the mirror, then made another stroke of the razor exactly parallel to the last. "Snooping?" he asked.

"Collecting cups and bowls for the dishwasher. Why did you get a severance check if they haven't fired you?"

He worked with careful concentration over his chin, then dipped the razor into the water again without looking at her. "Because I quit."

She angled her jaw. "Because of me? Was it a choice of your having to stop helping me or lose your job?"

He went to work on the few patches of shaving cream he'd missed. "They didn't believe me when I told them you wouldn't be receptive to a bigger and better offer. I got tired of arguing."

Having had enough of his nonchalance, she grabbed the razor, dropping it onto the counter and looked up at him, her eyes angry.

"Why didn't you tell me?"

He picked up a towel and wiped off the excess shaving cream. "Why should I? It really had nothing to do with you."

"You wouldn't come back to me with the second offer because of the way I reacted the first time. That has to do with me."

He folded thick arms over nicely rounded pecs and leaned a hip against the counter. Britt felt her breath congeal and her pulse accelerate in the humid little room. She made herself concentrate on his face.

"You think you scared me?" he asked with an amused little smile that both shamed and annoyed her. "I didn't come back with the offer because I understood that you didn't want to sell. That this was something you'd pulled together by yourself, and it had come to mean more to you than you probably even intended when you started out. I didn't come back with the offer because I respected that in you and I wanted you to have it without any more hassles.''

They were about a foot apart in the narrow space, and she felt his gaze like a touch. It was full of love and kindness and a curious hint of pity.

"But it cost you your job," she whispered.

He shrugged a square shoulder. "You meant more to me than the job."

"But the vice presidency...?"

"Relax, will you?" He straightened and reached for the bottle of Old Spice. "They've since approached me about coming back. Apparently the new vice president took a woman who wasn't his wife to a company conference weekend, ruining the family image Winnebago likes to present."

She watched him pat on the cologne. "Are you going to?"

"I don't know." He replaced the bottle and closed the cabinet. "I'm thinking about it."

"It's what you've always wanted."

"It used to be."

She reached out a hand to him, suddenly needing desperately to touch him, to talk this out, to explain everything she felt. "Jake, I—"

"Mom! Jake!" David bellowed through the door. "I have to go!"

"Use the other bathroom, Dave," Jake called back.

"The girls are in it doing their *hair!*" He gave the word scornful emphasis. "I have to go really bad!"

Jake smiled wryly and opened the door. David shot in as Jake led Britt out.

"Mom!" Matt called from the living room. "Telephone. Brick and Karen want to tell you good luck!"

Frustrated, Britt looked helplessly at Jake. "We need to talk about this," she said.

He pushed her gently in the direction of the living room. "Take the call while I put some clothes on. We'll talk later."

"But..."

"Mooom!"

CHAPTER SEVENTEEN

BRITT WAS PACING the greenroom minutes before she was scheduled to walk onto the soundstage, and she and Jake still hadn't talked. More friends and family had called to wish her well, then it had been time to get dressed. The children had talked excitedly, continuously, in the car on the way to the studio. Her nervous agitation had begun to develop a second head of steam anyway, and clear thought had been impossible since they'd closed the greenroom door behind her. Except that she knew something important remained unresolved in her life, and she didn't think she could take this important step without fixing it.

"The music's starting, Mom!" Christy called in a loud whisper. Britt had asked the children to remain quiet so that she could pull herself together. Their sotto voce exclamations of excitement and awe would have been comic had she been able to relax enough to laugh.

Then a production assistant appeared to take her onstage. She turned to Jake, her eyes desperate.

He walked her to the door. "You're going to be fine. Just remember you're the one whose accomplishments got Yes! Yogurt on the 'Oprah Winfrey Show.'" He tilted up her chin and pinched it. "Now, go do your thing."

She had a million things to tell him, but the production assistant was urging her through the door, so she communicated in the only way that was quick and sure.

She stood on tiptoe, hooked an arm around Jake's neck and kissed him with all the love she felt for him.

Then she was being physically pulled down a dimly lit hallway to a room filled with blinding light and inky shadows.

She was advised to watch her step as she was led over wires and cables until she could see an audience, and Oprah, a camera in close, announcing her lineup of guests.

Then there was applause, the theme music, and she was being pushed to a waiting position just beyond camera. Oprah turned to give her an encouraging smile before someone raised a hand for silence and began the countdown.

IN THE GREENROOM, Jake and the children sat in a cluster on the sofa, their eyes glued to the television.

"There's Mommy!" Renee pointed to the screen as Britt walked on.

Jake saw the signs of nervousness, but doubted that anyone else did. Britt moved with confidence, the sides of her hair swinging back like a veil, her posture perfect. Only he saw the terror under the smile she turned on the audience.

"She looks beautiful," David breathed.

"She *is* beautiful," Christy corrected.

Oprah gave the audience a brief history of Yes! Yogurt, telling about its staggering success and then, quite kindly, about the position Britt had been in only a year before.

"On the edge of bankruptcy," she said gravely, "she took an idea, developed it into a product to fill a need, worked that gorgeous body day and night, turned down an offer from a major dairy to buy her out and now sits on a very promising little empire in southeastern Wisconsin. And you'll never guess what else."

Oprah turned to the audience in her intimate, conversational way, then added significantly, "She has *four children,* ages six to almost thirteen." There was a communal groan that seemed to signify empathy and admiration, then resounding applause.

The camera closed in and Britt smiled and blew a kiss. It was for her children, Jake knew.

"Brittany, what we want to know," Oprah said, leaving Britt alone in a chair before the camera while she walked into the audience, "is how the rest of us can take what would seem like the lowest point in our lives and turn it into success."

LATER, Britt couldn't remember much about her time in front of the camera, except that she finally began to feel comfortable when the audience asked questions about her children, her household, how she juggled and coped.

It was easy to relax and answer, because that was who she really was inside. This woman in the elegant dress, talking before studio lights and cameras, was a fun if nerve-racking persona to indulge for a few hours. But the real Britt had a life that revolved around the people waiting for her in the greenroom. She was developing a love for goats and the curious paraphernalia of her business, and reaffirming her devotion to Lakeside Farm and everything it would always mean to her.

After all questions had been asked and answered, Oprah ended the segment by dispensing cartons of Yes! Yogurt to the studio audience. She then produced her own, reading the nutrition panel on the back, making a point of displaying the spoon attached conveniently to the carton and taking a bite.

"Wave your spoons if you love it!" Oprah cried.

The enthusiastic reaction caused laughter in the audience and among technicians on the set.

"And the best part," Oprah went on, "is that she also makes *frozen* yogurt, cheesecake, salad dressing and a cheesecake Danish they can't keep in stock in Tyler, Wisconsin. Let's hear it for Brittany Hansen."

The audience applauded and waved spoons as the program went to a commercial break.

In a kind of daze, Britt was reunited with Jake and the children in the corridor. The producer's assistant ran to stop them from leaving. She pressed a fistful of messages into Britt's hand.

"These are people who want to place orders!" she said. "Our phones are ringing off the hook. You were a hit, Brittany." She winked at Jake. "Thanks for putting us on to her."

As the woman hurried away, Britt felt a trace of her customary control returning.

"You arranged this?" she asked, her eyes wide. Now that the show was behind her, fear had finally dissolved and reality was trickling back. She looked up into Jake's eyes and knew finally, unequivocally, that she loved him with a power that staggered her. And she needed him. God, she needed him.

As that knowledge filled her and flooded her senses, she held herself apart from the joy that tried to take over. Had he arranged this for her, she wondered, because, as usual, he'd wanted to do all he could to help her, or so that she'd be in a completely secure position when he accepted the Winnebago vice presidency and walked out of her life?

JAKE WATCHED her blue eyes cloud and darken and felt something inside him snap. Patience, forbearance and understanding fled. He grabbed her arm and strode to the door, barking at the children to follow. Britt, protesting, was forced to run to keep up with him. The children hurried after them, exchanging glances.

He put the kids into the Explorer, closed the door on them and turned his back to concentrate on their mother. Still he was aware of four little faces pasted to the windows.

"What?" he demanded of Britt. She'd wrapped both arms around herself in the sudden chill of a fall-like afternoon. "What?"

"What, what?" she asked absurdly, her voice rising as her temper began to surface. "What's the matter with you?"

"Nothing!" he snapped back. "You're the problem here. One minute you kiss me as though you can't live another day without me, then you learn *I* set up your appearance and I get the same look you gave me the day I brought you Winnebago's offer. What do you suspect me of this time?"

She looked him in the eye, still huddled into herself. She reminded him of Matt the night Brick had brought him home. She had that film of hostility in her eyes that covered a vivid longing he'd have sworn was for him.

"That you did it—" her voice came out high and tight and filled with unshed tears "—so that I'd be in a secure and comfortable business position when...you walk out of my life."

He blinked, stunned, once again confounded by the workings of her mind. The urge to shake her or strangle her kept him completely immobile for a moment. Then he walked around the car to the driver's side, saying over his shoulder, "That's it. I'm leaving and I'm taking the kids with me. A crazy woman like you obviously isn't capable of caring for them. If you come to your senses, call me and I'll—"

She caught him as he put his key in the lock, and turned him around. He felt her fingers digging through the sleeves of his sports jacket, saw that the hostility was gone from her eyes and that her need for him now screamed from them. She pinned him to the side of the Explorer with a strength that surprised him. Out of the corner of his eye, he saw four small faces swing toward the driver's-side window.

"Tell me I'm wrong!" she demanded, the tears now pooling in her eyes, turning them aquamarine. "Tell me that wasn't why you did it."

The look in her eyes tore at him, but he made himself sustain the anger. "So that the next time I do something you choose to question, I have to reassure you all over again that I've no ulterior motive?" He shook her off and tossed the keys in his hand. "No, thank you."

She moved between him and the vehicle door to prevent him from opening it. The tears were spilling over now, large and swift.

"I'm sorry about the Winnebago thing," she said, her mouth trembling. "I'm sorry about *this*. But I know you wanted the vice presidency and—and..." Her face and her composure crumpled. "This just doesn't happen to a woman twice. It just doesn't!"

He felt his anger vanish as he realized what she meant, what had prompted that look in her eyes. She didn't doubt him, she doubted fate. But he had to hear it from her.

He took her chin between thumb and forefinger and lifted it. Her tears fell onto his hand. "What doesn't happen twice?"

Tense, exhausted, terrified she'd alienated him for the last time, Britt looked into his eyes and replied honestly, "The perfect man. The soul mate. The partner who can be husband and father, lover, friend." Sobs choked her. She swallowed and tried to pull herself together. "I had that with Jimmy," she said, "and when I lost it...I didn't think it could ever happen again. Then you came along." She laughed through her tears. "Dudley Doright in a suit." When nothing changed in his expression, she wept anew, sure she'd lost him. "I think I just...couldn't believe it."

Then, miraculously, his arms came around her and she was gathered tightly to his chest. "Believe it, Britt," he said, his voice gravelly and unsteady. "I'm far from perfection, but I adore you and the kids. I want to go home with you to the dog and the kittens and the goats and all the wonderful people in Tyler."

Britt clung to him, sobbing, as he promised to love her and the children forever, to devote himself to the land and the town that meant so much to her, to help her in the business and take it as far as it could go.

She drew back and looked up into Jake's eyes, all the promises she wanted to make alive in her own. But before she could speak, they were surrounded by children, laughing and hugging and wedging in between them.

Renee clambered up into Jake's arms. "What did Mommy call you?"

"Dudley Doright," Matt answered for him, his arm wrapped around Britt.

David leaned against his mother. "Who's that?"

"A guy in a cartoon," Christy, tucked under Jake's free arm replied. " 'Bullwinkle,' I think."

Renee looked gravely into Jake's eyes. "Then are you Jake or Dudley?"

Christy smiled up at him. "Now he's Daddy."

Everything stopped inside Jake for a moment as he let himself enjoy the wonder of love and acceptance and, at last, family. He looked at Britt, unable to speak.

"We love you," she said.

"Yeah." Renee giggled and hugged him fiercely. "Daddy Doright!"

JAKE TURNED off the dark highway into Tyler, following the double column of old globed lights that lit Main

Street. He headed through town toward the road that would lead to Lakeside Farm and his new life as a family man. A glance into the back seat assured him that the children were asleep, sated with pizza, soft drinks and a new contentment for which he knew he was partly responsible. The notion was humbling.

He glanced at Britt in the seat beside him. She was looking out the window at the town square and all the turn-of-the-century buildings that were now as familiar to him as downtown Chicago.

"What are you thinking?" he asked quietly.

She turned to him with a sleepy smile and reached a hand toward him. He caught it and brought it to his lips.

"How much I love you," she said. "How much I love this place." She squeezed his hand. "I know it's after nine, but would you mind if we stopped by the Ingallses for just a minute? I'd love to run in and give Judson a big hug and tell him how much his belief in me has meant." She leaned toward Jake to kiss his cheek. "Almost as much as yours. I won't be long, I promise."

Jake complied, turning onto Elm Street and pulling to a stop across from the Ingallses' regal Victorian.

As Britt stepped out of the car, she saw Judson and Amanda get into Amanda's car. Something about the slump of Judson's shoulders made her uneasy. Then she noticed Alyssa standing in the open doorway in an elegant silk robe, a hand over her mouth in obvious distress. She waved as the car pulled away, but when it was out of sight, she buried her face in her hands.

Britt ran across the street and up the walk to the house. "Alyssa, what's happening?" She held out her hands and Alyssa took them, collapsing into tears. "Where is Judson going?"

"Oh, Britt!" Alyssa replied unsteadily. "My father's been asked to turn himself in to the police. He's being charged with Margaret's—with my mother's—murder."

And now,
an exciting preview of

CROSSROADS

by Marisa Carroll

the tenth installment of the
Tyler series

Dr. Jeffrey Baron and Cecelia Hayes were high school sweethearts, but that was a decade ago. They haven't seen each other in years. Now, a series of near-fatal accidents at Worthington House Retirement Center brings them together again. Jeff and Cece must deal with their reawakening love for each other as they race against time to discover what or who is killing the residents of Worthington House.

CHAPTER ONE

"MRS. HAYES! Please hurry! Something's terribly wrong with Mr. Badenhop."

Cecelia Scanlon Hayes, R.N., known to everyone in Tyler, Wisconsin, as Cece, shoved the metal-backed patient chart she'd been studying into the circular file on the counter of the nurses' station. "What is it?" she asked, her crepe-soled shoes making little sound on the vinyl-tiled floor of Worthington House Retirement Center's extended care unit as she hurried along. "What's wrong?" She moved past the agitated nurse's aide who had called her and into the patient's room.

"I don't know," the young woman responded. She looked scared, unsure of herself, the way Cece felt so often inside her soul these days but couldn't let show.

She took a moment to give the aide a calming smile as she moved toward Wilhelm Badenhop's bed, her practiced eye taking in details of his condition as she spoke. "Take a deep breath and start at the beginning."

"He was resting comfortably when I looked in on him half an hour ago. When I came back to check his intravenous line, I noticed he was barely breathing. Has he had a stroke or something?" the aide asked very quietly as she watched Cece rapidly examine the old man.

"I can't tell yet," Cece admitted, being careful not to let any of her own anxiety creep into her words. She wasn't seeing any of the expected symptoms of pneumonia and advanced arthritic deterioration, the medical problems that had brought Wilhelm to the unit, and it threw her off balance. "He's having a lot of trouble breathing. I'm going to increase his oxygen flow." Cece opened the valve on the metal cylinder at the head of the bed. Respiratory distress wasn't unusual in a patient suffering from pneumonia, but Wilhelm Badenhop's breathing was unusually slow and deep, not quick and shallow as she'd expected.

"Is he going to die?"

"Raise his head," Cece instructed, ignoring the question. "Then get the charge nurse to bring the emergency med tray and get Dr. Phelps on the phone. I don't like his color or his pulse rate."

"He looks like he's going to die." The young woman, Tracie, a part-time employee and second-year nursing student from the university, stood frozen at the end of the bed.

"Not if I can help it," Cece assured her, but she felt far less confident than she sounded. "We may have to get a breathing tube down his throat. Be sure there's one ready when Dr. Phelps gets here." She kept her fingertips on the old man's thready pulse. "Mr. Badenhop," she said loudly. "This is Cece Hayes. Can you tell me how you're feeling?"

No response.

"Tracie, do as I said," Cece ordered.

"Dr. Phelps isn't a-available," Tracie stuttered, as Cece pulled her stethoscope out of the oversize pocket of her white lab coat and prepared to slip the tabs in her ears. "Didn't you hear?" Her pale blue eyes fixed themselves on Cece's face. "He eloped with Marge Peterson—you know, from Marge's Diner—over the weekend."

"I was out of town over the weekend," Cece said, checking Wilhelm's IV setup. The bag of fluid was nearly empty but the unit seemed to be functioning properly. In any case, the only medication in the fluid was an antibiotic, nothing that would cause the perilous condition her patient was in at the moment. She glanced down at the old man once more. His color was slightly improved since she'd increased the flow of oxygen through the mask covering his mouth and nose, but his lips and the flesh beneath his fingernails were still dangerously blue.

"Then you missed the excitement," Tracie went on, making no move to leave the room. "No one knows for certain where they've gone."

"Someone's got to be covering for Dr. Phelps at Tyler Memorial," Cece snapped. She was only half listening to Tracie. Most of her attention was focused on Wilhelm's labored breathing. "Who is it?" Cece turned on Tracie, her gray eyes flashing. There was no time for this. The aide was going to have to learn that when a superior gave her an order, she should carry it out immediately. "Someone has to be on call. It doesn't matter who, just get them."

"It's Dr. Baron," Tracie said. She finally moved to do the nursing supervisor's bidding. "Dr. Jeff Baron."

"Great. That's all I need—Jeff Baron," Cece muttered. She took a deep, steadying breath. Now wasn't the time to worry about awkward meetings with the boy she'd once thought she loved more than life itself. She took a deep, steadying breath. "Get moving, Tracie." She made the words an order. "Get someone from Tyler Memorial over here. Stat! There's no more time to waste—he's going into arrest."

DR. JEFFREY BARON pulled out of the staff parking lot at Tyler Memorial Hospital and headed home. It had been a long, hot Sunday night in the emergency room. They'd been understaffed, as usual, and busy with sunburns, a case of food poisoning, two minor car accidents and a stab wound victim from a fight outside a bar on Michigan Street. Even in a town as small as Tyler, there was a wrong side of the tracks. And since the recession had begun, it seemed to take in more and more of the town.

He rubbed the back of his neck and rolled down the car window to let in the still-cool morning air. He was dead tired, but he only had time for a shower and shave before he'd have to head back across town to see George Phelps's morning patients. He made a mental note to have George's receptionist, Anna Kelsey, rearrange the appointments after today, move them back to afternoons, or he'd be dead on his feet before Wednesday.

Jeff didn't mind doing George a favor; he just wished the older doctor had let him in on his plans to elope with Marge Peterson so he could have shifted his own duty schedule around to balance the load. Thank God someone else would have to be responsible for George's administrative duties at Tyler Memorial. As it was, Jeff didn't know whom he'd find to fill in for him at the free clinic tomorrow. He didn't like the idea of his patients there having to go all the way to Sugar Creek for care. But if he didn't get some financial help for the clinic—and soon—they'd be making the drive on a regular basis, not just for the two or three weeks that Doc Phelps would be out of town.

Life seldom worked out exactly as you planned it. And then again, Jeff decided with a wry twist of his lips that just missed being a smile, if you were as much in love as Doc and Marge you didn't always look as far ahead as you should. He certainly hadn't wanted to listen to anyone or anything but his heart four years earlier, when both his grandfather and his mother had warned him that his marriage to a wealthy Chicago socialite would never work out.

It hadn't. In spades.

And he'd learned the hard way about never letting your heart overrule your head.

The emergency channel radio scanner under the dashboard crackled to life. Jeff listened to the tersely worded request for emergency help at Worthington House and realized with a jolt that the patients at the retirement center were his responsibility as well, until George returned from his honeymoon.

"Hell, what a day," he muttered under his breath. "It isn't even nine o'clock in the morning."

He made a U-turn in the middle of Elm Street to head back toward the old brick mansion that housed Tyler's only retirement home. By cellular phone he informed the Emergency Medical Service that he would need an ambulance and wondered just what kind of situation he was going to find at Worthington House.

He could handle just about anything they threw at him from a medical standpoint; he had no qualms about that. He wasn't so sure he could handle being face-to-face with the facility's new nursing supervisor. So far during the course of the summer he'd been able to avoid one Cece Scanlon Hayes. This Monday in August it looked as if his luck had run out.

CECE PULLED the sterile wrap off an endotracheal tube and made preparations to insert it in Wilhelm Badenhop's airway. He'd stopped breathing almost a minute earlier. She knew if she didn't attempt to resuscitate him immediately, his heart would stop beating.

"Help me," she ordered Juanita Pelsten, when the charge nurse joined her uncertainly at the old man's bedside.

"You're not authorized to intubate." Juanita made no move to assist her.

"I know that," Cece said, positioning the old man's head herself.

"None of the nurses at Worthington House have that authority, including the nursing supervisor," Juanita went on in an agitated whisper.

Cece tried to hold on to her fraying temper and her fear. Inside she was shaking like a leaf; outside she was solid as a rock. This was her first real emergency situation since the earthquake that had leveled the hospital where she'd worked in Nicaragua, killing her husband. She knew she was operating outside the boundaries of her authority just as Juanita did, but she couldn't stop to consider the consequences of her actions now. Her patient's life was all that mattered. Mrs. Pelsten was twenty-five years older than Cece. She'd been trained at a time when a nurse never questioned a doctor's order or acted on her own initiative. It wasn't her fault she was hesitant to take the responsibility now.

"Mrs. Hayes, you'll lose your job. Maybe your license," the woman cautioned, putting her hand on Cece's arm in gentle restraint. "We both will. He's old and sick. People come to Worthington House to die. Let him go in peace."

"No!" Cece hissed. "Not as long as there's a chance to save him."

"Step back and let her work, Mrs. Pelsten."

It was a man's voice—deeper and more mature, perhaps, but a voice she'd know anywhere, any time, even though she hadn't heard it in ten years. Cece didn't look up when a pair of strong, well-shaped male hands reached forward and helped her secure a breathing bag to the tube.

"Bag him," Jeff Baron instructed. "Mrs. Pelsten, get that emergency med tray over here. What have we got, Cece?"

She ignored the use of her first name. She'd always liked the way he said it. She still did.

"One of the nursing assistants came in to check on his IV meds and found him unresponsive and in respiratory distress. He arrested about ninety seconds ago."

Cece took a moment to glance up from her patient. Jeff was frowning as he surveyed the array of medications on the wheeled tray Juanita pushed toward him. She'd only seen Jeff a time or two in the weeks she'd been back in Tyler. From a distance, he'd looked much the same as he had a decade before. Now she could see the subtle changes time had worked on his features, turning a handsome, earnest boy into a man.

"We can't give up on him, Doctor."

Jeff turned his head. She could feel him watching her from eyes so dark a blue they were almost black.

Lord, how she remembered those eyes, achingly blue, with absurdly thick black lashes that had set her adolescent heart beating so wildly all those years ago.

She looked him straight in the eye and felt not a twinge of reaction; her heart was already beating so rapidly she thought it might burst.

"Get me an ampule of epinephrine," he directed over his shoulder to Juanita Pelsten.

He gave Cece look for look. She broke eye contact first, glad for the excuse to keep her attention fastened on her patient and the situation at hand. She went back to counting respirations, gently forcing air into Wilhelm's lungs, certain that Jeff would do everything he could to bring their patient back from the brink of death. He grabbed the syringe Juanita held out to him and injected the contents directly into the IV tubing running into Wilhelm's arm.

"Mrs. Pelsten, get a bag of glucose and start it running. We don't want to lose this vein if we can help it. We might need it later. Come on, you old geezer," he said under his breath. "Breathe!"

"He's not responding," Juanita said, although she picked up a plastic bag of intravenous solution and moved around the bed, behind Cece, to make the transfer.

"Don't give up on him yet," Jeff answered gruffly. "Keep it up, Cece, until he comes around. Then watch out. He'll probably make a grab for the breathing tube."

"Yes, Doctor." For one of the first times in her life she was grateful for the protocols they'd drilled into her in nurses' training. It helped not to have to address Jeff by his given name, the name she'd scribbled in countless notebooks all through high school. *Jeff. Jeffrey.* And the most exciting, wonderful of all, *Mrs. Dr. Jeffrey Baron.* How silly and foolish—and so very much in love—she'd been then. Thank God she'd gotten over him a long time ago.

Wilhelm Badenhop's eyes fluttered open. He began to claw weakly at his throat with his one free hand. Jeff reached past Cece to restrain him and their hands brushed, for only a second, but long enough for Cece to realize what she'd been thinking just moments before wasn't altogether true. When he touched her her whole body tingled with awareness, just as it had the first time they'd kissed, after the homecoming football game their sophomore year at Tyler High. She'd come alive that night, in her heart and soul, in a way that no other man, not even Steve, had been able to reproduce. She certainly wasn't happy to know the chemistry between them, at least from her point of view, was still potent and alive.

She didn't want anything to do with Dr. Jeffrey Baron, personally or professionally. The latter circumstances she could do nothing about, as long as she was working at Worthington House; the former, she had every intention of accomplishing.

The ambulance is here, Dr. Baron," the aide, Tracie, announced in a not-quite-steady voice, as she stuck her head through the doorway.

"Tell them to wait." Cece relinquished her place by the bedside so that Jeff could remove the breathing tube now that Wilhelm was breathing on his own. "Dr. Baron will let you know when it's safe to transport Mr. Badenhop to Tyler Memorial."

"I want to make sure he's stabilized first." Straightening, he caught Cece's eye, his wry look telling her more clearly than words that he knew what she was doing—hastily erecting barriers of professionalism and medical etiquette between them.

"Yes, Doctor," Tracie replied and disappeared down the hall.

"Mrs. Pelsten, will you check Wilhelm's vital signs while Mrs. Hayes and I try to figure out exactly what happened here?"

"Yes, Doctor," the older nurse said, just as meekly as Tracie.

"Will?" Jeff asked in a gruff but friendly voice, a man-to-man kind of voice, as he bent over the bed rail and patted the old man's shoulder. "Did you wake up feeling bad this morning?"

"No." Wilhelm shook his head weakly. "Throat hurts like hell now, though."

"We had to put a tube in to help you breathe for a while. Do you remember anything about what you did this morning?"

Wilhelm closed his eyes, thinking. Cece reached over the railing from her side of the bed and smoothed his wispy white hair back off his high forehead. "He's very alert mentally," she said, interpreting the slight frown between Jeff's straight dark brows to mean he wasn't certain of their patient's ability to recall the morning's events with any clarity.

"I know that," Jeff responded, again catching her eye for a brief, disconcerting moment. "I've known Wilhelm all my life, just like you have, remember?"

"Pulse and blood pressure returning to normal," Juanita announced as she removed the cuff from Wilhelm's arm. Cece looked away from Jeff's compelling gaze, spared from making an attempt at a halfhearted apology by the older nurse's interruption.

"Wilhelm?" Jeff said more loudly. He gave the old man a gentle shake.

"Ate breakfast," Wilhelm answered immediately.

"Freddie Houser brought in his tray," Juanita informed Jeff. "She helped him with breakfast. She's slow, not quite right, you know, poor thing. But she's good at what she does. She would have come to me at once if he'd had any trouble eating, or choked on his food."

"Didn't choke," Wilhelm said in a thin, raspy voice. "Fed myself. Didn't spill anythin', even with my arm all wired up like it is. I ain't clear senile yet, Juanita Pelsten."

Jeff chuckled at the old man's show of spirit, and Cece bit her lip to keep from laughing out loud. Wilhelm took a deep breath, then another. Cece let out a tiny sigh of relief. It was a good sign.

"Do you remember anything else?"

"Got sleepy." The old man shook his head. "Sleepin' a lot, you know, since I got sick. Can't remember nothin' else. Just bad dreams. Couldn't breathe..." His words drifted off. He moved restlessly, looking up at Jeff with frightened, faded blue eyes. "What the hell happened to me? Is somethin' wrong with my heart?"

Jeff shook his head. "I don't think so, but for some reason you stopped breathing. I want to send you over to Tyler Memorial for a day or two so we can run some tests, try to find out what caused this to happen, okay?"

"I guess so." Wilhelm sounded uncertain. "Don't like hospitals much. You'd better check with my grandson, Bob. He's helpin' me take care of most ev-

erythin' since I got sick. Damned arthritis, ya know.''
He lifted one gnarled and twisted hand a few inches off
the sheet. "Slows a man down somethin' fierce.''

"I know, Wilhelm." Jeff patted his arm. "I'll talk
to Bob as soon as I leave here. You get some rest now.
It might be a bit of a bumpy ride getting you out of
here on the gurney."

"Most excitement I've had in weeks," the old man
said dryly, but he closed his eyes obediently. "You
won't get too far away, will ya, Doc, in case I go off
again?"

"I'll be right here," Jeff assured him. "Mrs. Hayes
and I are going to be taking care of the paperwork to
get you transferred to Tyler Memorial."

"Helps a body rest a mite better, not being alone."
Wilhelm's eyes drifted shut but his breathing was
quicker, more regular, and Cece relaxed a little more.

"I think we're out of the woods," Jeff said, reading
her thoughts. Straightening, he shoved his stethoscope
into his traditional black bag.

Cece wondered if it had been given to him as a gift
or if he'd bought it for himself. She'd always dreamed
of buying him one when he was accepted into medical
school—and he would have given her an engagement
ring when she received her nursing degree. But when
that day came they were hundreds of miles apart,
completely estranged, and they'd never seen each other
again. Steve had been the man who gave her a ring and
his heart, but she'd lost him after only six years together. Jeff had married, also, although from what her
mother said, the marriage had been short and unhappy. She was sorry for that. Life seldom turned out
the way you thought it would.

"You're certain there was nothing unusual to report
about Wilhelm's condition over the weekend?" Jeff
asked, as he flipped through the pages of the old man's
chart.

"Nothing that I'm aware of. It was my weekend off," Cece explained, pushing the intrusive memories of the past out of her thoughts to concentrate on matters at hand. "I was in Chicago, visiting my... visiting Steve's parents."

Jeff shut the chart with a snap. He looked at her and she couldn't break away from the compelling blue of his eyes. "I was sorry to hear about your husband's death," he said a bit stiffly, formally. "I... I was having some problems myself when it happened, but that was no excuse for not sending my condolences. I apologize."

"Please don't," Cece replied, more harshly than she'd meant to. Her throat ached with the effort not to cry. She couldn't seem to help it when people mentioned her husband's death, although in the past few months the horror of the earthquake and the pain of his loss were slowly fading away. "I know you meant well. And the mail is very erratic in the rural areas of Nicaragua. It's possible your letter might never have reached me."

"Still, you have my sympathy."

"Thank you." The words hung awkwardly in the air between them.

The sounds of voices and movement in the hall saved her from any further difficult conversation about Steve's death, or Jeff Baron's divorce, because she was certain that was the problem he'd been referring to. And she certainly didn't want the subject to progress into a discussion of their own past history.

She wondered what Jeff might think if he knew just how familiar she was with the events of his life. Her mother had made certain of that. Annabelle Scanlon, Tyler's postmistress, had inordinate faith in the ability of the United States mail to be delivered to the farthest reaches of the globe, and she'd bombarded Cece with long, chatty letters about Tyler's residents. Jeff's whirlwind courtship of a Chicago socialite and the short doomed marriage that followed had been the talk of the town, paralleling as it did some of the scandalous aspects of his grandfather's ultimately tragic marriage to Margaret Lindstrom a half century before.

Suddenly Cece found herself wanting to tell Jeff how sorry she was about his grandfather's ordeal following the discovery of Margaret's long-dead body. It was hard to imagine Judson Ingalls being in jail. It was even harder to believe he was a murderer. The idea didn't mesh with the image of the tall, dynamic, white-haired man she remembered so vividly from her girlhood. But the opportunity to mention it passed as the paramedics wheeled the gurney into the room.

In the bustle and confusion of the next thirty minutes, she didn't have a chance to speak privately with Jeff again. And perhaps it was better that way. What, after all, did they really have to say to each other beyond a few polite, strained pleasantries? Jeff seemed just as happy as she was to have the familiarity of medical routine keep a small distance between them. He asked that copies of Wilhelm's chart and medication schedule be sent over to the hospital, took a few minutes to help her explain the situation to her boss, Worthington House's administrator, Cecil Kellaway, and then he was gone. Back to Dr. Phelps's office to see his patients, he said.

It was only later, as she sat in her cubbyhole of an office beneath the carved walnut staircase on the main floor, filling out yet more reports, that Cece recalled how tired he had looked. He must have been on duty at the hospital all night, she realized, and by now would have been on his feet nearly twenty-four hours straight.

That was like him, she decided, chewing the end of her pen. He had always been earnest and trustworthy, handsome, smart, the all-American boy. It was only when it came to the dream they'd shared, or she'd thought they shared, that he had let her down and broken her heart.

"I BROUGHT YOU something to eat. I thought you might be hungry." Alyssa spoke from the open doorway of her son's bedroom.

"Sandwiches and lemonade. Great. Thanks, Mom, I'm starved." Jeff turned away from the window, tucking his shirttail into his jeans as he talked. He was barefoot and his hair was still damp from the shower. He smiled.

He looked a lot like his father when he smiled. He had Ronald's thick, slightly curly chestnut hair, which he never remembered to have trimmed unless she or Amanda reminded him, and his father's dark blue eyes. His nose—commanding, she liked to call it; big, Jeff always insisted—and strong, obstinate chin were exact duplicates of her own father's features. His personality was also more like Judson Ingalls's—bluff, direct, no-nonsense. Ronald had been more outgoing and fun-loving than his son, at least until near the end of his life. Jeff, like most children, was very much a mixture of his parents, and at the same time, very much his own man.

"Clara insisted I bring them up." Alyssa smiled, a little apologetically, in return. Clara Myers was her father's housekeeper. She and her husband, Archie, had been with Judson as long as Alyssa could remember. Clara had been almost a mother to her when she was growing up and was still trying to mother her now that she had moved back under her father's roof.

"Tell her thanks," Jeff said, eyeing the chicken salad sandwich on the tray appreciatively. "I don't think I have the energy to make it down to the kitchen. I'm beat."

"George Phelps should never have expected you to take over his practice on such short notice. You've got more than enough patients of your own to take care of."

"People don't generally plan elopements weeks in advance," Jeff pointed out, moving across the big, high-ceilinged room in three quick strides. "If you do that, it's a wedding, not an elopement, and you know what kind of a to-do weddings cause in this town. Everyone goes a little crazy. You ought to have figured that out yourself by now. Tyler has had more than its share of them lately," he added as he picked up half a sandwich and took a bite.

Alyssa ignored his comments on weddings in general. "I can't imagine what those two were thinking of," she said with a shake of her head. "They ought to know better at their age."

"I never knew there was an age limit on falling in love," Jeff said, sitting down on his bed. He reached up and took the tray from her hands, to place it carefully on the bedspread in front of him. He was watching her with a teasing sparkle in his eyes, but she continued to refuse the bait he dangled in front of her. Her feelings for Edward Wocheck were far too complicated and uncertain to qualify as anything even close to love. Not now, not yet.

"There's certainly no age limit on showing poor judgment," she responded tartly, moving forward to shut the drapes at the big double windows to block out the bright August sun so Jeff could sleep when he'd finished eating.

"C'mon, Mom. Admit it. No one in this town thought George Phelps had a romantic bone in his body until he fell in love with Marge Peterson."

"Well, no," she admitted with a smile, as she settled herself carefully at the foot of the four-poster cherry bed. "You'd think he'd shy away from becoming involved again so soon. But that's neither here nor there. I hope they're very happy together." She tucked one foot up under her skirt and watched her son eat. "Lord knows he spent a lot of unhappy years with Mary. Still, I hope they get themselves back here soon so you can get a decent night's sleep."

"I can't disagree with that," Jeff said, taking a long swallow of lemonade. "I could sleep for a week. But I have to be back on duty at the emergency room at eleven and I want to stop by the clinic before I go." He ran his hand through his hair. "And I want to get to the hospital early enough to check up on old Wilhelm Badenhop, too."

"Oh, dear," Alyssa said, frowning slightly. "What happened to Wilhelm?" She'd known the old man all her life. He was only a few years older than Judson. "Has he had a relapse? I thought he was recovering from his bout with pneumonia."

"It seems he was, until this morning. He nearly died of respiratory arrest. If it hadn't been for Cece Scanlon . . . I mean, Cece Hayes." He grinned ruefully, but the teasing glint had gone out of his eyes, leaving them dark and cold as a midnight sky. "She's a hell of a nurse. If it hadn't been for her quick thinking, we'd be paying our last respects to old Wilhelm at the funeral home tonight, instead of me poring over his lab tests at Tyler Memorial, trying to figure out what went wrong."

"I hope everything turns out well. I like old Wilhelm," Alyssa said. "And I agree, Cece's an excellent nurse. Worthington House is lucky to have her. But it must be quite different from the work she did as a midwife in Nicaragua."

"Midwife?" Jeff scowled, his dark brows pulled together in a frown that was so like Judson's, Alyssa had to lower her head to hide her smile. "I didn't know she was a midwife."

"You don't spend enough time at the post office. Annabelle keeps the whole town up to date on Cece's life."

"Well, for once Annabelle isn't exaggerating," Jeff said, taking a last swallow of lemonade before setting the empty glass on the tray. "She's smart and savvy and cool as ice under pressure. She's sure as hell wasting her professional skills at Worthington House. We could really use someone like her at the clinic."

"Worthington House's residents deserve excellent nursing care also," Alyssa reminded him, picking up the tray as she rose from the bed.

Jeff lay down and pulled a pillow onto his chest. He folded his arms around it, just as he had from the time he was a boy. He looked up at the ceiling. Alyssa looked at him.

"Why don't you ask if she's willing to volunteer a few hours of her time at the clinic each week?" she couldn't resist asking.

"No. And don't you go asking her on my behalf either, the next time you see her. I've got enough problems on my mind without adding Cece Hayes to the list." He closed his eyes deliberately, ending the conversation.

It was the first time he'd mentioned Cece since she'd been back in town. They'd been very much in love when they were younger. Alyssa often wondered what had happened to end the romance. Jeff had never talked about it, although she was certain in her own mind that it was his father's suicide and the financial hardships that followed that had been the cause of it all.

Wisely, she decided not to question her son further. He was a grown man, after all—thirty years old; he could look out for himself where matters of the heart were concerned.

At least she hoped he could.

His divorce had hurt Jeff deeply, Alyssa knew, although he tried to pretend that it hadn't. She hoped it hadn't scarred him so badly he wouldn't take the chance on falling in love again. Not that she had any intention of trying to act as a matchmaker for her son and Cece Hayes. She knew better than that. And she'd make sure Annabelle Scanlon didn't get the idea into her head to do so, either.

"I'll wake you at ten," she said, preparing to close the door behind her.

"Better make that nine-thirty," Jeff answered, his voice already husky with sleep. "I've got to juggle a few accounts around at the clinic to keep the wolves from the door another month."

"Nine-thirty," she repeated, shutting the door. He was asleep before the latch clicked shut. "Pleasant dreams," she whispered, starting down the stairs. Those were the words she'd spoken to her children every night when they were small, a talisman to protect them from the darkness and the unknown. It was still her wish for them now that they were grown.

Her own dreams were seldom pleasant, especially these past few nights since her father had been sent to jail. The reality of Judson's being accused of her mother's murder still carried the quality of nightmare. She couldn't believe it was true, yet she remembered so little of the night Margaret Ingalls had disappeared. She could barely distinguish actual memory from childhood fantasy and recent snatches of recollection. She had been so young then, and it was so long ago; she only wanted to forget. But that wasn't possible. Her father's future happiness, perhaps his very life, depended on her remembering everything she could about that terrible night.

Alyssa paused at the bottom of the stairway. She set down the empty tray on the walnut pedestal table that had sat in the foyer for almost a century and lifted her hand to her temple to rub away the dull ache of tension that echoed every beat of her heart. Most of the time she couldn't remember enough about the night her mother disappeared to answer anyone's questions, including her own. But sometimes, sometimes, she was afraid she would remember too much.

In her dreams the past few nights, dreams that had kept her awake for hours after their passing, she had seen a man. No one she knew or recognized, only a shadowy masculine figure running away from her mother's bedroom. Running away from her. Because in her dream she also saw herself, the child Alyssa, standing at the foot of her mother's bed, and that other, long-ago Alyssa was holding a gun.